A Hypnotic Suggestion

Allison Jones

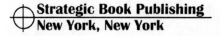
Strategic Book Publishing
New York, New York

Strategic Book Publishing
An imprint of AEG Publishing Group
845 Third Avenue, 6th Floor — #6016
New York, NY 10022
www.StrategicBookPublishing.com

ISBN: 978-1-60693-676-4
SKU: 1-60693-676-X

Printed in the United States of America

To Dad

Acknowledgments

Thanks are due to several individuals who assisted in various ways with the writing of this book. Thanks to my daughter, Debra, who provided me with resources to support my fiction writing. Thanks to Fred, Debbie, Donna, Janie, Judy, and Betsy for taking the time to read the book and give me feedback. Thanks to Suzanne and Kathy for continuous support to persist in this writing. Thanks to all other family members, friends, and colleagues whom I am fortunate to have in my life, whose words of encouragement were always appreciated. My special thanks to my editor, Pamela Guerrieri, for her superb way with words and her formatting and editorial assistance.

1

That August Sunday started innocently enough for Michael Freidan. He was up early, 6:00 AM to be exact, in order to be ready when his son-in-law, John Harkins, arrived at 7:00 AM. An organized man, he had already showered and dressed in the guest room to not wake his wife, Marjorie. With joyful anticipation of his golf game, he dressed in tan shorts and a pink polo shirt.

Down in the kitchen, Freidan's pleasant thoughts were altered as he thought about his son-in-law. "God damn wimp," he muttered while helping himself to the coffee his wife had set up the night before. John Harkins wasn't aggressive enough to suit Freidan. Wanting to work early in the morning was one of the few things Freidan liked about him. Freidan only used him as his accountant because it helped his daughter's financial well-being.

Michael Freidan was an aggressive man. It was one of the characteristics that made him a success in business. Freidan had started a small Internet server company during the dot-com boom of the late nineties. He had been bought out by one of the giants in the burgeoning information technology industry, but was kept on as the executive director of the North Carolina region in Charlotte. He was smart but honest, with neither a particularly good nor bad reputation. Somehow, he had managed to be successful, cutting corners when necessary, but never enough to cross the line to the other side of the law.

Now in his mid fifties, he was reaping the benefits of his early successes. He worked when he wanted and played golf when he wanted. This morning he had a 9:00 AM tee time with three of his associates. He wanted this early meeting with his son-in-law to be over in time for his game.

Freidan took his coffee to his den, his private place. Very few family members even entered the den without the expressed permission of Freidan. He had his own office at work, but this den was different. This was Freidan's space exclusively. The door was usually shut and sometimes locked. The lock wasn't really necessary, since few dared to enter.

On his way to the den, Freidan unlocked the front door and left the door to the den partially open. He decided this morning to work on his current tax structure. His son-in-law had some new approaches he wanted him to consider, but Freidan didn't totally trust Harkin's ideas, and wanted to do his own thinking about taxes first. He kept a close watch on his company and its finances.

He heard a car drive up and stop. He looked at his watch. *The wimp is early,* he thought. He made a mental note to stop thinking negatively about his son-in-law. After all, he was a good husband to Freidan's daughter and a good father to his grandchildren.

He heard a knock on the door. Freidan was grateful Harkins had remembered not to ring the doorbell, but to knock instead, as he had been instructed. He didn't want Marjorie disturbed during any of his early morning meetings at home.

"Come in, John," Freidan said. As he heard someone enter the den he said, "I was just looking over my current tax structures. I'm not…" He stopped as he looked up.

"What are you doing here?" he said surprised by the person who had entered the room. "I don't have you down for a meeting. Did you forget something?" Annoyance had entered Freidan's voice.

The visitor pulled out a .38 revolver.

The annoyance in Freidan's voice was now mixed with fear.

"What are you doing with that gun?" Freidan got up from behind his desk and headed toward his visitor.

"Give me that gun. What the hell do you think you're doing pointing a gun at me? Are you out of your mind?"

Freidan was about three feet from his visitor when the gun went off. He fell to the floor wounded and bleeding, but still conscious. Somehow, he had the presence of mind amidst his fright to lie very still, trying to look dead. His visitor bent over and put something in his hand, making this possum act difficult. Freidan remained limp. The visitor stood over him for a minute. Freidan held his breath, staying still. *Please don't shoot me again,* he thought.

He heard steps heading toward the front door. He exhaled deeply hoping his visitor hadn't heard the breath. He was panicking now. He could feel the wetness from his blood spreading beneath him. His thoughts were racing. He couldn't believe this had happened. He needed to focus on how to get help. Once he heard the front door shut, Freidan crawled toward his desk, trying to reach his phone, too weak to call out to his wife. He grabbed the phone line and pulled down the phone. He heard it crash, then slipped into unconsciousness.

When he became more alert, he realized instead of panic he now felt calm, even peaceful. He thought he was dead, but he wasn't sure since he still felt like who he had always been. Being dead didn't seem to have changed him much. He was in the corner of the room now, looking down on his body. He felt a detachment toward his body like it had been a covering he had just shed. He could have changed clothes with more feeling.

He saw his son-in-law, John Harkins, come into the room and bent over his body to check if he had a pulse. Freidan watched as Harkins picked up the gun the killer had used so he could turn him over to do CPR. It continued to not matter to Freidan that he had no pulse. What bothered him, though, was Harkins putting his fingerprints all over the gun. *Not only is he wimpy, he's dumb, too,* Freidan thought.

2

The grand house sure didn't *look* like a good place for a murder, thought attorney Tom Danford. It was a two-story stucco with a rocking chair porch on the main level and a veranda above, a modern Southern manse with antebellum echoes straight out of Tennessee Williams. The house was in the Meadow Lake division in Myers Park, an exclusive south Charlotte neighborhood. A small lake on the house's western view glimmered in the warm Sunday morning sun. As Tom Danford added his black Lexus to the sea of police vehicles and news vans that crowded the driveway at 220 Andrews Lane, he imagined Southern gentlemen in seersucker suits lounging in the wicker chairs on the porch, sipping fine bourbon and smoking big cigars as they solved the world's problems. Danford estimated the house at just shy of 4000 square feet. The owner—former owner, now—had done all right for himself.

As Danford got out of his car, he recognized the hulking figure of Detective Stan Lukowski, riding roughshod over the crime scene with his usual bluster. Lukowski was a big man: six foot three, 250 pounds. People generally assumed he had played football sometime in his life. Now that he was in his fifties, he might have more flab than muscle, but he still carried himself with the menacing authority of a linebacker. Lukowski was giving two uniformed cops Danford knew, Tony Strada and Joe Owens, the son of the police chief, a hard time.

"What are these news people doing inside the crime tape?" Lukowski barked from the porch. "Strada, Owens, get your asses in gear and move these civilians back." As he lumbered back inside, his muttered opinion of "God-damned reporters" could plainly be heard.

The two uniformed cops corralled the throng of reporters and ushered them with quiet authority from the porch. Owens spotted Danford and called warningly, "He's in rare form today."

"You got that right," Strada concurred. "I wish something would take the edge off him. He doesn't hesitate to write you up if things aren't just exactly the way he wants them. Be careful of him when he's in one of these moods. I got a week's suspension because the SOB said I contaminated evidence at a crime scene. All I did was go into the room where the vic was and give Lukowski an update. He can be a real bastard, but I guess that's how cops from Chicago act. I wish Lukowski had stayed there when his twenty-five years were up."

Danford nodded knowingly. "Gotcha. Bear on the prowl. Thanks for the heads up, guys. I appreciate it."

Danford enjoyed an amiable relationship with the police. Two years ago he had defended a uniformed cop falsely accused of murdering a popular and socially prominent woman in the community. In a sensational trial, Danford proved the woman's husband had been the actual killer and had set up his client. The cop was completely cleared and now Danford was the go-to attorney for practically the whole force, as well as their family and friends.

Danford heard Lukowski's bellowing voice as he strode into the air-conditioned house and followed it to the den, where Michael Freidan's body lay, blood trailing on the floor from the thick pool under his back.

"You CSI guys through yet?" Lukowski berated Dick Jennings, head of the Crime Scene Investigation unit. "I'd like to get this body out before Christmas, if that's not too much to ask."

"We're working as fast as we can," said Jennings calmly, delicately extracting a fiber from the dead man's shirt with tweezers.

"Well, it's not fast enough. We've got other things to do besides wait for you prima donnas. When are you going to be done?"

Jennings glanced up at the towering detective with mischief in his eye. "Stan, you know Michelangelo, the painter and sculptor?"

"Who don't know Michelangelo?" Lukowski spluttered, perceiving that his intellect had been challenged. "What the hell does he have to do with this?"

"The Pope kept asking him when his fresco on the Sistine Chapel ceiling was going to be done. Michelangelo said, 'When I'm finished.' So, to answer you, Stan, we'll be done when we're finished." Jennings didn't try to conceal his satisfied smirk as he continued to collect samples.

"What are you, some fucking fresco faggot? Just get it done."

As Lukowski exited, a barely audible "asshole" caused him to wheel around angrily. The CSI team stared innocently at him.

"Goddamn it, don't tell me you've got to be here, too," Lukowski complained, meeting Danford in the hallway. "Who ever thought it was a good idea to have lawyers at the crime scene?"

"Hi, Stan. Good to see you, too," said Danford sarcastically. Sparring with this surly Yankee detective was one of his job's perks. "Isn't our North Carolina civility ever going to rub off on you?"

"You know, if you weren't so buddy-buddy with that prick we have for a captain, you wouldn't be allowed here. What's up with you two anyway? You into wife swapping or something?" Lukowski smiled like a shark. "Oh, I forgot, you're a widower. Your wife was probably killed by some creep one of you lawyers got off. So you got a girl friend now? Is it that sexy witch lady who follows you around? Where is she anyway? I always like checking her out, particularly when she's walking away."

An uneasy silence filled the room. Everyone knew how sensitive Danford was about his wife Beth's death. If the attorney was bothered, he didn't let it show.

"Susan will be here soon and when she gets here, she'll put you in a trance you'll never wake up from," said Danford, wriggling his fingers sorcerer-like. "Isn't it just about coffee and doughnut time for you?"

"Yeah, yeah. Go see what your client did to his father-in-law. I'm going out for a smoke."

"Lukowski looked a little green, Counselor," laughed Jennings, looking up from the corpse. "I think you really got to him. Does he really think Dr. Kemper would do that?"

"He's superstitious. To him, hypnosis is akin to voodoo. I would never dream of doing anything to alter that perception."

Danford was glad to see Dick Jennings was on the case. No one, not even Lukowski, would keep Jennings from doing the meticulous work he was known for in the greater Charlotte area. "Dick, I understand my client is on the scene. You wouldn't know where Lukowski put him, would you?"

"I believe he's in what they used to call *the parlor,*" Jennings said with exaggerated gentility. "I'm supposed to swab him for DNA, directly. I think Freidan's wife, Marjorie, and his daughter, Ann Marie, John's wife is there, too."

"Thanks. I'll talk with John and the family after I've had a look around, if you don't mind."

"Don't mind a-tall."

Danford surveyed the murder room, jotting notes on a yellow legal pad, careful not to get in the way of the CSI team. His reputation as a lawyer of impeccable ethics made him a welcome figure at crime scenes, a privilege most of his colleagues couldn't claim. He knew he would get copies of the CSI pictures, but actually being on the scene always aided in the formulation of his defense. He was in luck this time. Only rarely was the victim's body still at the crime scene when he was called in to defend a murder suspect.

He knew his client, John Harkins, must be beside himself with worry, and who could blame him? The circumstantial evidence against the high-strung accountant was overwhelming, and Lukowski had immediately pegged him as a person of interest. The poor guy had surely seen enough cop shows and news bulletins to know that "person of interest" was police code for chief suspect.

Danford had done his best to ignore Lukowski's reference to his wife. Now, with the stench of death all around him, he helplessly recalled that tragic day. It had been three years since her death. He'd left for work the morning she died without a thought about anything but getting to his office. Beth had gone to the bank on routine business. Witnesses later said the robber entered directly behind her. He started waving his gun like a lunatic. Even though he wore a mask, the witnesses thought he was just a kid, nervous and scared. Beth had taken her checkbook out and was innocently returning it to her purse when the robber saw her. He shot her in the head and she died instantly. The only explanation was the robber thought she was going for a gun. As soon as the gun went off, the would-be robber bolted and made a clean escape.

The phone call came at eleven AM. Yes, the robber had escaped, but Beth was gone. "Just like that," Danford had reacted in disbelief to the news, too numb to say anything else.

"Just like that," he murmured aloud in the den, rousing Jennings.

"What's that, Tom?"

Danford said nothing. Yes, just like that, Beth was gone.

3

Rounding the corner toward Andrews Lane, Susan Kemper saw Tom Danford's Lexus and parked her silver Acura TL behind it. "Oh, damn," she said. She recognized Stan Lukowski standing near two uniformed officers. She knew he had seen her, too. Susan was well-respected as a psychologist and criminal profiler and was working hard to bring that same level of credibility to forensic hypnosis, but she knew Lukowski just saw her as an attractive woman and regarded the emerging field as so much hogwash.

Establishing credibility with the police force as a forensic hypnotherapist was an uphill battle. A big blow came to forensic hypnosis in the 70s when the Los Angeles police created what became known as the Svengali squads. Police officers were trained in hypnosis techniques but used them to plant suggestions in subjects leading them to confess to crimes they hadn't committed. Subsequently, any testimony obtained under hypnosis against a defendant became inadmissible in California and some other states, including North Carolina. Fortunately, in 1986, the Supreme Court said hypnosis testimony that benefitted the defendant could be admitted, thus supporting a defendant's rights and the field of forensic hypnosis.

"If you think you're going behind the police line, I got news for you." Lukowski challenged as Susan walked toward him.

"Don't give me a hard time, Stan," sighed Susan, hoisting the crime tape and passing under it. "I've already had my share today."

Lukowski grabbed Susan's arm roughly and pushed her back. "I said you can't go in there."

"Listen, Stan, you know I have permission to be at the crime scene if Tom is here. I'm working as his assistant."

"This is my turf—I'll do all the permission-granting. Now get behind that yellow line like a good little girl." Susan staggered as the detective strong-armed her past the tape.

"Let go of her or I'll have you up on assault charges," said Danford, emerging from the house. "It would be my pleasure to call Captain Owens and tell him what an ass you're being."

"That black prick don't scare me. Call him and see what he says. He has no business authorizing you two to be here. Let him be woke up early on Sunday morning. Serve him right."

Susan could feel Lukowski's grip relaxing on her arm, but he refused to let her go. She fought back tears of anger and humiliation. Danford whipped out his cell phone and located the chief's home number. No answer. The chief's cell was busy; he left a message for Jay Owens to call him back immediately.

Lukowski broke into a shit-eating grin and said, "Ain't letting her through until he calls and authorizes it." He crossed his massive arms on his chest and glared at Susan. "You try an' sneak in and I'll throw you in a jail cell so fast you won't have time to wiggle your ass."

The crowd of cops and reporters stirred in anticipation at the thought of Lukowski getting his ass kicked by Tom Danford. If a fight did break out, he was the odds-on favorite. Tall and muscular, he had been a boxer in college and still worked out at the gym nearly every day. Lukowski had it coming and Danford was the guy who could deliver the goods.

"Stay out here and get the information you need, Susan, and take your outside sketches," Danford said evenly, breaking the tension. "Jay will get back to me before long." Danford was too smart to jeopardize his career by getting into a fight with Lukowski, although he sure would have liked to. He had a hunch Lukowski knew he could bait him with little fear of physical retaliation.

Susan gazed at the always in control attorney. He wasn't quite movie star handsome, but with his intense blue eyes, cleft chin, and thick, dark hair, he was certainly easy on the eyes. His intelligence and sincerity only enhanced his attractiveness. She took her cue from him and controlled her emotions even though she was close to tears with frustration at not being allowed to do her job.

Lukowski released Susan and called over his shoulder to Joe Owens. "You keep all these people, including Dr. Kemper, behind that police line. I'll have your badge if you don't." He put special emphasis on the doctor's name.

"Hey, Dr. Kemper, sorry about Lukowski," said Owens. He and Susan were well acquainted through mutual police work. "He's giving everyone a hard time today. I'd like you to meet my new partner, Tony Strada."

Owens was one of Susan's favorite men on the force. He was a clean-cut man in his mid-twenties who had already distinguished himself as an intelligent and conscientious law-man. She was pleased to meet his partner.

"Glad to meet you," beamed Susan, shaking hands with the young officer, who looked all of twenty-one. He had a firm grip, a nice smile, and inquisitive blue eyes.

"Tony has never met anyone who does forensic hypnosis. Tell him about the kidnapping case you helped us solve. He needs to be schooled," Owens said, grinning and elbowing his partner.

"Are you going to make me cluck like a chicken if I talk to you?" Strada quipped, tucking his thumbs in his armpits and flapping his arms.

Susan laughed. She had heard all the jokes before. "No, that's a myth. A hypnotist can't make you do anything you don't want to do. What I do mostly is hypnotize witnesses and help them recall information they've mentally suppressed. When people witness a crime, their emotions often cloud their memory. Under hypnosis, sometimes they remember details covered up, so to speak, by those emotions."

"I thought hypnosis reports weren't admissible in court?" said Strada.

"In North Carolina, only information obtained before someone is hypnotized is admissible in court if it aids the prosecution. However, all information, even that obtained under hypnosis, is admissible if it aids the defendant. The police use me sometimes to enhance their investigations if they have no clues or leads. What a good forensic hypnotist does is videotape the subject both before and during the hypnosis session. In the pre-hypnosis videotape, the subject will describe their recollections as completely as possible, with no prompting from the hypnotist. Then the hypnosis session itself is videotaped, wherein the mentally blocked details can come out. That way, the judge and jury can see the hypnotist didn't give the subject any suggestions. I only ask broad, open-ended questions that aren't leading in any way."

"So what happened in this kidnapping case?" asked Strada, his curiosity piqued.

Susan was pleased to have a receptive audience. "Tom Danford was defending the gardener of Dr. and Mrs. Cassem. It was their nine-year-old daughter who had been kidnapped. The gardener had the means and opportunity to commit the kidnapping. He also had a lot of debt. The police assumed that was a good enough motive. One of the neighbors, Mary Ford, kept saying she knew there was something she saw the morning of the kidnapping that could help the case, but couldn't quite remember what it was. Under hypnosis, I helped her go through the events of that morning.

She remembered she had gotten up and made the coffee. She heard a thump outside and went out to get the paper for her husband, Fred. It was part of her morning routine. She complained to me that the newspaper boy always threw the paper anywhere but on their large drive-way. This morning it was in the gutter. When she bent down to pick up the paper, a van drove by almost hitting her. One of the men in the van called her an old bitch and told her to get out of the road."

Susan paused, checking on her audience. Owens and Strada were now engrossed in the story. "At first it was hard for her to see the van," she continued. "The emotion generated by almost being run over and sworn at had blocked some of the detail. I got her to picture the van in her mind on a television screen. That helped her emotionally distance herself from the scene. She remembered three significant details. One, there were two white men in the car. Two, the passenger was wearing a blue baseball cap turned backwards. And three, the most significant detail: the windshield had an orange decal with the letter E in the middle."

"Everett Concrete Company!" exclaimed Joe. "I remember. That's where they found those two guys."

"Correct. The police discovered these men had installed the side-walks around the Cassem house. Now that they had a witness who put these guys at the scene that morning, they tailed them and found the little girl, unharmed. I admit I cried watching the TV coverage of her being returned to her parents."

"So, what are you then, a doctor of hypnosis-ology?" Strada asked, grinning.

"Not exactly. I'm a psychologist. I have a private practice and teach criminal profiling at Bluffton University." Susan flicked at the crime tape. "And, if I ever get past this yellow barrier, I'll sketch out the murder room and take notes. When witnesses describe crime scenes, it helps if I've actually been there." She drew a heavy sigh. "It's all moot, unless that Nazi, Lukowski, can be put in his place."

Strada and Owens nodded sympathetically. If they had been at a bar off duty they would have said more about the insufferable detective.

"Here comes the chief," said Strada, jerking his head toward the street. "He'll take care of Lukowski."

4

Jay Owens had been police chief for nearly twenty years in Charlotte, NC. He was the first African American to hold that position. He'd seen the positive growth of the city along with the unfortunate concomitant increase in crime. He was a stand-up career cop who still got his hands dirty in the field with his men to keep the crime rate down. About six years ago, he had led a special task force in the capture of a serial killer. The killer had kidnapped four women under the ages of 40 from mall parking lots. He had raped and killed them in their cars, found later in the wooded areas outside of town. Because the murders were random, the police couldn't find the killer through a connection with the victims. The women in the town were afraid to go shopping at the mall alone, particularly after dark.

The only clue the police had came from a teenage girl who had seen a man in a brown uniform talking to a woman bent over her tire. When the woman's picture appeared in the paper as the killer's fourth victim, the teenager mentioned what she had seen to her parents and later to the police. Owens ordered a tail on the UPS driver who serviced the mall area. The tail paid off when two cops on his task force caught him red-handed in the commission of an attempted kidnapping. Owens was a bona fide hero, but he never put on any airs about it; he was still just plain Jay Owens, local boy made good.

"Morning, Tom. How's it going?" said the chief as he got out of his spotless

Crown Victoria. "Got your message and hurried over."

"I 'preciate it, Jay," said Danford, offering his hand. "Your man, Lukowski, has a burr up his ass about Dr. Kemper being allowed inside."

"That so?" the chief said, turning to Susan. "Miss Susan, you go right on in, you hear?"

Chief Owens raised his eyebrows and crooked his right index finger purposefully in Stan Lukowski's direction. The big man lurched over and stood before his superior like a chastised child. The onlookers were still disappointed that Lukowski and Danford didn't mix it up, but watching the detective get a good dressing down was the next best thing.

Susan hurried into the house. Behind her, she could hear Lukowski muttering meek apologies. She thought she heard Chief Owens use the words obnoxious and political. Susan could understand the chief referring to Lukowski's behavior as obnoxious but what could be political about what he had done?

"Hi, everybody," Susan chimed as she entered the den.

"So, you got past the gorilla outside? Good for you," said Jennings.

"Thanks to the chief," replied Susan, nodding her head toward Chief Owens as he headed toward the living room still having a one-way conversation with Lukowski, albeit a little more subdued since entering the house.

Susan got to work. She hated seeing Michael Freidan lying in all that blood, but she was glad the body was still there. She would be privy to the pictures the CSI team was taking, of course, but being physically in the room gave her a fuller perspective that aided her profiling and would prove invaluable if she later hypnotized a witness. In this case, she would likely be hypnotizing John Harkins, the primary suspect at this point. She removed her legal pad from her briefcase and started taking notes. The den was large. Susan guessed it was about eighteen by fifteen feet. The windows had dark green and bamboo pull-up Roman shades. Pricey, thought Susan, like the ones she had seen in her decorator's shop. The chenille dark green couch, placed under the window, matched the colors of the blinds. The throw pillows, in soft apricot and green, accented the colors perfectly and were neatly at attention at each end of the couch. Susan wondered if anyone ever sat on it. It was certain no one had come in or out that window with the couch in such neat condition.

Books, decorative bookends, and objects d'art filled the bookcases that lined two of the walls. Susan knew immediately the bookcases had been professionally decorated following the 1/3 role. She had been told by her decorator a bookcase should be 1/3 space, 1/3 books and 1/3 objects. One inconsistently arranged shelf caught Susan's eye. The books were spread out more on the shelf, as if to artificially fill a once full space. The shelf also had on it a round circle surrounded by dust, as if something had been in that spot. The rest of the room was as orderly as a military barracks ready for inspection. Given the care given to decorating the room and its general orderliness, it seemed unlikely the decorator would have purposely left the shelf so untidy. She put a question mark on her pad to inquire if anything else had been on that shelf.

Large and masculine, Michael Freidan's desk looked very expensive—probably made of hand-tooled walnut. There was a comfortable looking high back leather chair behind it and two small leather chairs in front.

Sitting behind the desk, Freidan would have seen the beautiful gardens in the back of the house. He could also have clicked on the 32-inch liquid crystal TV set in the armoire in the corner. Sitting in front of the desk, a person would have viewed the businessman against a backdrop of crossed Civil War swords and a rifle with a polished brass plate on the wall. The top of the desk had a leather blotter, pens in a wooden holder, and a stapler. The phone that once sat on the desk was now on the floor.

Susan put her profiling instincts into play. Based on the blood trail, she guessed the killer had shot Freidan in the chest while Freidan was standing in the middle of the room. After the killer left, Freidan had then crawled to the desk to reach the phone, pulling it down in the attempt. She surmised that the CSI team had bagged the murder weapon, if it had been left on the scene. There were no signs of a struggle between the killer and Freidan. He was standing when shot, probably turning to talk to the killer. Probably someone he knew, thought Susan.

Susan met Danford in the hall. "Who found the body?" she asked.

Danford shook his head and exhaled wearily. "Unfortunately, John did. He filled me in on the phone this morning and just now in the parlor. He had come over for breakfast to go over some tax documents with Freidan. The door was open and John found his father-in-law on his stomach. He says he wasn't sure if he was dead or alive. He called 911 because he could see the blood and a gun was lying beside the body. The gun was in the way, so John innocently but stupidly picked it up so he could roll Freidan over. His intention was to perform CPR, but once he got him on his back, he could see he was dead. Of course, now his fingerprints were all over the presumed murder weapon. When the police and ambulance arrived, John was standing there, covered in blood."

"Counselor, I think you'll want to see this," called Jennings from the den.

"One of my guys found this as we were taking one more look around the crime scene."

Together Danford and Susan examined a bloodstained photograph in a clear poly bag. The picture showed John Harkins and a blonde woman standing in a doorway, locked in an embrace and kissing with obvious passion.

"That's your client, all right," said Jennings. "Guess the blonde's his old lady, huh?"

Danford looked grim. "No, Ann Marie's—"

"A redhead," Susan interjected.

Jennings rolled his eyes. "Good luck with this one."

5

Danford allowed himself a rueful smile as he handed Jennings the bagged photo. John Harkins was innocent until proven guilty of murder, but he clearly wasn't innocent in at least one other sense. "Do you have a time of death?" he inquired of Jennings as they walked into the hallway.

"Medical examiner says somewhere around 7:00 AM. It looks like the shot in the chest was the cause of death, although his death wasn't immediate." Jennings motioned to the blood smear on the floor behind the body. "From the blood stains, Freidan was still alive for a few minutes after he was shot. He dragged himself to the phone leaving that trail of blood. Whoever shot him took off without checking if he was dead or not. He or she threw down the gun and left. Doesn't look like a robbery. Nothing seems to be missing. Freidan still had had a Rolex watch on his wrist and the LCD TV was left. Any robber would have been glad to take those items. The only disturbance was your client turning the victim over to do CPR. At least he used his cell phone to call 911 and didn't touch anything else."

"What about the shelf on this bookcase?" asked Susan. "The room is too well decorated to have spaces like that there."

Jennings looked toward the bookcase. "I'll check with Mrs. Freidan. She's in the living room with her daughter. We have to fingerprint them directly. We dusted the bookcase for prints and will compare them with members of the household." He looked at Danford shaking his head. "It doesn't help that your client picked up the gun, counselor."

"Tell me about it," Danford sighed, shoving his hands in his pants pockets. "Why do clients do such stupid things?"

"Ask your profiler there," Jennings suggested, nodding toward Susan. "We just collect the evidence."

Susan was thinking. The thing was, picking up the gun could have been either very stupid or very smart on Harkins' part. If he did indeed kill his father-in-law, he created a plausible explanation for why his fingerprints were on the gun by claiming he moved him in order to perform CPR. What jury wouldn't respond sympathetically to Harkins' concern for the welfare of his father-in-law? On the other hand, if he didn't pull the trigger, the thought of leaving of incriminating fingerprints on the gun would be the last thing on his mind.

"Anything else interesting in your bags of goodies?" Danford asked Jennings.

"Fibers, hairs, the usual stuff. Can't tell if it's important until we analyze it back in the lab."

"Has Lukowski seen the picture you found in Freidan's hand yet?" asked Tom.

"Not yet, but I need to show it to him before I leave the house. "I've swabbed Harkins for DNA and checked his fingers for gunshot residue," said Jennings. "He's all yours, if you want to grill him again."

"Thanks, Dick. Susan, you stay here. I'll round up John. We can talk privately in my Lexus."

Danford encountered Lukowski in the hall outside the parlor. "Mind if I have a word with my client, Stan?" Danford said in a cool, even voice.

Lukowski appeared subdued after his upbraiding by the chief. "Be my guest, your highness," he said, gesturing grandly toward the parlor door. "He's not under arrest. Yet."

Once they were alone in the car, Danford could see his client was a very nervous man; a loud "boo!" would make him jump out of his socks. As an accountant, John was used to an orderly world with rigid guidelines. He was definitely out of his element, but Danford couldn't afford to treat him with kid gloves. He would have to push the truth from him, if necessary.

"Well, John, the CSI will establish your fingerprints are on what looks like the murder weapon and, of course, you were here at the approximate time of death," Danford said matter-of-factly.

"All they need is a motive and I'm dead meat, right?"

Danford looked him dead in the eye. "It looks like they've got that, too. So who is the *blonde* you've been seeing, John?" he almost shouted.

"Blonde? What blonde? I would never cheat on my wife," Harkins shot back.

"Don't give me that bullshit," Danford said impatiently. "If I'm going to represent you, you need to tell me the truth. Your father-in-law had a picture in his hand of you kissing a blonde. It looks like he confronted you with it, and you shot him."

"No, no. I'm being framed. For Christ sake, I don't cheat on my wife. Where's the picture? I want to see it!" Harkin's voice was shrill and his forehead beaded with sweat.

"The CSI guys have the picture bagged and tagged. They'll be checking it for fingerprints and authenticity. Lukowski's got enough to charge you when they show him that picture, particularly when they confirm your fingerprints are on the gun. You definitely moved the gun, right?"

Harkins nodded his head.

"If this is a frame, it's a good one."

"Listen, the old man and I didn't get along particularly well, but I'd never kill him. You know me: I'm timid. My wife has to kill the spiders in the house. Can't say I'm sorry he's dead, but I swear I didn't do it."

Danford had a good bullshit detector. He knew some of what John Harkins was saying was true—just not how much of it. He probably wouldn't have the balls to kill Michael Freidan. Could he have an affair with a woman? Maybe.

"John, if you've been seeing another woman, you have to tell me," Danford thundered. "I can't defend you without the whole story, even it it's not pretty. You have to be perfectly honest with me at all times. They've got a *picture* of you kissing a pretty blonde. Trust me, it wasn't just a friendly peck on the cheek."

"No, no! Never would I cheat on my wife."

"Yeah, so you say. We'll get a copy of the picture soon. Maybe you can identify her, although her face is partially turned away. It definitely wasn't your redheaded wife. I want you to tell me again what happened when you found your father-in-law, but I want Susan to hear you, too. Okay with you?"

"Sure, sure," Harkins agreed. He daubed at his sweating forehead with his loosened tie.

Danford flipped open his cell phone. "Susan. Me. Won't you join us?"

Susan left the scene of the crime and walked quickly to Tom's car. She slid her long, shapely legs into the spacious back seat of the Lexus. "What's up, guys?"

"John's going to catch us up on his busy morning," Danford said, smiling at her. "All right, John, you're on."

"Okay. We had a meeting scheduled for 7:00 AM. He didn't answer the door when I knocked, so I tried the door. It wasn't locked. I called his name when I walked in, but there was no answer. I walked into the den and saw him laying face down on the floor with all the blood around him and the phone on the floor. I couldn't feel a pulse. I started to turn him over to do CPR, but first I had to get the gun out of the way. I don't know how, but somehow I called 911 from my cell while I was doing CPR. I also remember yelling for Marjorie, his wife. Then everyone showed up.

Lukowski was on me like a bulldog about why I killed him. I got nervous and called you right after I called my wife, Anne Marie, and broke the news to her. What a morning! I swear I didn't kill him. I found him just like you saw him." Harkins shook his head in wonderment and whistled. "Folks, I need a smoke."

"Sure, just take it easy, John," said Danford. "Susan and I are going back inside. You stay here until I tell you differently and don't stray too far from the car. And definitely don't talk to anybody without me around."

Hawkins got out of the car and lit a cigarette as Danford and Susan walked toward the house. Lukowski met them at the front door. "Owens! Strada! Grab that man and put him in handcuffs," he bellowed, gesticulating frantically at Harkins. "He's under arrest! Read him his rights and don't let him get away!"

Owens and Strada strode over to Harkins. His eyes went wild and his chest heaved. He flung his cigarette down and started to run down the sidewalk.

"Stop!" Danford cried. "Don't run, John, *don't run!*"

Lukowski unholstered his revolver and started toward Danford's Lexus in a fast shamble, yelling, "Shoot him if he doesn't stop!"

Danford grabbed Lukowski's arm. *"Are you crazy?* What the fuck's the matter with you? You don't order a cop to shoot an unarmed man!"

"Unarmed? How do you know he's unarmed?" Lukowski wrested his arm free.

Harkins had about ten yards on the officers as he sprinted down the sidewalk, glancing over his shoulder repeatedly in terror. Owens and Strada were catching up fast, their guns flopping on their hips. "Get him boys, whatever it takes," Lukowski bellowed coldly as he joined in the chase. Danford and Susan were close behind.

"I'm going to get your badge for this, Lukowski." Danford sneered, keeping pace with the detective.

"We'll see about that, counselor."

Harkins disappeared around a corner. Owens and Strada, guns still holstered, were just ten feet behind. Susan gasped as a drawn out squeal split the quiet morning air, followed closely by a sickening, flesh sounding thud.

Danford and Susan outpaced Lukowski to the scene. When they arrived, Owens and Strada were bent over the crumpled body of John Harkins.

6

"Did you call 911?" Danford panted.

Owens nodded. "He's got a pulse, but it's weak."

"Honest, I didn't see him," the driver, a young woman in her twenties, protested to Strada. Twelve feet away, her newer Camry sat against the curb with a badly crushed front end. "He ran right out in front of me. He's lucky I slowed down for a squirrel that was trying to decide whether or not to cross the road. I don't usually do that. It's too dangerous to slow down that much."

"I know, ma'am. We saw it all," said Strada evenly. "You won't be charged. He's lucky to be alive. Someone's watching out for him."

Momentarily, the ambulance arrived. Lukowski put his hand on the paramedic's shoulder and said, "Careful with this one, boys. He's a murderer."

Danford was in Lukowski's face. "Why, you sorry bastard!"

"Tom, don't," Susan implored. She put her hand on Danford's arm and felt it relax a little.

"Where will you take him?" Danford asked the paramedic.

"Carolina Medical Center. It's closest."

Danford turned to Susan. "Maybe we should go with him."

Susan smiled reassuringly. "Let's let the hospital take care of John. You're overwrought; you need to relax. Come on. Let's go back to the house." Susan took Danford by his arm and led him away.

"You two love birds run along," Lukowski jeered. "I'll make sure this scum bucket is taken care of."

In moments, Danford and Susan were sitting in the comfortable wicker chairs on the Freidan front porch. In the distance, a siren screamed as the ambulance headed to Carolina Medical Center.

"Why do clients do such stupid things?" Danford exclaimed, throwing up his arms in exasperation.

"We all do stupid things, especially in difficult situations," said Susan. She placed her hand on Danford's arm again and squeezed it reassuringly.

The gentle touch felt good to Danford. He felt a warm connection with Susan. He hadn't felt that kind of connection with a woman since his wife was killed. He had found Susan attractive since the first time he met her. He liked the way her long dark hair curled gently around her face down to her shoulders. When she became passionate about a case, she was so alive and so sexy. He had tried to think of Susan only as a colleague because she was married but it was tough.

After his wife's death, his will to live came from his passion to find the person who had killed Beth. For months after her murder—and it was just that—his depression had been deep. Mornings were the worse. He couldn't get up and face the day without Beth. She always had gotten up first and made the coffee. The good smell of it woke him up. A fresh cup was always waiting for him when he went into the kitchen. As soon as Beth saw him, she would yell "Yay!" and pump her arm like a cheerleader, as if his being awake was an event worth celebrating.

For a long time he was consumed by an unfocused hostility toward the shooter. It wasn't until he thought about what he could do constructively to find his wife's killer that he could face the day again. At first, he couldn't look at the bank video of the shooting. Watching Beth slump to the floor caused a pain so deep, his body was paralyzed from it. He knew he could kill the man who had shot his wife. But he wanted to make him suffer first. He wanted him to die a slow, nasty death. In his most gruesome fantasy he resolved to cut off the bastard's private parts, shove them in his mouth, and throw him in a vat of boiling water. He tried hard to rein in his violent urges, but it had been a constant struggle. He had to keep reminding himself that torturing and killing the shooter wouldn't bring Beth back. But he found a grim satisfaction in imagining the delicious ways he could make the bastard suffer.

As the days and years passed, the depression and pain gradually left him, but his desire to find and punish Beth's killer still burned like a furnace in his gut. He could now look at the bank video and suck up his pain. It weakened him, but his emotions no longer took over. He had grieved for Beth and now was ready to go on living without her.

The sound of Susan's voice snatched him back from his reverie. "Okay, counselor. What would you like me to do for you?"

Danford was feeling calmer. He couldn't resist smiling suggestively and wiggling his eyebrows Groucho Marx-fashion.

"You know what I meant," Susan said, laughing and punching him lightly on the shoulder. "By the way, my son, Jeff, would love to help investigate this case. He was begging me to let him come with me this morning. Did I tell you he's decided to go to law school, too, next year? Phillip wasn't up yet when I left, but I'm sure he'd like working for you, again, if you need the help. Can't believe at the end of this school year, once he passes the bar, he'll be a lawyer."

"I'm sure I'll be able to use all of you. This is shaping up to be a nasty case. I have an unconscious client on the way to the hospital and absolutely no information on the blonde in that incriminating picture. Who knows when, or if, John will even wake up? I suppose I could ask his wife if she knew." Danford bolted from his chair. "Oh, God, Ann Marie! She doesn't even know what happened to John!"

Danford instinctively touched Susan on her back as they hurried into the house. Susan felt just a small sparkle of electricity. Ann Marie Harkins was in the living room, comforting her mother. Both women were sobbing softly. Ann Marie looked up from the couch and met Danford's sober gaze.

"What's going on?" she asked cautiously.

"Excuse us, Mrs. Freidan," Danford said. "We need to talk to your daughter." Ann Marie looked at Marjorie Freidan, who nodded her approval wearily.

"The porch, we'll have some privacy there," Ann Marie suggested, leading them into a sunny, glassed-in Florida room. "Wh-where's John?"

Danford shot Susan a helpless look. "John's on the way to the hospital, Ann Marie," Susan said softly. "He got hit by a car and he's unconscious."

Instantly, Ann Marie became hysterical. "What? He was just here. That can't be true. How could a car have hit him? What would he be doing in the street? You sure it was John? Is this some sick joke?"

Danford took over. "You know John found your father and that he admitted to picking up the gun. When the police and ambulance arrived, John was standing over the body with blood on him. We know his fingerprints will be on the gun."

"I still don't get it. So what? He told me he tried to revive my daddy. He's a hero," Ann Marie said haughtily.

"There's more," said Danford. "The CSI team found an incriminating picture in your father's hand."

Ann Marie's tone became frosty. "Incriminating? What are you talking about?"

Tom took a deep breath. "Your father was clutching a picture of John kissing a blonde. When Stan Lukowski saw the picture, he ordered John arrested. John ran. He was hit by a car as he ran into the street with two cops in pursuit on foot."

Ann Marie nervously paced the room, wringing her hands. "This is crazy. How badly is John hurt? Which hospital is he in? He was having an affair? That can't be! John wouldn't do that. My father's dead, my husband might be having an affair and is unconscious in the hospital. It can't be happening. I can't handle all this." Ann Marie nervously paced the room, wringing her hands. "I have to go see John. I have to talk to him. Where is he?"

Susan took hold of Ann Marie's arm. "He's at Carolina Medical Center. I'll drive you there."

"My mama, I can't leave my mama. I don't know what to do."

"I'll stay with Mrs. Freidan," Danford said. "Is there anyone else I can call for her?"

"Yes, her sister, my Aunt Helen, will come over. She should be home. Where's a piece of paper? I'll write down her number."

Danford proffered a small pocket pad with a pen. "I'll call her and stay with your mother until your aunt arrives," he said, placing a calming hand on Ann Marie's shoulder. "Now don't worry, John will be fine. Meanwhile, Susan will take care of you. She's the best."

As the two women departed, Danford wished he were as confident as he tried to sound. *A helluva way to spend a Sunday morning!*

And it wasn't over yet. He still had Marjorie Freidan to interview.

Grieving widows did not for a restful Sunday morning make.

7

En route to Carolina Medical Center, Ann Marie was still a basket case. "I still don't understand what happened," she wailed. "Why did John run? Who is this blonde? My life is all turned around. This can't be happening to me. Everything is out of control."

Susan's professional instinct told her to help Ann Marie regain some emotional equilibrium. "Ann Marie, I have to ask you some questions, so I need you to take a deep breath and calm yourself down," she said patiently. "It might be helpful to start with what happened early this morning. Just fill me in as best you can."

Dutifully, Ann Marie placed her shaking hands on her knees and made a visible effort to steel her nerves. "Alright. John was to meet my father this morning for breakfast and go over some financial papers. I was still in bed when I heard the garage door open. It was around seven this morning. I went back to sleep after that."

"How did you know it was around seven?"

Ann Marie hesitated for a moment. "I don't know for sure. I don't think I looked at the clock. It must have been about ten minutes to seven. John was supposed to meet Dad at seven o'clock, and he's always punctual." At the memory of her father, the floodgates opened and Ann Marie began to weep pitifully.

Susan commiserated, but she had a job to do. "I know this is hard for you but you have important information that can be helpful. How did your father and John get along?"

"Alright, I guess. My father could be very aggressive and domineering. John's more on the wimpy side, I guess you could say. I think my father would have respected him more if he stood up to him."

"What financial papers were they going to review?"

"I think it was an investment option for my father that would help with his taxes, but I'm not sure. John had showed me some papers, but I don't get too involved with his business, so I really didn't pay much attention."

Susan made a mental note to follow up on the documents. She screwed up her nerve for the hardball question she had to ask. "Ann Marie, were you ever suspicious that John was having an affair?"

Ann Marie was indignant. "*What?* John? No, never!"

"Did he work late often?" Susan prodded.

"Of course he did. He's an accountant and investment banker. They work all the time."

"Did you ever worry some of those late night meetings were not all professional?"

Susan could almost see and hear Ann Marie's hackles rise. "Listen here. My husband would never cheat on me. He loves our children and me. How dare you insinuate such a thing?"

"I'm sorry, Ann Marie, but the police found that picture of John kissing another woman. It's very incriminating. It also points to a motive for John to kill your father. Do you know of any blonde he could possibly have been involved with, even on a platonic basis?" Susan knew the kiss was anything but platonic, but there was no reason to fan the fire of Ann Marie's temper.

"No, absolutely not. I have a blonde sister, Kathy, but she lives in Boston and would never..." She hesitated. "John was in Boston two months ago. I suggested he see my sister, but he said he wouldn't have time. It can't be, not those two. You're just making this up. You're trying to ruin my marriage. My life is in shambles! Isn't it bad enough my father is dead? What else could possibly happen..." Ann Marie's voice trailed off as she buried her face in her hands, sobbing like a woman bereft of hope.

Susan realized her question about the bookcase would have to wait. In light traffic, they had arrived at the hospital in less than twenty minutes. Carolina Medical Center always looked imposing and frightening to Susan. Maybe it was the weathered gray stone that framed the entrance. Maybe it was the building's angles, straight and unfriendly. Maybe it was because her husband, Frank, was a doctor here.

Once inside, Susan waited alone in the waiting room while Ann Marie sat at her husband bedside. Susan's thoughts wandered back to the morning, when she had told Frank she was going out on a case. She had gotten a call from Tom during her morning run. After a quick shower, she had put on her black slacks and red and black top, thinking they were flattering, but not too provocative. A spray of perfume, and she was ready.

She had gone looking for her husband and found him in the den, poring over his coin collection like a latter-day Silas Marner. She remembered thinking how much Frank Kemper looked like the doctor he was. He was always a picture of neatness and was obsessively fastidious about his clothes, his car, and everything around him. To his credit, he extended these same personal standards to the level of care he gave his patients.

"Susan, take a look at this new coin I got at an unbelievable price," he was saying as she entered. "Jennifer Houston found it for me. How many decorators would help find coins for their clients? Maybe she's got a thing for me, you think?"

Frank's coin collecting bored Susan. She got right to the point. "Frank, Tom Danford called. There's been a murder at Meadow Lakes. He wants me to meet him at the crime scene."

"You're going like *that?*" Frank said with an insinuating snarl.

"What's *wrong* with what I have on?" She regretted her question as soon as it left her lips. She knew Frank was using how she was dressed as justification to keep her home. He hated her going on out on assignment, and she knew he would try to stop her.

"You look like you're going to trap someone besides a criminal," Frank said smugly, pleased with his wit.

"Frank, don't start. I don't want to get into an argument with you."

"You can go, but you have to change your clothes. You can't be around Tom and those cops dressed like that," Frank insisted, his voice dripping with disgust.

"Frank, you're being ridiculous."

"You heard what I said. Change your clothes."

God, how the man could push all her buttons! "Who do you think you are, telling me what to wear? I am not a child."

"Who do you think *you* are," Frank exploded. "Coming and going with no regard for your family, and dressed like a hooker on top of it all?"

"Go to hell, Frank," Susan had responded simply and left. Damn, it felt good to have the last word!

Alone with her thoughts in the waiting room, Susan caught herself shaking her head. Even psychologists, she guessed, were entitled to a little family dysfunction. Lately, the dysfunction between her and Frank was growing from little to major. How could someone with his professional status be such a chauvinist? And so insecure?

She decided that, sometimes, the best medicine was the voice of a friend and took her cell phone out of her clutch purse.

"Peggy? Free for lunch tomorrow? I need some girl talk, bad!"

8

John Harkins' improbably young doctor looked sleep-deprived, Susan thought, with red-rimmed eyes, a disheveled mop of auburn hair, and a wrinkled and stained lab coat. As she listened to him counsel Ann Marie, she was reminded of how she detested everything about the hospital: the medicinal smell, the noise, the frenetic energy.

"How is my husband, Doctor?" Ann Marie implored.

"As well as can be expected," said the doctor, scanning the chart. "The femur in his right leg is fractured. As that's the largest leg bone, it will take a while to heal." The much-discussed femur was wrapped in gauze and what looked like to Susan a Velcro blue wrapping suspended in the air in a sling. "He also fractured some ribs," the doctor went on, seemingly enjoying his center stage position, "and one penetrated his lung on the right side. That is the most life-threatening injury. He'll require surgery to remove the wayward rib and set that right leg. These chest tubes are keeping his lung inflated."

The doctor lifted a tube and shook his head affirmatively at the pink fluid draining into a bag. "There'll be some blood for some time, so don't get nervous about it. By the way, he opened his eyes a short while ago, but then drifted back into unconsciousness. But he'll wake up soon. He probably had a mild concussion, but his neuro signs are good." More reassuringly he added, "Don't worry, Mrs. Harkins. He's not completely out of the woods yet, but he'll make it. Call me if you have any questions. The nurses know how to get a hold of me. Good day." With that, the doctor went briskly down the hall.

Ann Marie gave vent to a colossal sigh. "I guess I'm relieved he's going to be alright. Of course, if he was fooling around with another woman, he may wish he stays in the coma." She sat down at her husband's side and finger-combed his rumpled hair. "My problem is, I don't know what to say to him. I'm glad he's okay, of course, but did he kill my father, like the police think? Did he cheat on me with some blonde chick? Should I be nice to him or tell him to rot in hell? I feel like my life is all twisted."

Susan motioned her to step out into the hallway. Susan placed her arm around Ann Marie's shoulders as they walked. "The nurse at the desk was telling me one of their nurse researchers interviewed over a hundred people after they came back from a coma or unconsciousness. Supposedly, when people are unconscious, they may be able to hear, even though they can't respond. A lot of those patients heard what was being said about them, like being called a vegetable. I wouldn't say anything you don't want John to hear."

At the drink machine, Ann Marie declined her offer for a soda. Susan inserted a dollar bill and selected a Diet Coke. "Your conflicts are understandable, Ann Marie. This is a confusing time for you. But right now, John is still in a precarious health situation. The best course of action you can take is to say only things that will help him get better. Once he's recovered, then you can deal with these other issues."

Ann Marie nodded thoughtfully. "You're right. I'm going to go back in and be with my husband. My daughter can pick me up later. Thanks for bringing me here, Dr. Kemper."

"My pleasure, but please call me Susan." She sipped the tepid soda. "Ann Marie, before you go back in his room, I have a question. In your father's den, there was an empty space on the bookcase near the window. The space was on the second shelf down. It looked like there had been something there formerly, but we can't tell what it could have been. The missing item might be important in investigating your father's murder."

Ann Marie chewed her bottom lip in thought. "Gosh, I don't remember. My father didn't let people in that room unless he was in it, too. A decorator did the decorating, then he moved his stuff in, and we weren't allowed in. I don't know which are the decorator's touches and which are my father's. I bet I was only in that room two or three times. Sorry I can't be more help, Susan."

"Not a problem, Ann Marie. You've got a lot on your mind. We'll figure it out.

You take care of John *and* yourself, you hear?"

Susan hugged Ann Marie warmly and watched her go back into her husband's room. She took her cell phone from her clutch purse as she headed for the main hospital entrance.

"Tom? Susan. Hi! Got some good news from the hospital. They're taking John to surgery, but it looks like he's going to be okay."

"That's a relief. I'm going to talk with Freidan's wife, Marjorie, now but I'm heading back to my office to get ready for some clients I'm seeing tomorrow. How about grabbing a bite tomorrow night to go over the case?"

"Sounds good, as long as it's not hospital cafeteria food. I took a look and they have all this fried stuff and clumpy macaroni and cheese. My arteries started clogging from just looking!"

"How about Chips out on the lake? I could use some fish. It's supposed to be brain food. And the way this case is going, I'm going to need all the brain power I can get." Danford had been to Chips many times with Beth; this would be his first time there without her. Somehow, dining there with Susan felt right. He resolved not to overanalyze the situation and let it take its natural course.

"Love the place! See you there around six tomorrow. Bye." As Susan hung up, an ecstatic grin bloomed on her face. Lunch with Peggy and dinner with Tom tomorrow. Life didn't get any better than that!

9

Danford sat next to Marjorie Freidan on the living room settee as she continued to sob quietly. Even in her disconsolate state, it was easy to tell she was a handsome woman, probably in her early sixties, Danford guessed. Her hair was short, an attractive light blond color styled with not a hair out of place. Even under these circumstances, she was impeccably dressed. Tom remembered once going with his wife, Beth, to a store called St. John's. Beth thought the clothes to be too expensive, but Tom had been impressed with the understated elegance of those clothes. He was sure Mrs. Freidan was wearing a St. John blue top and pants. She impressed him as a gentile woman but accustomed to getting her own way and always being the best-dressed woman in the room, be it an upscale restaurant or a holiday ball.

"Mrs. Freidan, I know this is a tough time for you. But right now, your memories of today's events are the strongest they will be ever be. I apologize for this intrusion on your grief, but I need to ask you some questions, if I may?"

"Please, call me Marjorie. I don't know anything that could possibly help you," Mrs. Freidan sniffled. "I was in bed."

"Just tell me what you do remember."

"All right, I'll try. I knew John and Michael were having breakfast today and going over some tax papers. Michael always is up at six and turns on the coffee. I had left homemade apple coffee cake for them

37

on the counter, and there was fruit in the 'fridge. I like to sleep until around eight, so I let the men take care of themselves. I was aware of Michael getting up, but I fell back to sleep."

"That's good, Mrs. Freidan…Marjorie. Then what happened?"

"I heard a loud noise, like a car backfiring, then the noise of a car motor. I was half asleep and didn't think too much about it. Then I heard John's frantic voice on the phone, calling 911, and then him calling me. That's when I knew something had happened and I got up. When I came downstairs, John was checking Michael for a pulse. Then the police and ambulance came. I can't believe he's dead!"

Marjorie uttered a plaintive cry that came from her soul, blew her nose noisily and continued. "John wouldn't have done that to Michael. I'm adamant on that point. He's just not that kind of person. Besides, Michael always said he didn't have much backbone and didn't like him for that reason. But who *would* do this? Who would come to the house and gun my Michael down in cold blood? Oh, my God!" She collapsed against Danford's arm, sobbing hysterically.

Danford tried awkwardly to comfort the grieving widow and was relieved to see Marjorie's sister, Helen Quinn, in the doorway. She looked like a younger version of Marjorie, with more flamboyant clothes, black capris and a tied black and white striped shirt.

Danford rose to shake Mrs. Quinn's hand. "Mrs. Quinn, thank you so much for coming. Marjorie, just one more thing," Danford said, seating himself in a Queen Anne chair to make room on the settee for Helen. "One of the shelves in the den has a conspicuously empty space that seems to suggest something is missing. Do you have any idea what that might be?"

Marjorie glared at Danford in disbelief as she took her sister's comforting hand. "Mr. Danford, I don't *care* what is missing. Nothing was more important than my husband, and now he's gone."

Tom could feel her pain. For a moment it threw him back emotionally to the day Beth had died. How important could the missing item be? Perhaps very important, he reminded himself. But was it worth pushing Marjorie to find out? He couldn't lead her into the den, where her husband's lifeless body still lay. Being as specific as possible would be the best tack, he decided, in order to avoid that choice.

"Marjorie, I wouldn't be so insistent if I didn't think it might be crucial in tracking down Michael's killer," Danford said with equanimity. "There's an empty space on the bookcase nearest the window. It's the second shelf down."

"Mr. Danford, I don't *know* and I don't *care* what's on the second shelf down. Michael didn't like anyone going into his den. He had a lot of confidential papers there and locked the room when he wasn't using it. I simply don't remember what's in the den, and I *can't* go in there. I just can't."

Danford patted Marjorie's hand and strode into the hall. Away from the sisters' earshot, he allowed himself a muted *damn*. If the killer took what was on that shelf, it could be the most important piece of information in the case. But if no one recollected what was missing, the point was moot. Then an idea hit him.

Jennings was just closing up his bag as Danford entered the den.

"We're done in here, Tom. The body will be on its way to the morgue for an autopsy in a minute. Something I can help you with?"

"I'm trying to figure out what was in the empty space on that shelf," Danford said, nodding toward the bookcase. "Any clues there?"

"We took pictures and dusted everything for prints. Those shelves had a lot of regular household dust on them. Whatever was there, from the clean spot in the middle of the dust, the object had a round base about five inches in diameter. That's all I can tell you. How about the wife? Does she remember what was there?" Jennings asked helpfully.

"Nope, I drew a big goose egg there. She rarely goes in this room, and I couldn't very well force her to right now, under the circumstances. I thought I'd look around and see if there were pictures of people taken while they were in this room. Maybe the object shows up."

"Brilliant notion, counselor. I'll help you look."

Danford and Jennings started to search on opposite ends of the room. A picture of Michael Freidan standing near the bookcase with his arm around a young man of about twenty caught Danford's eye. He strained to identify an indistinct object that occupied the now empty space.

"Dick, here's a picture. Can your guys blow up whatever this is? It looks like a sculpture of some sort."

Jennings came over to Danford's side and nodded his head. "It does look like a sculpture, maybe a bust. Strange thing to be missing. Any idea who the kid in the picture is?"

"Favors Freidan—maybe his son," Danford said. He tried to remember what he knew about Michael Freidan's family. Somewhere in the back of his mind, he seemed to recall some scandal concerning the son, but the details were hazy.

"Thanks for everything, Dick. Will you send me over a blow up of that picture as soon as you can?"

"Sure thing, counselor," Jennings said with a genial salute as he removed and bagged the photograph. "Always glad to help."

Danford was hoping he could exit the crime scene without running afoul of Lukowski when he heard a familiar Chicago accent behind him.

"Leaving so soon, counselor? I thought maybe we'd have time for coffee," the detective roared.

Danford wanted desperately to say, "With you, never," but held his tongue. He didn't want to get on Lukowski's bad side—not that there was really a good side to speak of.

"Thanks for the invite, but I have a lot of work to do on this case."

"Suit yourself," Lukowski shrugged. He laughed smugly as a shark-like grin played across his wide face. "You know your boy did this. We're going to nail him. The victim's blood was on his shirt. I'm sure those are his prints on the gun. Picture of him and the blonde clutched in the old man's hand. Father-in-law caught him cheating on his wife, the vic's daughter. We got him cold. 'Fraid you won't get much of a fee out of this one. It will be a slam dunk for the DA. Makes life easy on us on the law side of the equation."

Danford was livid. "Don't tell me you're already closing the investigation, Lukowski. What about other people who might have wanted Michael Freidan dead? He wasn't the nicest guy in town."

"You want us to waste the taxpayers' money so you can collect your fat fees? Don't be ridiculous," Lukowski chortled. "We got your guy dead to rights. No sense beating a dead horse. The DA will have a field day with this one. Too bad for you."

Danford's fist itched. He knew he could fell the tree-sized detective with a hard left to his fat gut and a roundhouse right to his temple. The penalty would probably be instant disbarment. It would almost be worth the risk. It would be more satisfying to put on the gloves and whip Lukowski's ass in public. It was a spectacle Danford was confident that Lukowski's long list of enemies would pay good money to see.

"But Stan, you know as well as I do that the picture of my client and the mystery blonde could have been photo shopped," Danford protested.

"Didn't look like it. No sense in spending time and money checking either. Nope, it all points to your boy. See you in court, counselor," Lukowski crowed as he strutted out to his car.

It was bad news that Lukowski considered the case a done deal; it meant any further investigation would fall to his office. Danford realized his earlier remark to Susan about needing all the help he could get had been prophetic.

The attorney called Susan's home number on his cell hoping to reach her sons, Phillip and Jeff. Both had helped him out with investigative work before. "Phillip? You and Jeff got time for some detective work? Great. Meet me at my office at eight tomorrow."

10

En route to meeting Peggy for lunch the next day, Susan felt obligated to let Frank know he was on his own for dinner that Monday night. The Neanderthal notion of having to issue her husband regular phone bulletins regarding her whereabouts rankled Susan no end. For that reason, she didn't feel guilty about not telling Frank the entire truth about her working dinner with Tom. It was the only way to prevent Frank from having one of his childish conniption fits. Frank's office would be closed for lunch so Susan knew she could reach him on his cell phone. She pulled up that number on her cell and pushed send, resigned to yet another argument about her activities outside her home and office.

"Where are you?" As usual, Frank's voice was tinged with control.

"I'm having lunch with Peggy, seeing a few clients in my office and then heading over to meet Tom to go over the case I told you about last night." Susan hoped Frank didn't notice her elimination of where she and Tom were meeting. "I doubt I'll be home in time to make dinner tonight."

"Huh. Phillip and Jeff are meeting Tom at eight, too, in his office. Looks like he's taking over my whole family," said Frank sarcastically. "Meanwhile, Phillip's having dinner with Mark, and Jeff's having pizza with Judy. I've got half a mind to call a hot nurse for dinner, since my family's too busy for me."

"How about if I stop at Chips after I meet with Tom and pick up something for you?" *Shit, why had she gone and brought up Chips?* The half-truths were coming fast and furious. Susan had to remind herself of the innocence of her dinner date with Tom. It was strictly business, after all, wasn't it?

"Chips! That sounds good to me. How about I meet you there?"

Susan had to think fast. "I won't be that hungry."

"Okay, just don't be too late. You know how I hate a late supper."

"I should be home by seven-thirty," replied Susan.

"That's a little late. Can you make it six-thirty?"

Susan fought to quell the anger that these conversations always brought to the surface. "Frank, I'll be home as soon as I can," she said simply and powered off her cell. Part of her wished he would call one of the nurses.

300 East in the Dilworth section of Charlotte was a favorite lunchtime haunt of busy professional women like Susan and Peggy. When the weather was nice, Susan preferred to sit outside on the patio at one of the intimate tables with festive tablecloths and surprisingly comfortable metal chairs. The patio was lovely, with huge planters overflowing with bright pink impatiens. There was a bird feeder hanging from a large tree near a bubbling water fountain where, to Susan's great delight, a variety of birds frolicked. Today, however, Susan wanted more privacy. She asked to be seated on the right side of the restaurant, where the wide oak booths with high backs were perfect for what Susan called 'private conversational dining.'

As she waited for Peggy to arrive, Susan had an iced tea, since it was too early for a glass of wine, and ruminated about how much she liked the Charlotte area, the Dilworth community in particular. It was a friendly place, yet sophisticated, close to the Mint Museum, her favorite place for an afternoon change of pace. She particularly enjoyed the exhibit of the fashions during the 19th century. Of course, current fashions were always available for viewing and purchase at nearby South Park Mall at Nordstrom's, Neiman Marcus, Chicos and a host of Susan's other favorite stores.

She had not always lived in Charlotte. When she was born, her parents were living at Gulls Point, a beach community close to Mystic, in Connecticut. They moved to Charlotte when she was nine. Gulls Point was still in her blood, though. Every summer, she and the boys—and Frank, too, if he could be dragged away from his practice and his coin collection—spent a month there in a small beach house Susan had inherited when her parents died. It was rented out the rest of the year when possible.

Suddenly, Susan's thoughts went south. She was worried about her marriage; her fights with Frank had become more frequent and more intense. Their failing relationship preyed constantly on her mind. She thanked her lucky stars she had a friend like Peggy to share her troubles with. Even a psychologist, Susan knew, could benefit invaluably from a friend's perspective. Peggy knew her better then anyone and was always honest with her.

She had met Peggy when they were in prenatal class together as Susan prepared for the birth of her first son, Phillip. Characteristically, Frank was always too busy to be bothered to attend; he insisted he already knew the information. Peggy's husband, Bruce, who was also a doctor, was by Peggy's side for every class. Together, they acted as Susan's coaches and the three had become fast friends. Peggy was a nurse manager on a medical-surgical floor at Carolina Medical Center. She had a good handle on how to manage situations. She also knew Frank, personally and professionally.

When Susan saw Peggy standing near the maitre de's stand, her spirit buoyed. She hailed her friend from the booth with an exuberant wave of her hand.

"Hey, girlfriend," said Peggy. "Love your outfit!"

"Thanks, Peg, I needed that. Frank didn't appreciate it. He had a hissy fit about it. Said I looked like a hooker. Can you *believe* that?"

"Face it, Frank's a jerk," Peggy said bluntly. "Tell him to grow up and be supportive, instead of fighting with you at every turn. It's not like your house is a mess or you don't cook all the time. You just want to do something with your life. Remember when we went to the Vernon Grant exhibit in Rock Hill?"

"Sure. The illustrator who created Snap, Crackle, and Pop for Kellogg's. That was a fantastic exhibit."

"Definitely. He was a fantastic artist, and we were both affected by his passion for yearning to *do something* with his life. You have that passion, too, Susie-Q."

"You're right, Peggy. I remember hearing a speech once by Ann Richards—"

"Wasn't she the governor of Texas?"

"Right, back in the nineties. One smart and funny lady. Anyway, in one of her speeches, she had said she didn't want, 'I kept a clean house' on her tombstone. I want to make a difference with my life, too.

"Suze, you can make a difference with this forensic stuff. *Go for it!* Don't forget, you supported Frank through the tough times in his medical career. It's time for him to support you. What's wrong with that man? You want me to have Bruce talk with him? You know how supportive Bruce is."

"If Bruce wants to take a go at Frank, that would be fine. I'm desperate for a solution."

The waitress took their orders. Susan ordered a chicken sandwich. Peggy, always weight-conscious, ordered a grilled chicken sandwich. Both had unsweetened tea.

Her friend's straight talk reassured Susan, but even Peggy didn't know everything that went on in her marriage. If she did, Susan knew Peggy would tell her to leave Frank. Susan no longer went to church regularly, but her Catholic upbringing formed the core of her value system. Divorce was unthinkable.

"So what else is going on with you?" asked Peggy. "You sure looked troubled."

Susan sighed. "Well, there are two things. You know that I love my boys. I've loved every minute of raising them, but they're grown up now. Phillip is graduating from law school this year, and Jeff will be graduating from college. It was great fun decorating the house and planting the garden, but other than an occasional tweaking, all that's done, too."

She paused. Maybe it was time to confide in Peggy about something else. "It's not only that I like the forensic hypnosis, I also like working with Tom."

Peggy let loose a comical whoop. "Wow, girlfriend! You're interested in Tom Danford? That's news! When did all this happen? More details! You've been holding out on me."

"Cool your jets. Nothing's happening. I just like working with him, that's all. We get along well, we work well together, and we even have some fun. What I was trying to say before is, what held me at home is not there anymore. The boys are grown. The house is as perfect as it's going to get. I just don't feel connected with Frank. We fight all the time. He does his thing and I do mine. I don't know what to do about it."

"Tough problem. Knowing you, being Catholic is making you stay with him. I remember going to a workshop once when the instructor said in any given situation, you always have one of three choices; you can flee, flow, or fight. From what you've been saying, you and Frank have chosen to fight. To quote Dr. Phil, 'How's that working for you?'"

Susan laughed so hard, she nearly snorted. "Not well, not well."

Their lunches had arrived. Peggy put her palms together and said in a TV evangelist voice, "Good bread, good meat, good God, let's eat!"

"Peggy!"

"You said there were *two* things? What was the other one, Susan? Is it related?"

Peggy never missed a trick. "This is more difficult to talk about. I'm worried you're going to think I've flipped out."

"Put that to rest. I already think that, but I still love you and consider you my best friend."

Susan smiled. "Okay, here goes. Something different is happening to me now when I hypnotize witnesses. As you know, in a traditional hypnosis session, before hypnotizing a client I do an assessment to evaluate their problem. While in hypnosis, I help these clients visualize their lives changing in a more positive direction. Then, I give them suggestions about how their life is going to change. Many hypnotists also go into hypnosis with their clients. Here's the strange part, when I hypnotize these patients, I also go into hypnosis, but when I do, I see what they say. If I say, for example, go to a safe place, a place of comfort. I don't tell them where to go. I leave that decision to them, but I can see where they are. If they go to their grandparents' house, I know it before they tell me, because I've seen the place."

"I'm with you so far. I always knew you were a little psychic!"

"When I hypnotize witnesses, it's a slightly different situation. I tell them I'm going to put them into hypnosis, and then I'll bring them back to the time the event occurred. After that, it's the client that leads the discussion about what they saw or heard or smelled."

"So far it's not terribly weird."

"Okay, so here's the weird part. As I said earlier, I go into hypnosis when I put my patients under hypnosis. With the witnesses, not only do I go into hypnosis, *I also see the crime scene.* They're talking to me and describing what's going on, but they don't need to do that. As soon as they're transported hypnotically to the locale in question and start recalling the events, I have a shared vision of their experiences. In fact, probably because I have had more experience concentrating in hypnosis situations, sometimes I can see details they can't see."

Peggy was thoroughly intrigued. "Give me an example so I can be sure I'm getting what you are saying."

"Remember the kidnapping case?"

Peggy nodded.

"I hypnotized the witness who saw the van drive by her house the morning of the kidnapping. While she was describing the van, I could see the van and the men myself, as clear as day. She focused on the orange decal with the big letter E on the driver's windshield. She couldn't make out the writing on the bottom of the decal. However, I could read those words as clearly as if they were on a high-def TV. I knew the decal said Everett Concrete Company underneath the letter."

Peggy mimicked a few bars of *The Twilight Zone* theme. "Wow, Susie-Q, you have a gift! That's not weird, it's great."

"Yes and no. It's a gift no one will believe. In the case of the kidnapping, it didn't matter. The letter E on an orange sticker was enough for everyone to recognize it as the Everett company's logo. I didn't have to say I could read the text underneath the letter, even though the witness couldn't see it."

"Is there a scientific name for this ability?" Peggy asked excitedly. "Is anyone else able to do this?"

"Through the Internet I found these two parapsychology organizations in New York City. The people who work there gave me some good books to read and answered many of my questions. As far as I can tell, it's something like a shared consciousness or telepathy. Husbands and wives sometimes connect this way. Sometimes a mother and child can tell what the other is thinking. But this is a little different. Telepathy is thought transference. This is a visual phenomenon. One of the parapsychologists said to not be surprised if I have more of these experiences. Once 'a psychic center' opens up, people tend to have more and more of these experiences."

"I still don't see how this is a problem."

"I can't lead the person I'm hypnotizing by suggesting what to visualize at a crime scene, even though I'm seeing it with crystal clarity. All these sessions are videotaped. The courts will throw out the testimony if they see I'm leading the witness. So, if I see something that a hypnotized witness can't see clearly, ethically speaking, I have to tell the police or someone like Tom. And who in their right mind is going to believe me?"

"I feel your pain, girlfriend. I can just see you trying to explain that kind of vision to Stan Lukowski. He'd want you burned at a stake. Have you told anyone else about this?"

"I tried to explain it to Frank. He just went on about how his mother, when she was dying, saw his dead father. He said all this kind of talk just gave him the creeps."

"I'm assuming you haven't said anything to Tom?"

"God, no! I'm trying to establish some credibility with him and the police. I don't want him thinking I'm a wacko!"

"So far, has this ability caused any problems?"

"No, not yet."

"Then here's what I'd suggest," Peggy said, brandishing her fork for emphasis. "Consider this vision a gift from God. Some people, including me, would say it's a sign for you to continue your work in forensic hypnosis. You can help with crime investigation in a way other people can't. You know from your training when to draw the line at not leading witnesses when they're under your spell. When you *do* see something the witness can't see clearly and it's important, deal with that situation then. You and I are good at coming up with ways out of tight situations. We'll just deal with the problem then. How does that sound?"

"That makes sense." Susan felt her shoulders relaxing. She hadn't realized all the tension she'd been carrying around. "Thanks, Peggy, you're a good friend."

"How kind of you to notice! Now that we have that problem solved, I have another earth-shattering question."

"Yessss?"

"Are we splitting the fried banana roll for dessert?"

Both women laughed heartily.

"Definitely!" said Susan.

11

Susan's elder son, Phillip, and Mark Everett had been constant companions since grammar school. As close as brothers, they had only been separated when Phillip went off to college and Mark joined his father's concrete business, the Everett Concrete Company.

Both men were in their early twenties. At six foot two, Mark was the taller of the two, with dark hair and brown eyes so dark, unwitting women who gazed into them felt like they were slipping into an abyss. He had broad shoulders, a slim waist, and muscles bulging under his shirt. There were few young women in the Myers Park section of Charlotte that didn't know who Mark Everett was and who didn't want to date him.

Phillip was slighter than Mark but had a more energetic air. His thoughtful eyes were deep brown and alive like his mother's. Phillip was good looking, too, but in a more boyishly handsome way than Mark. After only a few minutes with Phillip, women formed the impression he was nice, smart, and trustworthy. Women might notice Mark first, but most soon saw Phillip as the better choice for a long-term, stable relationship. So far, neither had settled down with one woman.

Phillip was on top of the world as he guided his red Civic this evening into a parking space at Pollack's Restaurant. He was ecstatic to be working with Tom Danford again. The money was good, and the real-life experience was better than any moot court law school could provide.

Mark was waiting for him outside. Pollack's was a favorite eating place for their regular dinner get together. It had a rustic look, dark cedar shingles and huge wooden door at the entrance. Its specialty was casual dining and stick-to-your-ribs country cooking. The hearty beef recipes were a favorite with the men even on a hot August day like this one.

"You look particularly cheery," Mark said as they were seated. "Some woman take pity on you and agree to go out on a date?"

"I'd be doing cartwheels if that happened. No, I'm going to help Tom Danford with a case. Jeff, too."

"It wouldn't be that murder in Meadow Lakes, would it? Everybody in Myers Park is all shook up over it."

"That's the one. Let's order so you can tell me what's going on with you, too. Hey, they've got the short ribs special tonight!" Phillip said, spotting a tent card on the table. "I can taste them now with those mashed potatoes and gravy."

"Works for me!" Mark concurred.

Presently a well-endowed college girl arrived with menus and silverware. "Good afternoon, gentlemen," she cooed as she crouched beside the table, offering Phillip and Mark an unspoiled view of her breasts in a shirt that was too low cut for the manager's comfort. "See anything you like?" Her Southern accent was almost comically broad.

Mark took the bait. "Well, yes, but unfortunately, my friend and I are on a new-fangled diet," he drawled, imitating her. "We like what you're a showin' us sure 'nough, but I'm a-feared we can't have any white meat."

Phillip snickered. "That's right. But we might want some cantaloupe for dessert."

"Funny boys," said the waitress, standing up. "I meant, do you see anything on the *menu* you'd like to *order.*"

"Shorts ribs special all around and beer," Mark said. "And keep 'em coming. The beer, that is."

"Be out shortly," the waitress responded curtly and sashayed toward the kitchen.

"Nice rack, but no sense of humor," said Mark.

"Amen. Busy day today?" asked Phillip.

When they were younger, there had never been any need to prime the conversation pump with Mark. But sometime when Phillip was away at college, Mark had changed. He seemed more guarded, like he was holding something back. The spontaneity they had always had in their conversations was missing.

"For a change, yes. My dad's having a meeting today to firm up plans for the grand opening of a new phase of the business. For the last few years, he's been working on developing this new department. You know him. He's a steamroller when he gets going. We've been putting in sidewalks and driveways for ages. Now we'll be doing patios and hoity-toity stuff like birdbaths, concrete steps for the garden, and God only knows what else."

The waitress brought the beers, set them down unceremoniously, and departed.

Mark lifted his pinky as he slurped his beer. "Yep, we're moving into the decorating business," he said with a sissified lisp.

Phillip looked at his friend with mock seriousness. "So, do I call you Marcella now?"

"No, you call me president of Everett Design. They wanted to call it Everett Décor, but I stopped that fast. Can you imagine the ribbing I'd take?"

Phillip guffawed. "Congratulations, bro. That's a far cry from driving those concrete trucks! Don't tell me your dad is going soft these days?" He had worked for the Everett Concrete Company on summer break from college and knew what a tough man Mark's father could be.

"Ever since my mom died, Dad's been different. At first, he wouldn't talk to anyone. He only worked. Man, he was weird. He'd grunt a hello in the morning and that was it. Then one day—I don't think I ever told you this—he said he saw my mother at the foot of his bed. He said it wasn't a dream. I thought he'd lost it. She told him she was fine and that he needed to pay attention to the people around him. He changed overnight, became more human. I would have told him to go to a shrink, but he was nicer than he'd ever been. He'd always been a son-of-a-bitch, and now he was like a real father. He sat me down and said to forget about the past trouble I had gotten into. We had to move forward. Then he let me into the officer's club of the business." Mark shrugged. "Go figure."

Phillip sniggered ruefully. "I remember those youthful fuck-ups all too well. Remember when you and Tim dragged me into turning around the street signs at the beach? We were what sixteen? Seventeen? We must have turned twenty of them. The renters and visitors couldn't find the right streets. The police showed up at my place, telling my mother I was the ringleader. She was furious. She threatened to sell the beach house at Gulls Point. I thought my brother was going to kill me."

"She called my mother and Tim's," said Mark, taking up the story. "That was only the first or second time we all had rented a cottage there to be together that summer. I was grounded for a week, but I think Tim got the tongue-lashing of his life and was grounded for the rest of the summer. Man, his mother was scary, wasn't she? The only thing the three of us were allowed to do that week was to turn those street sign back the way they were supposed to be.

Phillip grew serious. "Tim went on to bigger and better things, didn't he? I can't believe he got into kidnapping with that jerk from Texas. What was his name? Justin? Jason?"

"Jason Strongweather," offered Mark.

"Yeah, that's it. That summer I worked for your dad and Jason was there working too, I knew he was bad news. Why Tim hung around with him I'll never understand."

"He and I still did things together, but I was dating Sue and wasn't around as much. When he lost the job at the supermarket, I convinced my father to hire him to try and help him out."

"God only knows what you two did when I was away at college." Phillip puffed out his chest and continued teasingly, "I always thought I was the 'restraining force'—or was it the 'voice of reason'—where you two were concerned."

Mark wasn't smiling now. A troubled look clouded his eyes. "Let's just say I did some things I wasn't proud of."

The waitress brought the dinners and asked glacially, "I hope everything is satisfactory, *boys?*"

"Looks fine, doll," Mark drawled again. "We'll moo for you if we need anything else."

Mark and Phillip were silent as they dug into their meals with abandon. When their plates were nearly clean, Phillip leaned back in his chair and said conversationally, "I always thought you acted weird that day of our last camping trip. You were nervous as hell."

"What are you talking about? What camping trip?"

"About three years ago, we went camping in Sesquicentennial National Park and then you drove me to college. I could have sworn you got up in the middle of the night and took the canoe out."

Mark grew visibly nervous. "Where to begin? You have to promise this is between you and me and no one else. Do we have lawyer/client privilege?"

Phillip laughed. "You have my word I won't say anything, but since I'm not a lawyer yet, we don't have privileged communication. Sorry."

"Your word is good. Did you ever hear of the Dismas Houses?" asked Mark.

"Isn't that a rehab facility for juvenile delinquents? St. Dismas is the patron saint of prisoners, if I remember my catechism lessons correctly."

"Yeah, that's the place. There are a number of houses across the country with housefathers that supervise these kids. In Charlotte, they call these places the St. Dismas Houses since they are not connected to the national organization. No one knows who the big guru is behind the organization here in Charlotte, but there's a rumor that in some cases these kids don't get rehab instructions. Some of the housefathers give them lessons in larceny, you might say, setting up these young dudes to commit petty crimes. It's been a problem sorting out the good houses from the bad ones. No one knows who's who in the organization."

"I've heard some rumors about the group. But what's that got to do with you? You didn't ever live there."

"I didn't but Tim did. He and some other kids lived in this one house with a housefather that made them steal and commit other crimes. That's how he got into that kidnapping scheme."

Phillip looked startled. "I can't believe it. Our Tim involved with this group? How did that happen?"

"What Tim told me was, he had lost his job as a clerk at the BI-LO supermarket when it closed. He had no money to pay the rent and he broke into a liquor store after hours. The dumb shit tripped the alarm, of course, and the cops caught him. Since it was his first offense, he was told he could go to prison or one of these Dismas Houses. Tim said it seemed like a sweet deal. He got his own room, three squares a day, and access to a huge rec room with a pool table and a humongous TV. Unfortunately, he was told he had to do some jobs for the guy in charge, or he'd say he wasn't obeying the rules and they'd send him to jail."

"Out-and-out blackmail," Phillip sighed regretfully. "I wish we had known. Maybe we could have done something."

"Wait. It gets better. Before the kidnapping, the group had planned a bank robbery. Tim swears he wasn't involved. But someone in the group shot Tom Danford's wife in the bank."

Phillip's eyes widened as he sat bolt upright. *"What the hell?"*

"Remember, you swore you wouldn't say anything!"

Phillip's face grew ashen. "Right. Go on."

"Tim was told to get rid of the gun used in the robbery—attempted robbery, I should say. That was his initiation task to show he could be a trusted member of the group. Tim came to me with his panties in a wad. He had no idea how to get rid of a hot gun."

"I'm way ahead of you. The camping trip, right?"

Mark nodded. "It was the perfect opportunity. While you were asleep, I took the canoe out and dumped the gun in the middle of the lake. Who would suspect two upright young lads like us?"

"*Us,* did you say *us?*" Phillip's said angrily through gritted teeth.

"I didn't mean it that way. You had nothing to do with this, of course."

"*You* know it and *I* know it, but who else would believe it?" asked Phillip, his anxiety mounting. He leaned across the table and said whispered urgently, "Mark, do you realize what you did? *You're effectively an accomplice to murder.* You could be accused of the crime just as easily as the person who pulled the trigger."

"What?" Mark protested. "I had nothing to do with it."

Phillip continued to speak sotto voce. "Legally, you had a *lot* to do with it. YOU HID THE MURDER WEAPON. That's a felony. Tim is the one who is off the hook. You're the one in trouble and maybe by association, so am I."

"What should I do? You're not going to tell anyone, are you?"

"No, of course not. Let's think about this. Tim's already in jail so he doesn't have anything to lose. But there's plenty at risk for you. Me, too, probably. Usually, I'd talk this over with Tom, but we're talking about the gun that killed his wife. No way in hell he could be objective about all this."

Suddenly Phillip threw his hands down on the table, making a loud smack that drew stares from nearby diners. He looked around sheepishly and hissed at Mark in a seething whisper. *"What were you thinking, Mark? This is a mess!"*

"You don't think I've had my share of angst over this? I wanted to tell you, but I promised Tim I wouldn't say anything. Now that he's in jail, I figure it won't hurt him. I don't see how this is a problem. We'll just leave the gun where it is."

"*We'll* just leave the gun?" Like a two-ton boulder, Phillip could feel the responsibility of his friend's mess being heaped on his shoulders. He was completely innocent, but who would believe he didn't know Mark had had the gun? Who would believe Mark had acted alone in disposing of the gun in the middle of the night, without his best friend's help? *Shit, his law career might be in jeopardy because of Mark's idiot decision!* Phillip's mind raced to possible solutions. If they let sleeping dogs lie, maybe no one will find out. But it was the gun that killed Tom Danford's wife. If the police had it, that might help them catch the murderer. They were honor-bound to follow an ethical course of action.

"Mark," he said finally, "we have to tell Tom Danford what you just told me. It's the best thing—not to mention the right thing—to do."

"No way, man. You just said I could be arrested. No one knows where that gun is but me. No one will ever find it. Let it be."

"I know where it probably is," Phillip reminded Mark. "Maybe we can dive for it and then leave it where the police can find it. That way, they can examine it for evidence—and hopefully even tie it to Mrs. Danford's killing—and we're free and clear."

"How are we going to find it? And if we find it, where are we going to leave it?"

"We'll just have to think it through," Phillip said wearily. His stomach was in knots. "Right now I've got to pick up Jeff and meet Tom at his office."

The waitress appeared, slammed the dinner check on the tabletop, and began collecting the dishes noisily as she recited what sounded like a well-rehearsed speech. "I just want you smartasses to know I'm taking baking and pastry arts at Central Piedmont Community College, my mama's an assistant manager at Wal-Mart, and my daddy's a part-time school bus driver!" She stormed off, leaving a trail of dirty napkins in her wake.

Phillip and Mark looked at each other and burst out in helpless laughter as their tension melted.

"Now what do you suppose put a burr under Elly May's saddle?" Mark deadpanned.

12

Chips was a popular lakeside restaurant on the north side of Lake Norman. Being Monday night, the crowds were thinner. There were still boaters pulling up to the dock after a day on the water for a cold beer and an order of deep-fried catfish. It had a nautical sea motif with shells dominating the landscaping in the front of the building, where most restaurants in the area would have plants or pine needles. The inside sported paintings of boats and weathered fishing gear. Danford arrived before Susan and ordered his usual dry Beefeater martini straight up with ice on the side. He sipped it slowly as he looked out from his booth over Lake Norman. It wasn't dark yet, but the sun was starting to set. He had always felt a strong affinity with the lake and loved being near it, day or night, in sunny or stormy weather. He and Beth had come here almost every Friday night to ring in the weekend.

A flood of memories washed over his weary mind. *The case,* he reminded himself, *I must focus on the case.* So much was still up in the air. What do we know unequivocally? What do we still need to ascertain? He took out his pad and pen and started to write.

Facts:

1. Freidan was killed around 7:00 AM, probably with a bullet from a .38 caliber revolver.

   (Check with ME for time of death and COD, who owned the gun if registered?)

2. Freidan and Harkins had financial papers to discuss.

   (Check with Harkins about nature of papers. Where are they? Was there a briefcase at the scene?)

3. Freidan had a picture of Harkins kissing a blonde woman.

   (Check with crime lab. Fingerprints on picture? Was picture doctored? Who is the blonde? Any background info? (Assign to Phillip/Jeff?)

4. Vacant space on bookcase

   (What was there? Anyone know? What is the image in the picture from the den?) (Assign to Phillip/Jeff?)

5. Personalities (consult with Susan)

   John Harkins—could he kill someone?

   Michael Freidan—relationship with other people? Wife? Daughter? John? Business associates?

As Danford scrawled out his notes, he saw Susan walk in the front door. There was no ignoring the fact that she was a bona fide knockout. Her shoulder length, dark brown hair curled just a little around her heart-shaped face. Her eyebrows nicely accented her almond-shaped blue eyes. She had high cheekbones, exquisite as a super-model's, and full lips other women secretly envied. She was tall and slim with firm, perky breasts and a shapely derrière that drew appreciative glances from men wherever she went.

Smiling broadly, Danford waved her over. It was the first dinner with an attractive woman he had had since Beth died. It felt a little like a date. Maybe it was just the martini, but he felt excited and a little flushed. He knew he'd better be careful. Susan and Frank had their problems, sure, but she *was* still married.

As she sat down, Susan was mesmerized by the exquisite view of the sun sinking into the horizon. Above the shimmering water, a tapestry of pinks, blues, and reds played across the sky. The scene, so achingly romantic, reminded Susan of the Impressionistic paintings she loved so much. A sailboat was crossing in front of a small island, catching the wind just right to ride gracefully into the inlet as twilight gave way to the night.

Susan felt relaxed and pleasantly tired. Being here with Tom felt so natural. She ordered a glass of Pinot Grigio and held it across the table. "A toast, counselor, to a brilliantly successful case," she said.

Danford chinked his martini glass against hers. He didn't want to work. He just wanted to sit and have a pleasant chat with Susan, but this was supposed to be a working dinner. After all, he was on Michael Freidan's dime and the discussion should only concern the case.

"Did you learn anything helpful from Ann Marie?" Danford asked perfunctorily. The waitress appeared. Susan ordered the salmon. Danford chose fish and chips. Susan resisted a strong urge to tease him about the perils of fried food—way too wifely. She plunged into the task at hand. "Ann Marie didn't believe her husband could be having an affair. She detected no signs that anything like that was happening. She also said they were close. She didn't think he could have killed Michael Freidan. My sense is his personality does not fit the profile of someone who would cheat on his wife or conspire to murder anyone.

In technical parlance, I believe the phrase is: He's too wimpy." She flashed her dazzlingly bright teeth. "But I need more info before I can definitely say that. I need to talk to him myself and gauge his potential for violence."

Danford laughed appreciatively; Susan was not only beautiful, she had a great sense of humor. "By the way, I called Phillip. He and Jeff are meeting me in the office later to go over the investigation. Anything about John Harkins you think they should check out?"

"Frank told me Phillip and Jeff were going to meet you. Let me think about how to best profile John. That reminds me, I got a call from Ann Marie on the way over here on John's condition. The docs patched up the fractured femur and the rib that punctured his lung, but he's still got a chest tube in. He regained consciousness after the surgery, but he's still extremely groggy. The doc said tomorrow, maybe, we can talk to him."

"Good. Let's hope I can keep him in the hospital or rehab so Stan Lukowski doesn't get a hold of him. He'd put him in jail, tubes and all."

The waitress arrived with their meals.

"I'm starving!" Susan exclaimed and set upon her food with relish. She felt comfortable. The lake, the good food, the good company—maybe it was too good, she thought guiltily. "Oh, I almost forgot," said Susan, aware she was talking with her mouth full. Frank would have berated her mercilessly; with Tom, it didn't seem to matter. "Ann Marie couldn't identify the mystery item missing from the bookcase."

"By the way, that was a nice pick-up on your part," said Danford, liberally coating his chips with ketchup. "Neither the lab guys nor I would have noticed there was anything special about that shelf. But I got a little lead on it. Thankfully, there was a picture in the den with the object in the background. Dick Jennings said his lab would try to get a blow-up. He's going to call me when it's ready. I'm also hoping he's going to check the picture of Harkins and the blonde to see if it's authentic. That's if Stan Lukowski doesn't stop him. I'm going to see if Phillip or Jeff can find out who she is."

"Ann Marie did say she had a sister in Boston who's a blonde. John had been to Boston not too long ago. I hesitate to show her the photo; could be rough going."

"I'll do that when I get a copy," Danford volunteered. "It's better if you play the nice guy. I can be the heavy. If you have the time, I can use you to profile Michael Freidan, too. I want to know if he'd made any enemies who were pissed off enough to want to kill him."

"Glad to. I can talk with Marjorie. Freidan. She would probably be the best source."

Absorbed in the shoptalk and the pleasure of each other's company, Danford and Susan were unaware of the tense figure standing at their tableside.

"Well, well, well, isn't this cozy," roared an irate Frank Kemper. "My wife having a romantic dinner with another man."

13

The accusatory look in Frank's eye was at once horrifying and repugnant. He stood beside the table, weaving slightly. Danford caught a whiff of whisky and noticed an amber stain on the doctor's shirt. *Great,* he thought, *the bastard's already three sheets to the wind and looking for trouble.*

"It's not what you think," protested Susan. "We're just going over the case."

"So, why did you say you were meeting this prick at the office? I had a hunch you were lying on the phone. This doesn't look much like an office to me. Wine, martini, dinner. Some work you're doing. Bringing me home something from Chips, my foot."

Frank grabbed Susan's wrist roughly. "Let's go. I'm sure Perry Mason doesn't mind paying the bill. You're going home with me."

"Get your hands off me," hissed Susan with a fury she didn't know she had in her, wrenching her arm free. "You sit down and talk like a reasonable human being or get the hell out of here." Her voice shook with anger, but at the same time it was firm, controlled, commanding. She had no idea what Frank might do and was surprised to realize she was past the point of caring.

Frank's gaze traveled coldly between Susan and Danford as he sat down clumsily at the table. "Get me a scotch on the rocks," he yelled at the waiter. "Make it a double."

Susan knew booze wasn't going to help the situation. She knew from hard experience that Frank became belligerent and domineering under the fortification of alcohol. She suspected he probably had a few drinks before he left the house. "You see this?" Susan said, yanking the case notes from under Danford's elbow. "Here's what we've been talking about. We're planning an investigation, not a romantic getaway."

"Humph. You two were looking mighty cozy to me," said Frank. "I haven't seen you smile and laugh like that for a long time. Something's going on between you two, I can smell it." He gulped down the scotch and snapped his fingers for another one.

Frank disgusted Danford. He often wondered why Susan stayed with him. "Maybe if you were less of an asshole, Susan would be happier with you," he said evenly. "You're nothing but a suspicious drunk who takes no responsibility for his own behavior."

"Listen, counselor, even drunk I'm a better man than you. When was the last time you saved a person's life? I do it everyday. All you do is cheat poor saps out of their money." Frank sized Danford up. Physically, he knew he was no match for the hard-bodied lawyer, but he could more than hold his own in a war of words.

Danford would not be baited. "Susan, are you going to be OK with him? I need to be at the office by eight, but I want to make sure you're safe." Danford was loath to leave Susan with Frank, but he feared his presence was only making the situation worse.

"Sure, counselor, take off to meet with my sons," Frank piped in. His face was florid and puffy, his speech slurred. "Guess you've got no compunction about muscling in on a man's family. Would you like the house, too? That way you can have my entire life. Too bad you're not a doctor; you could have my practice, too."

Susan's spirit fell into an abyss of darkness. Her wonderful evening was on the verge of disintegrating into a barroom brawl. Frank's drinking over the years had gotten worse. She hated that Tom was a witness this part of her life; she hoped it wouldn't damage their working relationship. "You go, Tom," she said gently. "I'll be fine. I'll talk with you tomorrow."

Tom stood up, avoiding further eye contact with Frank to avoid a scrap. He was forced to go against a strong instinct to protect Susan, not to leave her. "Bye Susan, I'll talk with you later."

"No, you won't. She's not talking to you again. She's through with this forensic bullshit and through playing footsie with you."

Frank gulped down the rest of his scotch. "Another!" he demanded loudly, pounding the table with his empty glass. Susan shook her head and mouthed "no" at the waiter. He acknowledged her and returned momentarily with the check.

Susan knew her wisest tack would be to prey on Frank's vulnerability. The doctor-patient relationship was holy to him; he would be mortified if his marital problems became fodder for local gossip.

"Frank we're going home," she said decisively. "You're creating a scene. I'm sure you don't want your patients hearing about your dirty laundry in public."

The ploy worked, as Frank visibly relaxed. But too late, Susan saw Danford reach for his wallet.

"Look, you son of a bitch, I pay for my wife's dinner, not you," Frank bleated. "I'll be goddamned, though, if I'll pay for you. Give me that bill," he cried, snatching the check from Danford's hand.

Danford kept his cool. He tossed thirty dollars on the table and walked casually toward the exit.

"There he goes, Susan, your lover boy," Frank crowed. "Not even willing to put up a fight for you. You have lousy taste in men."

Susan felt her gorge rise; she felt on the verge of vomiting. "Yeah, and you were the worse choice I could have possibly made," she muttered, adding two twenties to the pile of money. Frank allowed himself to be hefted from his seat. Susan led him, staggering, to the door.

In the parking lot, Frank fumbled in his pants pockets for the key fob to his blue BMW. "I'll see you at home," he said, trying to activate the keyless remote.

"You're drunk, you fool. I'll drive us home."

"Are you saying I can't handle my liquor? I'm just not good enough for you, am I Susan?"

Susan's conscience toyed momentarily with the decadent notion of letting Frank get in his precious Beemer and kill himself. She maneuvered his weaving bulk to the passenger side of her Acura and installed him in the seat.

By now, the alcohol had hit Frank full force. "There's a good movie with Tom Hanks playing at the Winchester Theater. You wanna go see it?" he said sedately as if nothing had happened.

Susan rolled her eyes. "Let's talk about that tomorrow."

"What was that early movie of his where he was a kid but looked like a grown-up?" said Frank in a childish tone.

"*Big*, Frank," said Susan exasperatedly. "The name of the movie was *Big*."

"Yeah. That was a good 'un. But I think his best movie was *Philadelphia*," Frank giggled.

"Yes, Frank," said Susan patronizingly as she got behind the wheel.

Minutes later, as Susan pulled into her driveway, she remembered how excited they had been to find this two story brick house with the four elegant white columns in front. She had fallen instantly in love with the semi-circular driveway and the magnificent foyer with its cathedral ceiling. The four-bedroom house with its lovely den and welcoming great room, marble fireplace and all, had been part of their dream. How could the early promise of their lives have gone so terribly awry? Maybe it had been the young woman who had died in the hospital one night Frank was on call. He had missed the signs she was bleeding. No one blamed him since her primary doctor misdiagnosed her with appendicitis instead of a bleeding ulcer. But to a conscientious doctor like Frank, her dying on his watch was an unforgivable mistake.

Like a dutiful wife, she got Frank ready for bed. As she was tucking him in, she felt his hand on her waist, pulling her down beside him.

"I love you, Susan," he murmured, kissing her neck. "Let me show you how much."

Susan freed herself with ease. "You love me, alright," she hissed. "You probably ruined the best work opportunity I've ever had. You're a selfish bastard. All you care about is yourself." Her anger came in torrents now. "Having sex is the last thing I want to do with you. Marrying you was the biggest mistake of my life."

Her angry words were lost on Frank. As he snored contentedly, Susan could smell his rank breath polluting the room. To her inexpressible disgust, Susan noticed Frank's flaccid penis peeking out of the fly of his boxer shorts, looking for all the world like a mutant Vienna sausage, comical and defenseless. "Frank," she whispered, "if I weren't afraid of the legal entanglements, I'd show you my best imitation of Lorena Bobbitt right about now."

Susan turned out the light and walked to the guest room.

14

As he drove to pick up Jeff for their meeting with Tom Danford that Monday evening, Phillip's mind was torn in hundred different directions. No matter how he looked at it, the situation with Mark Everett and the incriminating gun was fraught with risk. If he got involved in the gun's recovery, he might as well write off his brilliant law career before it had even started. On the other hand, he owed it to Tom Danford to help him find closure, at last, in the death of his wife. Tom was a great guy—one of the best. He knew his mom was fond of him, too. Phillip knew one thing was certain: He had to pour his guts out to someone or he would lose his mind. Talking with his father was out of the question; he'd just get the usual lecture. *The boy is bad news,* he'd pontificate in that smug way of his. *If I've told you once, I've told you a thousands times to steer clear of that working class trash.*

Phillip pulled in front of Jeff's girlfriend Judy's house and honked his horn. He was still deep in thought when Jeff rapped on the window. Phillip hadn't unlocked the door on the passenger's side.

"Boy, someone is in outer space," Jeff observed. "What's with you, anyway? You look like you're so far out as to be irretrievable." He smiled complacently at his usage of the jaw breaking word.

"Wise ass," said Phillip, punching his brother hard on the arm.

"Now that you've mentioned it, though, there is something on my mind. A big something. You're the brains of the family; maybe you can help your big brother sort out a problem, Mr. 168."

Jeff laughed at Phillip's reference to their scores on the Law School Admission Test. Phillip had scored a 167, which put him in the ninety-sixth percentile of his exam group. Jeff's score was 168, which ranked him in the ninety-seventh percentile and gave him bragging rights. Phillip had teased Jeff about being the brains in the family ever since. Jeff was the life of most parties. He was about 6 feet tall, slender, blonde hair and blue eyes, with a quick sense of humor.

"Okay, big bro, I'm all ears," said Jeff.

Phillip gave Jeff a detailed account of his earlier conversation with Mark Everett.

"Let me see if I have this right. You have legal and ethical concerns about your involvement. If you don't do anything, you've let a suspected murder weapon remain hidden. It doesn't seem like you have a legal responsibility to report what Mark said, since you're not an officer of the courts yet. But, ethically you should do something. If you help Mark find the gun and move it, you *might* be legally culpable for concealing a murder weapon. On the other hand, since you would be moving the weapon from a concealed location to an open one, technically you wouldn't be hiding the weapon. You'd be exposing it. As a legal technicality, how would that fly?"

"Good question," responded Phillip. "I'd have to check it out."

"I have an idea," said Jeff, grinning. "And don't say 'Oh, no' like you usually do.

"Okay, shoot. At this point, I'll even consider one of your dipshit ideas."

Phillip felt his anxiety waning. He didn't want to get Jeff involved, but having a close peer to talk to made him feel a lot better. He trusted Jeff's innate logic and book smarts, not to mention his brotherly love and ability to keep his mouth shut.

"Why not send the police an anonymous tip and tell them where the gun is?" Jeff suggested. "Let them go dredge it up. That way, there's less exposure for you and Mark, the police get the evidence they need, and Tom can get some closure if it helps solve his wife's murder. Everybody's happy."

He paused, his expression grim. "Is there anyway the police could know or find out you and Mark were camping in that area around the time of the bank robbery and the murder of Tom's wife?"

Phillip shook his head. "I don't know how. No one saw us the whole time we were camping. We didn't even decide until we got there where to pitch our tent. Afterwards, Mark took me straight back to school. I don't think he told anyone exactly where we were that night. But that's not a half-bad idea. If we went up there with scuba equipment—even if we could somehow get hold of some—someone would be bound to get suspicious. But if we tip off the police, they can play Jacques Cousteau themselves."

"Not we, bro. Let Mark do it. You need to stay as far away as possible and just cover your ass. Advise him and see what he says. Now all you have to do is think about how the tip should go down. I say Mark's got to type up a message and send it to the cops."

"I don't know about that. Personal computers and printers leave too much of a trail. How about doing it the old-fashioned way? Cutting text out of a newspaper? He can do that at home with gloves on. Newspaper is nondescript and it's just about impossible to trace."

"It's always worked for serial killers and kidnappers, so I'm sold," said Jeff. "But what are you going to have him say?"

"How about something like, '"Gun in lake off Sumner Point at Sesquicentennial State Park. Used in shooting.'"

"Perfectamundo. But don't write it out for him," warned Jeff. "Tell him in person or over the phone, but don't leave a message. You don't want to do anything to implicate yourself." Jeff reveled in the legal ring of his statement.

"Who should he send it to?" asked Phillip. "I'd like to avoid that prick Stan Lukowski getting a hold of it."

"How about Jay Owens, the chief of police? He always seemed pretty stalwart."

Phillip chuckled. "*Stalwart?* What did you do, swallow a thesaurus? Good thought, though. Thanks, Jeff, for helping me think this through. It means a lot to me. Making a bad step in a mess like this could screw up my life."

"True that, dawg," said Jeff good-humoredly.

"Mark, it's Phillip. Call me when you get this message. On second thought, I'll be busy for the next two hours. Call me after that. Later."

Jeff had always kept his opinion of Mark to himself. He had put his dislike of him down to a nagging jealousy of his brotherly friendship with Phillip, but there was also something *insidious* about the guy. Now he realized his instincts had been right.

Mark Everett was trouble with a capital T.

15

Tom Danford's office was downtown Charlotte on East Trade Street close to the courthouse. Some referred to the general area as Vampire Lane since there were many lawyers in the area. Tom was lucky though to have a one-man office with a suite of three rooms. The cheery reception area and his office, which he had decorated with a few of his favorite Winslow Homer wood engravings, had the same off-white, grass cloth wallpaper. It was the library, though, that his clients always commented on. The deep cherry wood paneling, with bookcases on three walls, gave the room an ambience of comfort and peacefulness. A large conference table stood majestically in the middle of the room, surrounded by distinctly masculine wooden chairs with black leather seats and backs.

Danford arrived ahead of Phillip and Jeff at 7:45. He was glad to have a few minutes to compose himself before they arrived. The confrontation with Frank had unnerved him. Was he really guilty of subconsciously trying to take over the Kemper family, as Frank had suggested? If so, Frank was only fighting for what was rightfully his, and who could blame him?

He liked Susan and the boys; he had always just thought of them as part of his work life. Still, there was no denying that his dinner with Susan had had all the ingredients of a great first date. He liked her smile, her laugh, the way that one strand of hair fell over her eye.

There had even been that electric tingle of excitement when their hands touched as they traded documents. *Red flag on the play, counselor!* Guiltily, he acknowledged to himself that he was playing with fire with another man's wife, and damn it all, it was exciting as hell!

He heard voices in the hall and ushered Jeff and Phillip into the conference room.

"Hi, guys. Good to see you," he said warmly, shaking their hands. "Ready to get down to work?"

"Ready, willing and able. What do you have for us?" said Jeff enthusiastically.

"Ditto, counselor," said Phillip.

"Great. Y'all know that Michael Freidan was found shot to death this morning. What you don't know are some of the other pertinent details, so I'll bring you up to speed. John Harkins, the deceased's son-in-law, hired me to defend him. John found Michael, moved the gun to turn him over to do CPR. It was too late for heroic measures, so he called 911.

When the police arrived, he was smeared with the victim's blood and his fingerprints were on the murder weapon. The worst part of it, though, is a picture of John kissing a blonde, discovered in the dead man's hand. Stan Lukowski, the detective in charge, ordered John to be arrested. John panicked and was struck by a car as he fled the crime scene. He's in the hospital, semiconscious but expected to recover. I had time to ask him if he was having an affair before he was hit. He denied it. I have to admit, I believe him. I didn't have a copy of the picture at the time to show him."

"Wow," said Phillip. "This is messy."

"Damn straight," agreed Tom. "I need you fellows to get answers to some questions. Here's what we need to know: One, who is the blonde in the photograph?

Two, is the picture a composite or a true image? And three, presuming John Harkins' innocence, who actually would have a motive to kill Michael Freidan?"

"Gotcha," said Jeff. "Anything else?"

"Yeah, there's one other thing. There's an object missing from the bookshelf in the den where Freidan was killed. Your mother was the one who noticed that. The crime lab has a picture with said object in the background. The techs are going to enlarge it for us. Neither Michael's wife nor his daughter could recall what this object was."

"Is Dick Jennings from the crime lab involved in the case?" asked Phillip.

"Thankfully, yes. It was bad luck drawing Lukowski on this deal, but hopefully Dick Jennings being involved will offset that disadvantage. Lukowski said he'd stop the crime lab from 'wasting the taxpayers' money' on further investigation, since he's sure John Harkins killed Michael Freidan."

"Lukowski just wants to mark this one closed," Phillip interjected. "He doesn't seem to care *how* he wraps up a case, just as long as he gets credit for doing it. He'll block any investigation that might lead to evidence that's contradictory to the conviction of his suspect."

"So it seems, so it seems," Danford smiled. He admired Phillip's astuteness. "Whatever is going on with Lukowski, we have our work cut out for us. You both know your mother is working on this case, too. I'd like to coordinate what we're all doing so we're not tripping over each other. Your mother will be talking with John Harkins to prepare a profile on him. So far, he doesn't seem to have it in him to commit murder, but all the same she needs to talk to him.

We're also looking for witnesses she can hypnotize. Michael Freidan's widow, Marjorie, was in the house and heard some noise. Your mother will be talking with her about what she heard this morning and about her son-in-law's relationship with her husband. She'll also be talking to John Harkin's wife, Ann Marie. As she accumulates information, she'll feed it back to me. There may then be more work for you two later, depending upon what we learn. Capeesh?"

The Kemper brothers nodded in agreement.

"In the meantime, though, we can start in other areas. Phillip, since you have your investigator's license, how about finding out what you can about the blonde in the picture? Right now, Dick Jennings has it. Even Lukowski can't stop him from giving us a copy, but he may try to hinder Dick from checking on its authenticity. Dick said he'd check it out, but that was before Lukowski saw it. Let me see if he's in the lab now. Maybe you could pick up the copy and any reports about the picture."

Danford made his call. "Dick Jennings, please. Hi, Dick. Tom Danford here. Glad I caught you. Any chance you duplicated that picture of John Harkins and the blonde? I 'preciate it. Phillip Kemper will be down to pick it up tomorrow. How about its authenticity? Gotcha, being verified now. How about the blow-up of the mystery object on the bookcase? That ready, too? I owe you big for this. See you later, Dick." Danford grinned and gave Phillip a thumb's up.

"I'll go first thing tomorrow morning," Phillip said.

"Great. Jeff, your assignment is to check out the object that was on the shelf. Get the picture from your brother. I want to know everything about it. What is it? What's it worth? Who bought it? Your mom might find out more about it, too, from her conversations with Marjorie Freidan and her daughter once we positively identify it."

"Sure thing, boss."

"The usual retainer still work for you guys?" Danford asked as he took out his checkbook.

"Counselor, you know we'd work gratis for you anytime," Jeff said jokingly, delighting in his lawyerly vocabulary.

"Is that so?" Danford grinned. "In that case—"

"Uh, excuse me, Tom, pay no attention to my *little brother*," put in Phillip. "As the saying goes, sometimes he's got shit for brains."

Danford chuckled. He drafted two checks for a thousand dollars each and offered them to the brothers.

Admiring his check, Phillip grinned broadly. "Not too shabby."

"Indubitably," said Jeff.

16

The formidable two-story county courthouse on East Trade Street in Charlotte was built in a neoclassical style popular in the early 1910s. It had cleaner lines than the old Victorian buildings but this building was very impressive with its twelve mammoth concrete columns that ran the length of its façade. The complex housed the police station, a small holding area, a criminal library, and the crime lab. When Phillip and Jeff arrived, early Tuesday morning, Dick Jennings was waiting for them in his office.

"Here's your order, Phillip," quipped Jennings as he handed him a large manila envelope. "One picture of John Harkins smooching with an unknown blonde and one enlargement of that the thingamajig on the bookshelf."

"Any info on the authenticity of the picture? Could it be a composite?" asked Phillip.

"Don't have that answer yet. Kevin is checking it out, but we won't know for a few days. We did run the blonde's picture through our databases, though, but we scored a great big goose egg."

"No criminal activity then," frowned Phillip. "Too bad. At least we would have something to go on."

Jennings yawned luxuriously and dug his fists into his baggy eyes. "Tell me about it. We're being run ragged around here by a rash of domestic robberies. On the face of it, the Freidan murder looks like a murder by somebody with a personal motive. But it could even be a run of the mill robbery gone bad."

Phillip and Jeff exchanged are-you-thinking-what-I'm-thinking glances. Phillip was about to comment when an all too familiar voice froze him in his tracks.

"What the fuck are you punks doing here?" Stan Lukowski bawled. "The public's not allowed in here. Get the hell out."

Phillip let the envelope Jenkins had just handed him hang out of sight by his side before turning around to face the detective. "We're Tom Danford's investigators on this case," he said boldly. "We've got every right to be here."

"Only lawyers and paralegals can pick up evidence here. Bullshit on allowing that privilege to pimple-faced buttinskies." Lukowski turned his wrath on Jennings. "Did you tell them anything?"

"Nothing to tell, Stan, old boy." Jennings looked pointedly at the brothers. "Ta-ta, boys. So nice to have you. Have a good day."

Jeff and Phillip took the hint. The sound of Jennings getting his ass chewed out followed them into the hallway.

"What a prick!" said Jeff. "Is he always that way, or does he just have it in for Tom?"

"It's just his marvelous good nature. Hold up, I want to see what else he says to Jennings. Maybe Lukowski has information he'll let slip."

A safe distance from Jennings' office, the brothers hugged the wall as Lukowski's ranting echoed down the hall.

"You gave those little fucks copies of the pictures? Whose side are you on, Jennings? And don't give me this truth crap. This case is political and you know it. I'll catch those sons of bitches if they haven't left yet."

The brothers bolted for Phillip's Civic. "I wonder what Lukowski meant by this case being political," Jeff mused.

"Dunno," Phillip sighed heavily. "Poor Jennings! But at least he threw us a bone."

Safely in the car driving away from the courthouse, the brothers continued their conversation. "Yeah," said Jeff. "Like he said, the rash of robberies and Freidan's murder might be connected. And that connection might be?

"The Dismas House. We'll look into that later. Right now, you take a look at those photos."

Phillip passed the envelope to Jeff. "The blonde chick looks a little familiar, but there's nothing I can put my finger on."

"How about the sculpture in the bookcase one?"

Jeff examined the photo. He had always liked art. When he was younger, he would visit art museums and galleries with his mother. He took a lot of ribbing from Phillip for taking an elective arts history course last semester. "Looks like the bust of a solider. A nice objet d'art, to be sure, but it doesn't look like it would be worth stealing."

"Thank you, Prof. Culture."

The sharp blast of a police siren made them jump.

"Shit!" exclaimed Phillip. In his visor mirror he saw Lukowski's scowling face as his unmarked detective's car rode the Civic's bumper.

"Talk about objects in mirror being closer than they appear," Jeff deadpanned. "Jeff, stow those photos. I'm pulling over and calling Tom."

Danford's office line was busy. Phillip dialed Danford's cell phone but was interrupted by Lukowski banging on the window. Danford's voice saying his customary "Tom Danford here" could be heard as Phillip dropped the phone on the seat hoping Tom would overhear the conversation with Lukowski without the detective knowing it.

"Hand them over," Lukowski demanded.

"Hand what over?" said Phillip innocently.

"The pictures you stole from the crime lab."

"That's bogus and you know it. I didn't steal anything."

"Get out of the car so I can search your vehicle."

"Let's see your warrant first."

"I don't need a warrant when I'm pursuing a criminal from the scene of a crime." Lukowski drew his Glock 9mm from his holster and brandished it in Phillip's face. "Get out of the car. I'm not going to ask again."

"You'll lose your badge over this one, Lukowski," said Jeff. He enunciated carefully, hoping Danford was listening on the still engaged cell phone. "The corner of *Race and Broad* is not a good place to have a conversation with a loaded gun in your face."

Lukowski glanced quizzically at Jeff as he snatched open Phillip's door and dragged him out of the car by his shirtfront. Jeff exited on the passenger side. "You two get over to the front of the car and put your hands on the hood of the car while I call for back up. One move and I'll shoot—don't doubt it for a second."

Just then, Jeff sneezed and involuntarily reached into his pocket for his handkerchief. Out of the corner of his eye, Phillip saw the blur of Lukowski swing into combat stance and level his weapon.

17

The phone rang in Danford's office early Tuesday morning. The caller ID indicated the call was coming from the Kemper household. Danford desperately wanted to talk with Susan. He couldn't deny their "date" had titillated him; he had spent a restless night wrestling with the complex feelings Susan awakened in him. But he wanted to avoid talking to Frank Kemper. The good doctor was probably hung over and still spoiling for a fight. He took a chance and answered. "Tom Danford here."

"Hi," said Susan sheepishly.

"Hi, yourself."

"Tom, I am so sorry about Frank. I can't believe he showed up at the restaurant like he did." Susan was thankful for the anonymity of a phone conversation about the incident. Not that apologizing on the phone was easy, but facing him in person would have been uncomfortable beyond words.

"Don't worry about it, Susan. It wasn't your fault."

"In some way, it was. I know sometimes Frank gets jealous. I told him we were meeting at the office. I didn't mention dinner. I was just trying to avoid an argument. *That* sure backfired. I hope you're not sorry now you asked the boys and I to assist you?'

"Absolutely, not!" Danford was surprised how emphatically he responded. "Given my line of work and some of the crap I have to deal with, Frank's temper tantrum was just a tempest in a teapot." He paused. Unbidden, the words formed on his lips. "I like working with you Susan, in so many ways."

Susan could feel herself flush. "I feel the same way, Tom."

There was an awkward silence. To their mutual discomfort, the proverbial cat was out of the bag.

"Anything new on the case?" Susan asked finally, changing the subject.

"I gave the guys their assignments. They should be at the crime lab as we speak. I had talked with Jenkins this morning. His crew worked all night on this case. The cause of death was the gunshot wound to the chest and the gun at the crime scene had John Harkin's finger-prints on it. No surprise there. Here's the big news: the gun was regis-tered to him."

Danford stretched and took a gulp of black coffee. "It's not looking good for John. To pick up from what we discussed over dinner, I have some specific chores for you, too, if you're up for it?"

"Of course. Go ahead."

"Would you interview Michael Freidan's wife, Marjorie, and hyp-notize her if she's willing? She was in bed when her husband was shot but she heard a noise: in her words, something like a car backfiring followed by a car motor. Crucial information, but we need more details. I'd also like to know more about the relationship between Michael and John Harkins. Finally, continue your profile on John Harkins. I know Lukowski's going to present John as the killer to the DA's office. I'm going to need you to determine if he has personality traits associated with a potential killer."

"My pleasure," said Susan. She could feel her adrenaline begin to pump at the prospect of exercising her craft.

Danford's cell phone rang. "Susan, excuse me, I've got another call on my cell. Hold on." The caller ID said it was Phillip's cell phone. "Tom Danford here," he said out of habit. No answer. "Phillip, are you there?" He could hear Phillip arguing with someone. The voice was unmistakable: Lukowski! Presently Danford caught the words "Race and Broad": Jeff's voice. Phillip's voice again, distant now. Lukowski yelling. *A gunshot.*

Danford thought quickly; no sense in sharing this with Susan now. "Better go. Talk with you later, Susan."

Forsaking the slow elevator, Danford sprinted down the two flights of stairs and was on the road in his Lexus within three minutes, grate-ful he had parked on the street and not in the garage today. Sirens whistled through the cell phone that was still documenting Phillip's call. In light traffic, Danford gunned the Lexus and arrived at the intersection of Race and Broad in five minutes. His heart skipped a beat at the sight of an EMS van.

Danford raced up to Phillip. "What the hell is going on?"

"It's that prick, Lukowski. He tried to shoot Jeff," said Phillip hands shaking, face drained of color. A paramedic was treating a nasty bruise on his right hand. "I jammed my hand against his gun so he would miss. Now he wants to arrest *me* for resisting arrest. He's a crazy person, Tom. Totally out of control."

"Back up a little. Why would he want to shoot Jeff?"

"Dick Jennings gave us copies of the photos. Lukowski found out, chased us, then pulled us over, saying we had stolen material from the crime lab. He wanted to search the car. Jeff sneezed and went for a handkerchief. I saw Lukowski take aim at him. I don't know if he was really going to shoot or not, but I wasn't going to take any chances. When I hit his arm, the gun discharged into the ground."

"You did the right thing, Phillip," Danford said, patting his shoulder. He spied Jeff. "Are you alright?"

"Yeah, I'm fine. Thanks to Phillip. Can you please sue his ass?"

"You got it!" said Danford with relish. *God, this must be my week for idiots!* He thought. *Lukowski and Frank Kemper should be locked up together; they deserve each other.* "You've really done it this time, Lukowski," Danford said, spying the detective by his car.

"Save your sermon, counselor," scoffed Lukowski. "Those two belong in jail. They stole material from the crime lab."

"The only person going to jail is going to be you. This time you've gone too far. I have you for unlawful detainment, unlawful search, and discharging a firearm without cause."

"Whaddaya take me for, a kid killer? I wasn't going to shoot the punk. The older kid caused my gun to discharge. Luckily the round went into the grass."

"You shouldn't have drawn your weapon at all," Danford said coolly. "And what was the safety doing off? Lots of questions here. Cops have such a good time in prison, Lukowski. You'll deserve every minute." Danford savored the look of panic on Lukowski's flabby face.

"Good morning, Tom."

Danford wheeled around. He was surprised to see Chief Jay Owens.

"Hey, Jay, back on the street again, I see."

"I wish that were the case. Dick Jennings called and said Lukowski was acting inappropriately. I'm following up. I hear he pulled a gun on the Kemper boys. Are they working for you? Are they pressing charges?"

"Both of the boys are working for me. As you know, Phillip has an investigator's license and has all the legal right to pick up info for me at the crime lab. As you can appreciate, my clients want to see Lukowski fry," Danford said, indicating the Kemper brothers. "Lukowski could have killed either one of them. What the hell is wrong with him?"

"Wish I knew, wish I knew. Anything I can do, Tom, to make this go away?" the chief said shrewdly. "Lukowski's only got eighteen more months until retirement from here. I can keep him in tow, but I can't cover up this incident if your clients press charges."

"Let me talk with them and see what they want to do. In the meantime, you'd better put a leash and muzzle on Lukowski. He's a loose cannon."

"Couldn't agree more," nodded Owens. "Don't worry, we'll keep a watch on him."

"See that you do," said Danford, grinning. He went back to the EMS van.

"The paramedics say my hand's not broken, just bruised," said Phillip. He held an ice pack against his hand, luridly purple now and swollen.

"That's good to hear," said Danford. "How're you holding up, Jeff?"

"I'm okay. Just a little shook up." Jeff's voice lacked its usual confidence.

"What's with Lukowski, anyway? He always was an ass but this is way over the top, even for him."

"I don't know, but I agree with you," said Danford. "Lukowski's got a chip on his shoulder these days that must weight a ton. Something's going on here and I can't put my finger on it." He put his arm around each of the boys' shoulders. "Jay Owens wants to know if you guys are going to press charges. Lukowski has eighteen months to go before he retires from here with a full pension. Jay promised to sit on him so an episode like this doesn't happen again. It's entirely up to you."

Danford was conflicted. He knew if the boys pressed charges, the case would be harder to work. If they didn't press charges, the police department would bend over to help. It was always good to have that kind of wind behind your back. He couldn't influence the brothers; it was their choice.

Phillip and Jeff looked at each other and simultaneously shook their heads no.

"We would lose more than we would gain if we pressed charges, as much as I'd like to," said Phillip.

Always the philosopher, thought Tom. *Susan had certainly raised two fine boys.* "Okay, then let's get to work. I'll tell Jay you are not going to press charges, but we expect full cooperation on this case and no more interference from Lukowski, or we drag his ass to court. How's that sound?"

"Works for us," said Jeff. "Man, my nerves are fried. I could use a shot of whisky."

Phillip laughed. "Yeah, if you want to get sick as a dog. You don't drink, remember?"

"A ciggie?" said Jeff hopefully.

"You don't smoke, either, dip wad," said Phillip, nudging Jeff good-humoredly.

"Guess I'm shit out of luck," said Jeff mournfully. "Hell, if I'd known criminal law was going to be like this, I'd have become a male model a long time ago."

"In your dreams, little brother."

18

Tuesday afternoon found Susan relaxing on her back glassed in porch, drinking sun-brewed iced tea. She and Frank had decided to expand the kitchen area by enclosing the porch to a warm, relaxation area. Her decorator had referred to the area as a Lanai but Susan found that description pretentious. The family still called it the porch.

Susan had decorated this area with white wicker furniture, including an eating table and chairs, and palm trees that loved the warm sun. Her white wicker lounge chair with its colorful flowered cushions was her favorite loafing place. The porch overlooked an idyllic English garden that Susan had designed with the help of a talented local landscaper.

This August day the garden was in full flower, a lush feast for the eye. The garden's centerpiece, a white octagonal gazebo, was the apple of Susan's eye. Monday afternoons, Susan had found, were unpopular with her therapy patients. She left the office at noon on Mondays and generally used her free time for personal appointments. With no pressing engagements, she had the whole afternoon to leisurely plan her week and maybe her life, she thought grimly.

"Hi, honey, I thought I would find you here," said Frank sweetly. He put his hands on Susan's shoulders and brushed her cheek with a kiss before sitting down beside her.

"Afternoon, Frank," replied Susan glacially. She didn't bother to look up at him.

"So, I'm going to get the cold shoulder because I caught you having dinner with another man, is that it? Let me tell you, you are my wife. You belong here at home, not out catting around town." His voice grew shrill, almost falsetto. "Haven't I provided for you well? Don't I deserve more respect?"

"Don't start, Frank. I don't need this. You get angry at everything lately. What has happened to you?" said Susan wearily, desperate not to relive the previous night's events. She was grateful when Jeff walked in. Her youngest son was eternally upbeat and positive. His warmth and good cheer never failed to uplift her spirit.

"Hi, parental units, how are you this afternoon?" said Jeff, unplugging his iPod from his ears. "What a great day for a run! Wait until I tell you guys what happened this morning." Animatedly, he described the details of the morning's drama, with special emphasis on Phillip's act of heroism. "I tell you, the dude's a regular Jack Bauer!" said Jeff, beaming with brotherly pride.

As if on cue, Phillip joined everyone on the porch with this comment.

Frank threw up his arms in a gesture of frustration and stood up. "This has got to stop!" he yelled, trying to control the creeping hysteria in his voice.

"What's got to stop?" remarked Phillip mildly as he entered the porch.

"I won't have my wife having dinner with other men, and I won't have my boys being shot at by the police! All of this has gone too far." Frank's face had become an ugly mask of rage as he pounded the patio table for emphasis. "ALL OF YOU STOP this crime crap today. This is the END of it. You hear me?"

"Hey, Dad, chill," said Jeff jovially, patting his father's shoulder. "We were never in any danger. Tom makes sure we only do his legwork and steers us clear of the perps."

"Don't you mention Tom Danford to me," Frank growled menacingly. "*He's* the one with whom your mother is having an affair! *He's* the one who's exposing my sons to danger. I don't want to hear his name in this house."

The brothers gawked at their mother with surprise and a hint of admiration. Susan dispelled their smirks with a firm shake of her head.

"But Dad," Jeff persisted, "we like what we do and the experience will help me with law school next year."

"I tell you what," said Frank menacingly. "If you don't stop working with Danford, I'm not paying for you to go to law school. Make your choice."

Jeff's eyes began to cloud with tears. "You can't do that: That's blackmail. You can't dictate what I do and don't do with my life. I'm not a child; I'm twenty-one years old. You're just being a jealous ass! It's no wonder Mom likes Tom better then you. Who wouldn't?" He bolted from the porch. Presently he could be heard leaving in his Jeep.

Susan was livid but determined not to sink to Frank's level. "Don't take it out on the boys because you made a supreme jackass out of yourself last night at Chips." Susan noted the puzzled look in Phillip's eyes. "Instead of being sympathetic to Jeff after his ordeal, you've alienated him. Who's next? Phillip? What have you got to say to him? Are you going to threaten to kick him out of the house just because he's twenty-five? You pretend to ride on a pretty high horse, Frank, but you're not that pure. If we went to court, you know I'd bring you down. We're pretty close to that edge."

Susan grabbed her glass and walked quickly to the kitchen, taking angry, deliberate steps. She held the glass over the sink for a few seconds, weighing its heft in her trembling hand to estimate how much force it would take to shatter it. No, the bastard wasn't even worth breaking a glass over. She placed the glass carefully in the dishwasher and decided to take an emotion deescalating ride.

When she had gone, Phillip tried to talk with his father. "Alright, Dad, what's going on here? I feel like I walked into the middle of a hurricane without any warning sirens. Start with what happened at Chips."

Frank sighed heavily. "I went to Chips and saw your mother and Tom Danford having dinner together. They're having an affair. I just know it."

"Do you have any proof? I thought they met to go over the case?"

"I don't need proof, damn it. I can tell. I confronted them in the restaurant, but I don't remember much of what happened because I-I had a few drinks. I know your mother drove me home."

"Dad, you can't accuse Mom of something like that in a public place. It's embarrassing for both of you. It was a working dinner, that's all," said Phillip reasonably.

"I can do whatever the hell I want. She's my wife. If I don't want her having dinner with another man, I can tell her to stop. She has no right to do that. She's married to *me*. She's supposed to be here with *me*. Who does she think she is, anyway? She's a cheat and a liar. A poor excuse for a wife and mother."

Phillip felt his hackles rising. "Don't talk to her about Mom like that. You have no proof."

"Fuck your proof. I know what I saw."

"You're an asshole, Dad. I never want to hear you talk about Mom that way again."

Frank smirked. "Or you'll do what? Hit me?"

"Don't give me any ideas."

Phillip stalked away to his room. Maybe he should move out, too. He'd been thinking about "batching it" for some time. As this was his last year of law school, he'd be moving out next spring anyway. Why not get the hell out now? The way things were going, he might have Jeff for a roommate. That wouldn't be so bad.

"Poor Mom," he sighed aloud. "You'd be better off with Tom."

19

When Susan arrived at her office Wednesday morning, she was still shaken from the previous day's family brouhaha. She had had one therapy client that morning, a session she felt she had not handled with her usual professional aplomb. Before she profiled John Harkins, who was conscious now and conversant, she knew she had to put her family issues behind her and focus on her work.

Susan desperately needed the serenity that only a self-induced hypnosis could provide. Placing herself in a state of deep contemplation, she let her mind wander to a peaceful garden. She could see daisies in a rolling meadow and birds on the wing in an azure blue sky. Susan felt her cares melt away in the sweet trilling of the birds' song.

Suddenly the sky turned black and the peaceful notes became a shrill cacophony. With a frown, Susan realized her cell phone was ringing.

"Please, don't let it be Frank," she said aloud. With a sigh of relief, she saw it was Tom's office. "Dr. Kemper here," she answered professionally; it might be Tom's receptionist.

"Hi, Susan. It's Tom."

She felt her pulse race at the sound of his voice. "Hi, Tom. Jeff told me about the incident yesterday with Lukowski. I can't tell you how much I appreciate you handling everything with your usual cool. I'd have been a basket case if I'd known the truth."

"That's me, your friendly neighborhood knight in shining armor."

Susan smiled. "They seem to be okay now, but it scares me, Tom, to think they could have been hurt."

"Totally understandable. I gave them the option of quitting the case. To their credit, they want to keep plugging away. I insisted, though, they only perform virtual investigative work, on the computer, and stay out of the field. I don't want anything to happen to them either."

"That's a good plan. Thanks, Tom." Susan tried to sound professional, but it was impossible to keep a note of affection out of her voice. She liked it that Tom was protective of Jeff and Phillip. He was protective but not smothering or manipulative like Frank.

"We do have some news," said Danford. "Now that John is alert, the police have officially charged him with the murder of Michael Freidan. They've posted a uniformed guard outside his hospital room. For all intents and purposes, the cops have already closed the book on this one. John will be arrested as soon as he's out of the hospital. Hopefully I can get him out on bail until the trial."

"I'm conducting John's profile this afternoon. I'll get back to you on my assessment after I see him. When's a good time?"

"How about coming over to my office at one tomorrow? I'll have my receptionist Terry pick up some lunch."

Susan smiled. His reluctance to dine with her in public again was understandable. "Let me check my book. Okay, I'm free from 12:30 until 2:30 tomorrow. Sounds good. See you then. Bye"

§ § § § §

"Hi, John. How are you feeling?" Susan asked as she entered John's hospital room. With his broken right leg in a cast and elevated on several pillows, John Harkins looked miserable and lonely.

"About as good as can be expected, I guess, itching like someone who ran through a poison ivy patch. I shouldn't complain, though; at least I'm alive. Tom told me to expect you."

"I'll try to make this as painless as possible for you," said Susan, extracting a piece of paper from her briefcase. "Let me explain what I do. I investigated the crime scene and based on how the murder was committed have some probable descriptions of the murderer. Forensic psychology, I have to warn you, is not an exact science. It's been around since the late 1880s when two physicians tried to make predictions about Jack the Ripper's personality. However, psychologists still argue about how it should be done.

"What I'm going to do today is ask you some questions about your personality and see if I can show you are no match to the person who killed your father-in-law. You know that Tom will only use the information if it presents you in a positive light. However, the prosecutor can call me in to testify. I have to tell the truth even if that truth describes you as fitting the profile of the murderer. I have a consent form here for you to sign saying you understand what I just said and you agree to be questioned. I also need to talk with your family and others who know you. If I find your personality and the way the murder was committed are not a match, that's good for your case. If I find you are a match, that's not good for you but it's not conclusive proof. Make sense?"

"I get it. I could be helped or screwed by what you say. Since I'm innocent, I'll take my chances."

After Harkins signed the paper, Susan put the form in her briefcase and took out her questions. When Susan investigated the crime scene she came up with several conclusions about the murderer based on the FBI's profiling process called the organized/disorganized continuum. Organized criminals plan their crimes carefully. They rarely leave clues at the crime scene. They are usually antisocial and unremorseful. In Susan's experience, they are also emotionally cold although clever criminals can fake emotional warmth. Disorganized criminals are often impulsive and leave fingerprints and other evidence. Young kids and drug addicts are the most common disorganized criminals. Criminals of both types often witness crimes growing up as part of their culture. What was most striking to Susan about Freidan's murderer was he or she shot him while looking at him straight on. That takes an emotionally cold person, more likely to have been a male then a female. This murder was well planned out. Someone knew Harkins was coming to see Freidan at 7:00 AM and got there early enough to set up Harkins for the murder. Planting the picture of Harkins kissing the blonde and placing it in Freidan's hand was also planned. This murderer is definitely the organized type.

What Susan had to do in this interview with Harkins was to see how emotionally cold he was, how methodical he was and how antisocial or unremorseful he could be. She also had in her head the outline of a potential for violence inventory. She was going to start with some nonthreatening questions. "How much education do you have, John?"

"I graduated cum laude with a bachelor's degree in accounting from the University of North Carolina. I also have a master's degree in business from Queens University."

"How did you get along in school?"

"I kind of kept to myself a lot. I'm not much of a party person. I did my homework, got good grades and graduated on time."

"Have you ever been unemployed?"

"No. From the time I was sixteen, I've always had a job of some sort."

"Any problems at your jobs?"

"No. I always tried to do a good job. I usually left because I'd finished a degree or certificate and could get a better job with more money somewhere else."

"If you had a boss that said nasty things about you but you knew saying something would cost you your job, what would you do?"

"Oh, I'd just walk away. You know that old saying, sticks and stones can break my bones but names can never hurt me. That's my motto."

"Would you describe yourself as organized or disorganized?"

"I'm very organized. I like everything neat and tidy. I can't stand mess."

"Would you describe yourself as someone who plans your activities or are you a spontaneous person?"

"You have got to ask my wife that question. She's always on my case about wanting to plan everything. She says I don't have a spontaneous bone in my body. Sometimes at the last minute she'll want to go out to dinner and I'll have trouble even doing that. I have to plan on being spontaneous even."

Susan laughed. "Did you ever see anyone in your family hurt another person?"

"I used to hear my father talk about a cousin who got drunk and ended up in jail because he took a swing at a cop. That's about it."

"Did you ever hurt a person or an animal when you were younger, even if it was by accident?"

"I ran over a squirrel once with my car. I felt so bad. I even stopped the car and got out to see if there was anything I could do for him. I was sorry I even looked, he was so mangled. It took me a week to get over doing that to some helpless animal."

If this was true, Susan thought, that was a good sign. She noted to check this story with his wife. "Do you use drugs or alcohol?

"No drugs, but I'll have an occasional beer. My wife thinks it's unsophisticated to drink beer, but that's all I ever have. Usually I like it when we have pizza."

"Do you have any weapons in your house?"

"Not anymore. Had a gun a while back, but it was stolen in a robbery. I was glad not to have it in the house any longer. It made me nervous. We put in a security system after the robbery. I'm more comfortable with that."

"Are you angry at anyone right now?"

"Maybe that cop that ordered me arrested. He seemed like a jerk. What was his name?"

"Lukowski. Would you think of hurting Lukowski?"

"Are you kidding? I'm in enough trouble already."

Susan laughed at the thought of Harkins taking on Lukowski. "How did you feel when Michael Freidan showed you the picture of you and the blonde woman kissing?"

"I know you are trying to trick me with that question, huh? He never showed me any picture."

Susan nodded her head.

"My father-in-law was dead when I arrived. I don't know what blonde everyone is talking about. I love my wife. I don't need to get involved with another woman. Can you imagine all the trouble and stress that would create? Not for me, thank you."

"All right, John. I have all the information I need," said Susan as she started to put away her pad and pen.

"So, can you tell them I didn't do it?"

Susan was a picture of professional decorum. "I still have to talk with your family and co-workers to complete my report. Tom will let you know the results."

Harkins was starting to sweat. "You can't tell me anything now? You're not going to sell me down the river, are you?"

"I'm not in the habit of doing that, John."

Harkins hesitated for a minute. Susan observed closely as his tense facial muscles gradually relaxed. "I know, you're just doing your job. What happened to Michael had nothing to do with you. You're just trying to help."

She smiled at him and said, "Hope your legs feels better soon. I'll finish this as soon as I can, but don't worry." With that statement, Susan gave Harkins a friendly tap on his shoulder. She wished she could tell him she knew he was no murderer but she still needed evidence to support that conclusion.

In her car, she thought about her session with Harkins. *If I can back up what John told me, it's highly unlikely he's a murderer. The question is who did kill Michael Freidan?*

20

As Phillip climbed into the Honda Civic his father had brought for him two years ago when he first started law school, he wrestled with his ambivalent feelings toward his father. There was no denying he and Jeff had had a cushy life, thanks to him. His mother had a good income, certainly, but it was his dad's money that enabled the lifestyle to which the family had become accustomed. He had seen their joint income tax returns a few years before looking while looking for forms for law school his father had left on his desk. His father grossed $432,000 that year and his mother $87,000. Even though his father's overhead and taxes were higher then his mother's, it was his father's money that had paid for their enviable educations: private high schools, good colleges, law school. They both had their own cars and would be graduating debt free from school. Their mother had inherited the beach house where they had spent their summers and learned to swim, play tennis, sail, and relate to other kids of means. Financially, at least, they always had it easy. Through it all, though, Dad had been an enigma.

It was hard to know what made Dad tick, Phillip reflected. It's not so much what he says, Phillip constantly reminded himself, as how he says it; there was a "my shit don't stink" pomposity at the core of his personality that rubbed people—including his own family—the wrong way. Phillip despised the way his father threatened people, controlled them, put them down. He had seen him treat nurses and interns like dirt one minute and adopt a doting bedside manner with patients the next.

Phillip loved his father. He knew Jeff did, too. He just didn't like him very much. Mom must, too, in her way, or she wouldn't have stuck with him this long. Her disparaging remark about his father's "purity" troubled him. Could Dad have had an affair with another woman? It didn't seem likely, but he had heard some rumors. He had just assumed there were always rumors about doctors getting involved with nurses at the hospital with little basis in truth.

Poor Mom. The phrase kept echoing through his head. On impulse he phoned his mother's cell and got her voice mail. "Hi, Mom. It's Phillip, calling from my mobile office. Just checking in to see how you're doing. Sorry Dad is being a jerk. You know I think you're great. I'll be out looking for a blonde today. For the case, that is. Don't worry; I'll keep tabs on Jeff, too. I might have pizza with Mark, but then I'll be home. Talk with you tonight. Love you."

Phillip sighed. He wished he could tell his mother that, far from being a boy's night out with Mark, they would be meeting to hammer out the details of what to do about the gun that, in all likelihood, had killed Tom Danford's wife. Whoever said, "Oh, what a tangled web we weave when first we practice to deceive" had sure known what he was talking about.

Phillip had always been family oriented. The recent dysfunction made him feel overprotective of his mother and Jeff. He speed-dialed his brother and was surprised at his gloomy sounding hello. "Hey, dude, why so down?" asked Phillip. "Where are you, anyway?"

"Aw, I'm driving around in my car trying to decide what to do. Dad's such an ass. I don't think I can live there any more. I didn't even want to sleep there last night."

It pained Phillip to hear his normally upbeat brother so downcast. "Maybe this will cheer you up. I've decided to stay until I go back to school in a few weeks. Why don't you do the same? We can get together with Mom and talk. We've been here before, remember?"

"Too many times. At least you're almost done with school and will be out of the house anyway. But okay, if you're going to stick it out until school starts, I'll do the same. I'm still working on the case. We'll just have to agree not to say anything to Dad. I'm sorry I said anything today."

"Live and learn, Bro. Live and learn."

"Thanks for checking on me. Lousy father but great brother! Later."

Phillip could tell by his tone that Jeff was up again. Mission accomplished. *Now to earn my keep for Tom Danford.* Phillip dialed Dick Jennings at the crime lab. His report on the mystery photo was not encouraging.

"Sorry, Phillip," said Jennings, "the photo was pulled for the DA's evidence file before we could look at it. Between you and me, they don't *want* to know if it's a composite or not. The higher ups have put the kibosh on further investigation; they're convinced they've got a slam dunk case against John Harkins. Without the original, my hands are tied."

"I appreciate you telling me. We'll see what we can do about looking at the original on our own. Have a good day, Dick."

As soon as he hung up, Phillip's phone rang. It was Mark.

"Hey, dude. What's happening?"

"If you had a week, I'd tell you. Are we on for tonight?"

"No can do tonight, but Friday's good. My place at six? You sure this note is a good idea?"

"Right now it's about the only thing I'm sure is on target. See you tomorrow."

"You're bringing the pizza and beer, right?" teased Mark.

Before Phillip could answer "You cheapskate," Mark hung up.

21

Susan arrived at Danford's office promptly at one o'clock on Thursday. Meeting Danford in his office was always a good experience for her. Today though, Susan still was tense although excited. Of course, now she wasn't sure if the excitement was due to the work or the presence of Tom.

The entire office was pleasant. Healthy green plants were in evidence throughout the suite. Stunning landscapes of the low country, by a local South Carolina artist, graced the walls. Susan particularly liked a large painting with a single egret standing at the edge of the water near the tall grass. It reminded her of the scenery around Beaufort, South Carolina, one of her favorite places to escape the hugger-mugger of her workaday world.

Danford's receptionist, Terry, recognized her immediately and ushered her into Tom's office. "Lunch is waiting," she said with a pleasant smile.

"Hi," said Danford. He stood up as she entered and motioned to the conference table where their takeout lunch was waiting for them. She recognized the Chips logo and was immediately taken back to that awkward dinner with Frank.

"You okay? You seem stressed out."

"It's Frank. He blew up at the boys this morning. He was understandably upset about the incident with Lukowski and the boys. I try to tell myself he's just a concerned father, but he gets so controlling and aggressive, it's hard to see beyond that."

Just leave the bastard, Danford thought. "I'm sorry he's not easier to live with," he said. "I just talked with Phillip and he seems good. He's right on target with the work I gave him. I haven't heard from Jeff, though."

"I haven't talked with Jeff, either, but I know Phillip did. I'm sure he's all right. He's been through his father's rampages before, unfortunately."

Susan's voice trailed off. There were so many bad memories of Frank exploding at the boys. She had listened to Phillip's message on the way over to Danford's office. She was relieved he was none the worse for wear and keeping a brotherly eye out for Jeff.

"I wish I had a glass of wine for you, or maybe a shot of whiskey," said Danford.

Susan laughed and touched his hand lightly. Tom was a complex person. He had the reputation of being a tiger in the courtroom, but she had come to know him as a sensitive man with a softer side, too, and a dry sense of humor. "Thanks, Tom, not while I'm on duty," she said, playing along.

Danford paused, remembering the takeout Terry had gotten from Chips. "How un-chivalrous of me, I completely forgot to offer you lunch. I thought I remembered you liked Caesar salad with salmon?"

Susan was surprised Tom had noticed; no wonder she liked working with him so much. Chips was a fair distance from the office, too. "I do have something to report. I did an assessment on John Harkins. I can testify that he does not meet the standard criteria for a person with violent potential. He says there is no family history of violence nor has he ever acted violently himself. I still have to meet with his wife and mother-in-law to confirm his remarks."

Susan stopped long enough to take a few bites of her salmon Caesar salad. "Thanks for this by the way. It's delicious," she said warming to being alone with Tom. In a more professional voice, she went on about her profiling. "Whoever killed Freidan, was an organized, cold killer. Everything was well planned out. Harkins has an organized personality and, if he had killed Freidan, he would have planned it to the last detail. He wouldn't have left the incriminating picture in Freidan's hand, nor would he have gotten his fingerprints on the gun. He's methodical but he's emotionally empathetic. He even stopped once when he ran over a squirrel. If that can be verified, there's no way he'd shoot someone face to face. I just need to verify that event with his wife, too."

Danford listened thoughtfully to Susan's findings. "In your experience, is there anything that might push him over the edge?"

"He would have to perceive a situation as threatening to someone extremely important to him. He wouldn't act upon road rage, for instance, but if his life or the life of someone he cared about was in danger, he would be moved to violence in order to protect them. That's healthy. Would he kill his father-in-law if he were threatening to ruin his career and his marriage? I can't answer that for sure, although I doubt it. However, I can tell you it's highly unlikely he would do it without a plan. He's too methodical. He'd think it to death first. No pun intended there. One other thing. I don't think he saw the picture clutched in his father-in-law's hand. And I did believe him when he said he walked into the room and found his father-in-law dead."

Danford smiled. "Very good. Now it's my turn. Phillip said he showed John the picture of him and the blonde and he reluctantly identified the woman as someone who once worked for him. He denied having an affair with her, but Phillip wasn't convinced he was telling the truth. I think I need to go talk with John, too. He's got to tell us the truth; otherwise, we'll be blindsided in court. I got bad news from the crime lab, too. They identified the gun as being registered to John, and, of course, his fingerprints are on it. John said the gun had been stolen in a break-in at their house about six months ago."

"He told me that he had had a gun that was stolen, too," Susan interjected.

"Now for the good news: John tested negative for gunshot residue on his hands. If the GSR test had been positive, I'd be looking to plea bargain."

"I'll talk more to John's wife and mother-in-law. I did talk with Ann Marie when I drove her to the hospital to see John. She was convinced he could never have killed her father. I doubt there has been any physical abuse in that marriage, but I want to know what she thinks could push his buttons."

As Susan spoke, she reflected dismally on verbal abuse in her own marriage. She tried in vain to focus on the case but knew the strain must show on her face.

As if he could read her mind, Danford placed his hand on hers.

"You're going to be fine, Susan. I know you. You'll figure out how to handle this situation with Frank. You're a strong person and you've got a good head on your shoulders. You know I'll do whatever I can to help you, too."

Danford's supportiveness brought Susan to the verge of tears. "Thanks, Tom," she sniffled. "I appreciate that. I'd better get to work before I start blubbering all over. Thanks so much for lunch."

Susan stood up awkwardly and walked to the door. Feeling Danford's strong arms on her shoulders, she paused and closed her eyes. As a thin trail of tears trickled down her cheeks, he turned her around slowly and pulled her close into a warm, cocooning embrace.

22

Susan left Tom's office on cloud nine. She had been surprised when he had taken her into his arms and just held her. Even now, she felt warm to the core of her being, just thinking about it. It had been all she could do to leave; she wanted to stay in his embrace, she wanted more. The "more" was what frightened her. So far, she and Tom had not crossed the line from colleagues/friends to lovers, but it sure as hell looked like they had bought their tickets for that train, as Peggy would say. *But she was married.* For better, for worse, in sickness and in health, until death do us part, she had promised on her wedding day, and her Catholic faith told her she must keep that promise, no matter what. *Deal with those feelings later,* she told herself. *Right now just feel good about someone caring about you and DON'T feel guilty about it.* She looked at her watch. Good—she would just make her 2:30 appointment.

Ann Marie Harkins answered the door and led Susan into an exquisite foyer with beautiful marble flooring and a round antique table decorated with a magnificent bouquet of fresh cut flowers. The foyer was opened up by a grand oil painting of a window in an austere room looking onto an open field. On the window ledge was a tiny moth. The painting was so realistic, Susan felt as if she could open the window and step out into the barren landscape with its subtle flourishes of color lending a hopeful aspect to the bleak scene. "Is that an

Alexander Yelagin?" asked Susan. She had long been an admirer of the Russian painter of Siberian scenery who now lived and worked in the United States.

"Yes, it's called *The moth*. I never heard of him until our decorator suggested one of his paintings for that spot. Do you know his work?"

"Yes. I was always interested in art. My son, Jeff, took a course in art history and I devoured all his textbooks. When we were in New York City, we visited a gallery that featured some of Yelagin's paintings. I was always captivated by his work: so forlorn, yet so peaceful. It's a wonderful piece for your foyer." Ann Marie smiled and led Susan into the living room. "Simply beautiful," gasped Susan. She had seen a room in one of the magazines that was decorated in Banana cream and chocolate brown and accessorized with tangerine orange pieces. This room had the same colors with a chocolate brown wall behind the fireplaces with a banana cream mantel. The couch was the same banana cream colored flanking the fireplace facing two brown chairs. There was a beautiful arrangement of orange tulips on the glass coffee table in front of the couch. Orange, brown and cream pillows were sprinkled on the couch and chairs. "It takes a genius of sorts to make a room both aesthetically pleasing and livable. "Who is your decorator?"

"Her name is Jennifer Houston. I'll be happy to give you her phone number before you leave. We were extremely pleased with her attention to detail. She did a little work with my parents, too, although my mother didn't always appreciate her suggestions. My father's home office had more of her touches."

"I know Jennifer. We had her come to our house, too." Susan thought Jennifer might be able to shed some light on the piece missing from Michael Freidan's office. "I'd better get down to business, Ann Marie. Tom Danford asked me to profile John, which I have done, and my professional assessment of his personality traits will be officially presented in court. However, the profile isn't complete until I talk to people who know the subject. That's why I'm here."

"I understand. I'll be happy to answer any questions."

Susan took out her pad and pen. "How would you describe your husband's disposition?"

"Well, he's somewhat on the nervous side, but he's good-natured and goes with the flow. Not much ruffles him; he just shakes things off. My father goaded him all the time about his golf game. Dad was very competitive, with a fifteen handicap. John has a handicap of about, oh, twenty, twenty-five. He's always thrilled when his golf score is under a hundred. Dad and John used to play golf once a week. My father always, *always* would tease him, 'Well, John, think you can keep yourself under a hundred today?'"

"Did he get angry?"

"No, he'd just say something like, 'We'll see what happens.' He walks away from confrontation. My father would say he was wimpy. When we get into an argument, John just says, 'Whatever you want, dear.' He's the poster child for non-violence."

"Has he ever raised his voice to you or your children?"

"Let me think. It would be rare. One time, our son, David, had taken John's car out at night. Someone vomited in the backseat and David hadn't cleaned it up. When John got in the car the next morning, he was angry. He got David out of bed and made him clean it up then and there. He was pretty mad then."

"Has he ever struck you or your children? I saw a picture of two boys on your father's desk with you and your husband. Are those your only children?

"Yes, we have two boys and no, John never punished the boys in any way. He's usually so passive, it's been a problem. I always had to discipline the children. He would just walk away, telling me to take care of it."

"Anything else you can add about your husband?"

"No, just generally speaking, he's a passive person who avoids confrontation. He doesn't argue much about anything."

"Anne Marie, I saw the police leaving here when I pulled up. Have they shown you the picture of the woman with your husband? Did you recognize her?"

"Yes, that's Mary Lou. She worked in John's office."

"Do you think they were involved with each other?"

"No way. Having an affair would be so out of character for John; it would make him a nervous wreck. Besides, he cares for our family and me too much to throw it all away for—a little piece on the side." Ann Marie paused, embarrassed. "You know, there's something about that picture that's familiar, as strange as that sounds. I keep thinking I've seen it before, only bigger. I wasn't shocked when I saw it, when I should have been. It was like I *knew* about them kissing. Strange, huh? I wish I could remember. It's like it's right there on the tip of my brain, but it just won't come through."

Susan thought she could help Ann Marie, if she was willing, retrieve this memory using hypnosis. She hesitated suggesting it without checking with Tom first about the legal ramifications. "Ann

Marie, have you ever been hypnotized? Sometimes hypnosis can relax the subconscious mind to a degree where supposedly forgotten events or information are revealed and augmented. Would you be willing to have me hypnotize you?"

"Sure, if it would help John, I'm game. I had a good experience with a hypnotist who helped me stop smoking."

"Great! Let me talk with Tom to make sure it will be helpful to the case. I have to forewarn you, I usually videotape legal interviews and what you say could end up in court."

"Just let me know when. I know John didn't kill my father. My father could be controlling and even nasty at times, but John just rode that wave. He took his abuse, shrugged it off, and stayed away from him as much as he could."

So Michael Freidan was verbally abusive, thought Susan. John Harkins might have ridden the wave, as Ann Marie put it, but who else could Freidan's vocabulary have turned from a normal person to a cold-blooded murderer?

23

For the hundredth time that Friday morning, Jeff Kemper scrutinized the crime lab's enlargement of the art piece missing from Michael Freidan's den. The photo showed a bronze casting of the head and neck of a rugged, mustached man with small eyes, high, proud cheekbones, and a square jaw. He wore what looked like an oversized cowboy hat and had a knotted kerchief around his throat. The visage sat atop a simple, rectangular pedestal about two-thirds as large as the sculpture itself. The sculpture reminded Jeff of General George Armstrong Custer. "Okay, cowboy," Jeff mused aloud, "let's see if we can't track your macho ass down."

Fortified by a cup of microwave coffee, Jeff Kemper sat down at his personal computer and began scouring the World Wide Web. His initial Googling of "sculptures of soldiers" returned over 1,300,000 hits. "Original sculptures" narrowed the search to 426,000-odd sites. "Twentieth-century sculptures" returned 463,000 possibilities. He hadn't expected the search to be a cakewalk, but this was ridiculous.

Supremely frustrated, he scanned the photo as a high resolution JPEG file and e-mailed it as an attachment to Professor Maxwell, the arts history professor at the University of North Carolina, with a message pleading for any information that would aid in its identification. After enduring an annoying registration process, he sent the same image to the personal shopper at Sotheby's, the international auction house in Manhattan, with the message: "Looking for a match to the attached photo. Thank you in advance. Sincerely, J. Kemper, prospective buyer."

Several hours and dozens of fruitless searches later, Jeff was just about to take a break with a run to clear the cobwebs in his brain when the doorbell rang. Through the den window, Jeff could see two men with the telltale aura of plainclothes cops standing on the front porch.

Jeff crept out the backdoor, stole through the neighbors' yard, and made it to the sidewalk, where he started jogging. A comfortable distance down the block, but with the house still in sight, he called Danford on his cell phone.

"Tom, it's Jeff. There are two guys who look like cops standing at the front door of my house. I was alone and didn't think it was a good idea to open the door, so I snuck out the backdoor. I'm just down the corner from my house and so far they aren't pursuing me. What should I do?"

"Stay put—I'll be right over. I'm at the office so I'm not too far. I'll meet you at the corner of Worthington and Mt. Pleasant. If they are cops, they'll probably be waiting in a parked car for someone to return. Don't go back to the house yourself."

Jeff jogged to the corner Tom had indicated. Fifteen minutes later, he was relieved to see Tom's black Lexus approaching. "Boy, am I glad to see you," said Jeff, getting in.

"You did the right thing calling me. What's the latest?"

"I don't see anyone at the front steps now, but there's a Crown Victoria parked down the street with two men in it. Do you have a plan, counselor?"

"Yes, we are going to go to your house like nothing has happened and see what they do."

In moments, Danford pulled into the Kemper's semicircular driveway. He and Jeff casually walked around back to the unlocked back door. Within minutes, the front doorbell rang.

Danford and Jeff answered the door together.

"We're looking for Jeff Kemper," said the first officer, showing his badge. "Is he home?"

"I'm Jeff Kemper. What's this about, officer?"

"Can we come in?"

"Not a good idea, gentlemen. You might get the misguided notion you're welcome to start poking around without a warrant. I'm attorney Tom Danford, officer. Jeff works for me. Why don't you tell me what this is about?"

"I'm Martin Kelly and this is Tony Colonis. This is just a friendly visit, but we can get a warrant, if we have to. We just want to ask Mr. Kemper here some questions about a Remington sculpture he's been asking about."

"A *Remington* sculpture?" asked Jeff. He recognized the name. "What about it?"

"We'd rather talk inside or down at the station, whichever you'd prefer."

"There's a table on the deck in the back. How would that be?" suggested Jeff.

The officers glanced at each other and shrugged. "That'll do. For now," said Colonis.

On the deck Kelly asked, "So, where did you get the sculpture you have?"

"I don't have a sculpture," answered Jeff. I just have a picture of one."

"When you e-mailed Sotheby's, you said you were looking for a match to the sculpture you had."

"I was hoping to hear back from them, but I didn't quite expect this. I just e-mailed them a picture of the sculpture. I thought I would get a quicker response if I told them I was looking for a match. You know, like a prospective buyer."

"This sculpture was missing from a crime scene that we're investigating. Jeff is helping me find out what this sculpture is," clarified Tom. "I'm asking for the last time, what's this about? If you can't give us an answer, you need to leave."

Kelly shot Colonis a relieved look. Both men visibly relaxed.

"This sculpture was purchased at auction from Sotheby's about a year ago," explained Colonis. "It's an original sculpture by Frederick Remington called *The Sergeant*. The buyer paid $28,000 for it. Six months later, it was stolen from the buyer's house. We've had an increase in robberies in the area, and this was one of the more expensive and notable pieces. Your turn to talk. Whose house was it missing from in your investigation?"

Danford debated the risks of revealing too much information about his case. He decided it was worth it, if it led to the agents letting something useful slip. "Michael Freidan's. He was murdered Sunday in his home office. We know from a vacant space on the bookcase in the office that the sculpture had formerly occupied that space. We managed to get a fix on the sculpture from a family photo taken in the office. Stan Lukowski is the officer on the Freidan homicide. You can check with him for a copy of the picture."

"We'll check out your story. Don't leave town," Kelly said, pointing a finger at Jeff.

"From whose house was this Remington originally stolen?" asked Danford hopefully. "The information was a matter of public record."

"I suppose you'll find out anyway. It was from Judge Avanti's house in Myer's Park. Unfortunately, that area has been hit with a rash of burglaries. All the major auction houses are on alert in case someone tries to sell it through them. It's not likely but if this is a bunch of kids, they may not know how tight the art world is."

Jeff was curious. "I'd think a Remington sculpture would be worth more then $28,000. Why so cheap?" asked Jeff in his art collector voice.

"From what I've gathered, the Remington sculptures of horses are much more valuable. This is a small sculpture, around 10 inches high and it doesn't have the 'energy' I've been told the horse sculptures do. If I were you, Mr. Kemper, if you're in the market, I'd spend the $100,000 grand or so on the horses," Kelly said with a smirk.

Danford and Jeff watched the two cops leave.

"Well, Tom, at least you know you can count on me to stir the pot and make the action flow."

Tom tossed Jeff's hair. "You know that line from the old Elvis song, 'A little less conversation, a little more action, please'? With you I'd like more conversation and a whole lot less action."

Jeff grinned his sheepish grin.

24

Phillip's destination, Carolina Medical Center, loomed before him. He had to beg Danford to let him go to the hospital. He insisted the hospital would be safe and he wouldn't be in any danger. Besides, there was a guard at Harkins' door. What could possibly happen? The bureaucracy of the hospital turned out to be the biggest obstacle. Because of Harkins' schedule of doctor visits, nursing activities and restricted visitors, Phillip had to wait until this Friday afternoon to see him.

He hurried inside with the incriminating photo of John Harkins and the mystery blonde in the attaché case his parents had given him when he started law school.

Phillip did his best to hide his squeamishness when he saw the pinkish fluid draining from the tube in Harkins' chest into a drainage bag on the side of the bed. He adopted a professional demeanor and extended his hand cordially to the miserable looking patient. "Good morning, Mr. Harkins. I'm Phillip Kemper. I'm an investigator working with Tom Danford. How are you today, sir?"

"Kemper? Are you related to Dr. Kemper?"

"Depends on which one you mean. My father's a doctor on staff here and my mother is a psychologist. She's also working with Counselor Danford."

"Your mother. She was here about an hour ago. Pretty woman."

"That she is and very good at her job." Phillip took a letter-size folder out of his attaché. "Mr. Harkins, I know you've heard about the picture Michael Freidan had in his hand when he died. I need to show you a copy of it to you to see if you recognize the woman. The picture might be a composite, meaning it was doctored. You're the best one to judge that possibility."

Phillip proffered the photo and observed Harkins carefully. Harkins' eyes moved upward and to the left when he looked at the picture, which Phillip knew from his training was an indication there was a memory associated with the picture. Conversely, when a person is trying to create an image and lie about it, rather than recall it, they look upward and to the right. Harkins' eye movement wasn't ironclad proof he recognized the woman, but it was a start.

"I never saw that woman in my life," Harkins said. "That looks like me, all right, but I have no idea who she is. You don't have to show this picture to my wife, do you? She's upset enough."

Hot on the scent, Phillip ignored his question. "Take another look at the picture, Mr. Harkins. Perhaps you remember seeing the woman someplace."

As Harkins studied the picture, his eyes traveled upwards and to the left once again. "Nope, nothing comes to mind. Afraid I can't help you, sonny."

Phillip drummed his fingers on his lips. "That's too bad, Mr. Harkins. Perhaps your wife, your daughter, or your mother-in-law will recognize her. I'll be seeing them this afternoon."

With an inward glee, Phillip saw a flash of panic play briefly across Harkins' face. "Wait, let me see that picture again," Harkins demanded. "Yeah, she does look a little like someone who once worked in my office. It might be Mary Lou, but her hair is different. But I never kissed her. We never had an affair."

"Does Mary Lou have a last name?"

"Benton, Mary Lou Benton. She left about a year ago. I don't know if we have an address or any info on her. I think she moved out of state."

Of course she did, thought Phillip. "That's very helpful, Mr. Harkins. I'll check with your office staff."

"I swear, I never kissed that woman or had an affair with her!" Harkins protested shrilly. "I love my wife, I would never do that. And I didn't kill Michael, either; he was always good to me. What a mess!"

Harkins' agitation triggered an alarm on one of the diagnostic devices. As a nurse arrived to investigate, Phillip headed for the door.

"Very well, Mr. Harkins. Sorry to have upset you. We'll keep working on this. You get better now, you hear?"

Back in his car, Phillip called Danford. "Tom, glad I caught you. I got news on the picture. John identified the woman, but there's more. He lied about her at first and then told me her name and that she worked at his office until a year ago. I'm going to his office to see if I can find an address. John says he didn't have an affair with the woman, but I have my doubts. The original picture is now with the DA. The crime lab didn't have time to check it to see if it was a composite."

"Outstanding, Phillip," said Tom. "Keep up the great work. Can you meet with me, your mother and Jeff at Starbucks around four?"

"Wish I could. I'm across town and then having pizza with a friend. I'll have Mom and/or Jeff fill me in."

Phillip swelled with pride as he pulled up to the drive-through window at the bank to deposit his retainer fee into his anemic checking account. He couldn't decide what was more satisfying: the fact that he was earning the money through hard work or Danford's confidence in his abilities. *Great work,* Danford had said. Phillip reflected darkly that his own father had never paid him such a compliment.

25

Susan arrived at the Starbucks on North Tryon Street at 3:55 PM that Friday afternoon, five minutes early. When she had phoned Danford about her meeting with Ann Marie, he suggested a quiet rendezvous where Jeff's proud discovery about the statue could be showcased to full advantage. She found a secluded table in the back and savored a few minutes of down time with her hazelnut coffee. Her thoughts drifted to her personal life. Her marriage was disintegrating and her relationship with Tom seemed to be progressing beyond the platonic stage. *Is this what you want to happen?* she asked herself. Things were moving so fast; she wished she had more time to think things over.

Danford and Jeff arrived, shooting the bull and grinning ear to ear. Jeff was always easygoing, but she noticed that when he and Tom were together, her son had an even brighter spark about him. Tom stopped off at the counter to place their order as Jeff, beaming like a lighthouse, dropped into the seat across from Susan.

"Hi, Mom. You'll never guess what happened and what we found out. You know that sculpture in the picture? It was sold at auction at Sotheby's for $28,000 and then stolen from the buyer's house. The police came to our house looking for *me*."

"What!" said Susan in distress. "Why would the police think you stole the sculpture?"

115

"Let me backtrack and give you the whole skinny: I was trying to
see if the personal shopper at Sotheby's in New York knew about this
sculpture. I implied I had one. When he got my e-mail, he contacted
the police. The sculpture had been sold at auction but then had been
stolen, according to the police. The police said there's been a rash of
robberies. Usually though the robbers would take objects they could
fence easily not art objects. They thought I was involved. But then
Tom and I outlined our investigation and they were cool with our
explanation."

"Thank God for that," exhaled Susan. It was clear Jeff was feeling
his oats; she didn't want to spoil his fun by teasing him about his
pointed use of "*our* investigation."

Tom joined them with two grande lattes. "I see Jeff has been regal-
ing you with his adventures," he teased, tousling Jeff's hair. "Here's
my two cents: Whoever Michael Freidan got the sculpture from is
probably involved in all the recent robberies. Do you concur, co-
counselor?"

Jeff attended to his mussed hair. "Yeah, sure, but lay off the 'do,
will ya? I've got an image as a sex symbol to uphold in this town, you
know."

Susan smiled; their easy banter warmed her heart.

Tom laughed heartily. "So, what do you have to add to this pow-
wow, Susan?"

"I'm afraid my news is not as exciting as Jeff's. By the way, where
is Phillip?"

"He finally got through the hospital bureaucracy and got into see
John Harkins today to show him the infamous picture. He reluctantly
identified the blonde as his former receptionist, a Mary Lou Benton.
He out and out denied having an affair with her and Phillip said he
believed him. By the way, he's not coming home for dinner, Mom.
He's having pizza with a friend."

"Thanks for the supper update. I've got three pieces of information. First and foremost, from Ann Marie Harkins' description of her
husband, I think it's highly unlikely he killed Michael Freidan. He just
doesn't fit the profile for a killer. He has excellent control over his
anger and would walk away from a situation rather than confront
someone. Second, the picture of John kissing his former assistant
didn't upset her. She thought she had seen the picture before, or
something like it, but she couldn't put her finger on where. In her gut,
she knew it was an innocent kiss but doesn't know where it happened.

"She agreed to be hypnotized to try to access that memory, but I need to know if you think that would be an okay thing to do, Tom. And last, but not least, I have the name and number of Ann Marie Harkin's decorator, who is the same woman who decorated Michael Freidan's office. She may know something about the sculpture."

"Good work, Susan!" said Danford. "Jeff, how about you follow up with the decorator and see if she was the one who got Mr. Freidan that sculpture? She may be the key to finding out where they came from." Jeff nodded enthusiastically. "Susan, I'm all for you hypnotizing Ann Marie. Any tidbit of information she can share with regard to that photo will stand us in good stead. Just make sure you videotape the session to prove it was on the up and up."

"Sure thing, I'll set a date up with Ann Marie."

Danford reared back on his chair and downed the rest of his coffee. "Anyone want to do dinner?"

"I'm game," said Jeff. "How about you, Mom?"

It was so tempting, but she couldn't leave Frank to fend for himself while she had dinner again with her purported lover—if Frank found out, he would surely go off the deep end! So, this was the eternal triangle! And she was in the middle of it. She decided she needed to slow things down and sort out the players and their roles. "Jeff, you go. Phillip is not going to be home so Dad would be alone."

"Suit yourself," said Danford, trying to hide his disappointment. "We'll talk with you tomorrow. What say, Jeff, we take in the steak house on College Ave?"

"Do they serve fish?" Jeff deadpanned.

Susan watched them fondly as they departed. Danford tousled Jeff's hair again and they both laughed uproariously. *Thick as thieves,* thought Susan, *thick as thieves.*

§ § § § §

As she drove homeward, Susan decided she would fix one of Frank's favorite dishes, poached salmon, for supper. She prayed that, for once, they could have an intimate dinner together without any drama. It was a remote possibility, if they spent some quality time together, she might remember why she had married him in the first place. Doubtful, but she owed it to herself to try.

When she opened the front door, Frank was standing in the foyer with a drink in his hand. "Where have you been?" he groused, clearly tipsy. "How come supper isn't ready yet? Have you been out *meeting* with that rat-bastard Danford?"

Susan looked at him with mingled pity and loathing. She was neither afraid of him nor intimidated by him. She had an epiphany; she realized she didn't know if she wanted to live with Frank any longer. There was no getting around the fact that their life together had become a loveless contract, existing on paper only. The specter of divorce was almost too terrible to contemplate; just the thought of it sent a cold shiver down her spine. There was finality and shamefulness to divorce that was fundamentally at odds with her Catholic faith. She had had theological discussions with her patients about Catholicism and the guilt of divorce, but they had seemed so abstract. Now that she was herself poised on that precipice, the words took on a profound new meaning. "Supper will be ready in thirty minutes, Frank," she muttered stoically. "Go sit and relax and watch the news."

"Okey-dokey, honey," Frank cooed drunkenly, putting his arms around her. It was all she could do not to recoil from his touch. The memory of Tom's strong embrace earlier that day got her through dinner and the rest of the long, lonely evening.

26

Mark Everett's jaw dropped that Friday evening when he answered the door and saw his fully encumbered friend with a pizza in one hand, a six-pack of beer, in the other and a backpack on his back. "Phillip, how the hell did you ring the doorbell?"

Grinning, Phillip cocked his elbow and walked into a bachelor's paradise. Phillip had been to Mark's apartment many times and never failed to envy his sweet setup. His room at home and the apartment he shared with two other guys at law school were comfortable enough, but he just didn't have the privacy and freedom he desired. Mark's end unit apartment on the second floor had two bedrooms with spacious walk-in closets, one and ∫ baths, a full kitchen and laundry area, and a living room/dining room combination. Sliding glass doors opened on a patio off the living room, where Mark kept a barbeque grill. He also had a garage and a storage room downstairs, under the master bedroom. There was even a small park at the front of the building and woods in the back.

"You're living large like this, yet you make me bring the pizza and suds," Phillip complained good-naturedly. "You always were a mooch, Mark."

"You're late," Mark grumbled.

"Mr. Congeniality, as always. What, cleaning lady didn't come today?" Phillip chided, sliding a mass of empty soda cans and chip bags to one end of the coffee table to make room for the pizza.

"I've been thinking more about this gun thing," said Mark contemplatively as he set out paper plates and napkins. "The more I think about it, the more I want to leave it where it is. My ass is covered. No one but you knows what I did, and I know you won't say anything."

Phillip cringed slightly, knowing he had conspired with Jeff about the gun dilemma. "Listen, Mark. I came up with a way where your ass is still covered but you can also live with your conscience. Covering up evidence in a crime—particularly one that led to the death of Tom Danford's wife—has got to be weighing heavy on you. You wouldn't have brought it up to me otherwise." Mark's face told Phillip he had struck a nerve. "Tim's in jail already and not getting out any time soon. This isn't going to affect him. But maybe the gun will help the police catch the rest of the crooks. Now here's the thing! You send an anonymous note to the police telling them where the gun is. It's up to them to go dredge it up. The only possible way they can track a note to you is if someone knew we were camping at Sesquicentennial State Park. Phillip was well aware he mentioned this to Mark before; he was double checking his friend's veracity.

"No way anyone would know," said Mark emphatically. "I had even told some people we were going camping at Dreher Island State Park. We changed our minds at the last minute to go to Sesquicentennial, remember?"

"Right. Okay, that's covered. Now all we need are some rubber gloves, an old newspaper, regular typing paper and some common glue. That way, the police have no fingerprints, no unique characteristics to trace the note back to you."

With that, Phillip opened his backpack and pulled out a package of rubber gloves, an unopened *USA Today* newspaper in a plastic bag, typing paper and a glue stick. "Voilà! Now, what do you want the note to say?"

"Shit, Phillip, I don't know. I just have this bad feeling. I never should have told Tim I'd hide the gun in the first place. But I can't do anything about that. But if I just let the gun be, I'm safe. Who knows who else is involved in this shooting? Tim said he didn't do it. *Then who did?* I don't want them coming after me. Doing the right thing is one thing; staying alive is another."

"But that's the beauty of all this. Tim won't tell anyone you hid the gun—he was supposed to do it himself. He'd get in trouble if anyone knew he passed that job onto you. Does he even know where you disposed of it?"

Mark shook his head no. "He was arrested before I could talk with him about it. I visited him in jail a few times, but we never talked about it."

"Good," said Phillip, taking a huge bite of pizza. "Not to worry, Mark: The tip-off will be totally anonymous; it's practically foolproof. But you're not completely out of the woods. If someone finds out you hide that gun, you'll be hauled in as an accomplice."

Mark groaned and slid down in chair, arms limp. "Okay, okay, I give up. But I still have a bad feeling about this. So, what are we going to cut and paste? This is like kindergarten all over again."

"Here's a draft I typed up. What do you think?"

Gun from Bank of America robbery of 10/23/04. ???? feet from Jagged rock in SESQUICENTENNIAL State Park.

"You don't want to say what town the bank robbery was?" asked Mark.

"They can figure that out from the date and the name of the bank. I don't want us to appear too slick and professional. How many feet from shore would you say?"

"I don't know, three hundred maybe? Of course, who the hell knows where it is now? Maybe they won't even find it."

"Aw, quit your bellyaching and put your gloves on and let's get this done. You take the first seven words and I'll take the last seven, plus the numbers. I'm faster than you anyway."

"We'll see about that, Speed Racer."

When they had finished, they admired the jumble of letters mounted on a piece of paper:

Gu$_n$ F$_{rom}$ ᴮ☐ᵇ of America Ro**b**bery of
10/23/04
300 feet from Jag$_{\text{♪}ns}$ Rock
SESQUICENTENNIAL State Park.

"Well, what do you think?" asked Phillip.

"Crude but effective. Should we say it's in the water?"

"Maybe. Or we could let the police figure it out. I don't want them knowing what smart guys we are."

"Smart guys wouldn't be involved in this. What a mess. How about adding 'in lake' after Jagged Rock?"

"Sure, we can do that. Here's the envelope. I wiped it for finger-prints and it's a self-sealer. The question now is: where to mail it. How about Columbia, South Carolina? We'll send it to Jay Owens mailed from a Columbia mailbox. Agreed? Let's do the letters for Jay's address."

The friends amended the note to reference the lake and prepared the envelope for mailing. "Ta-da! We're done," said Phillip. He stowed his gear in his backpack and donned his coat. "Let's go, dude."

Mark hadn't budged from his chair. His face was pale, his eyes wild and staring. "I'm still am not sure I want to do this, Phillip. Sup-pose I get found out? Those St. Ditmas House gangstas could come looking for me—I could get shot! And if the cops trace the gun back to me, I could go to prison."

Phillip's patience was at an end. "Look, Mark, there is *no way* any-one can connect this letter or the gun to you. Fact one: No one knows you had the gun. Fact two: No one knows we were camping there that night. Fact three: No one can trace this letter back to you or me. Con-clusion: Nothing's going to go wrong. Trust me. I'm an attorney. Almost."

Mark slipped on his jacket with the slow, deliberate motions of a doomed man savoring every moment of freedom. "You win, counse-lor. But I still have a baaaaaaaad feeling about this."

27

Tom Danford awoke Monday morning feeling refreshed and rein-vigorated. As he shaved, he was amused to see the face that looked back at him in the mirror sported a mule-eating-briars grin. With no appointments until ten, he fixed himself a bacon and cheese omelet and lingered over three cups of coffee, savoring the robust flavor as he idly flipped through the morning shows on TV—something he couldn't recall doing for years. Something was definitely different. In a flash, he knew what it was: His relationship with Susan and the boys. It was homey, that was the closest he could come to describing it. Frank's worry that he was trying to move in on the good doctor's family seemed to be a self-fulfilling prophecy. It bothered Danford very little that it was happening. He was happy, Susan was happy, the boys were happy. The hell with Frank Kemper.

The phone rang. Danford took his sweet time lowering the footrest on his worn La-Z-Boy recliner and sauntered to the nearest phone, in the kitchen. Oh, well, the machine would catch it if he didn't make it. He answered with a comically chipper "Tom Danford here," then his face went white. "Oh, no, Susan. Jeff has been SHOT?"

"Yes, Frank called me. Jeff's in the emergency room at Carolina Medical Center. That's all I know. I'm pulling into a parking space now."

"I'm on my way," said Danford.

Susan's heels clicked across the tiled hospital floor as she rushed to Frank's side. "Frank, Frank! Tell me, is Jeff all right? Please, is he all right?"

Frank stared at her with a look of cold, hard contempt. "He's in surgery. He lost a great deal of blood, but fortunately his vital organs appear to be unharmed. This is all your fault, Susan. I hope you're happy now. Our son was nearly killed thanks to the insipid sleuthing you and the lover you think is so goddamned important."

Suddenly Frank grabbed Susan's shoulders and shook her like a rag doll. His eyes were pits of fire. "You did this to Jeff, you selfish bitch, you and that high and mighty ambulance chaser. So help me God, I'm going to make sure nothing happens to Phillip because of your stupidity."

Crying hysterically, Susan flailed her fists in Frank's face. "Stop it Frank, you're hurting me!"

Within seconds a burly security guard approached and wrested Frank away with sharp tug on the back of his lab coat. "Calm down, Dr. Kemper," he said evenly. "Remember where you are."

Frank brushed the guard's arm away and barked insolently, "You can't tell me what to do. I'm a doctor here."

The guard put his hand on his holster and unsnapped the leather catch. "I'm going to ask you nicely—once—to please leave the ER, Dr. Kemper."

Frank's eyes smoldered. "Okay, okay. I'll go check on my son," he muttered as he slunk away. A safe distance from the guard, he jeered over his shoulder, "You're a rotten mother!"

The guard escorted Susan to a bench and gently sat her down. She was crying inconsolably. Presently, a heavyset nurse with a kind face came over and put her arms around Susan's shoulders. "I couldn't help but overhear Dr. Kemper's outburst," she said. "You need to know the whole story. The bullet entered your son's right shoulder and is lodged there. Jeff has been taken to surgery to remove the bullet, but the wound is not serious. He's going to be fine."

Through her despair, Susan vaguely comprehended the nurse's comforting words. "Fine, did you say he's going to be fine?"

"Yes. Your son may need physical therapy, but he should make a full recovery. And he'll have a beauty of a scar to show off to his friends."

"Oh, thank you, thank you," said Susan, hugging the nurse. "You are very kind."

"Sometimes your husband isn't, Dr. Kemper," said the nurse sheepishly. "You helped my mother through a difficult time in her life after my father died. This is the least I could do. You can wait here in the ER, if you'd like, or there is a waiting room upstairs in surgery. I can tell the surgeon where you are."

"I'd like to stay here, if that's all right," said Susan. "I don't want to run into that—that *bastard*."

The nurse smiled as she led Susan to an empty waiting room. "You'll be comfortable here. Just call me if you need anything."

As the nurse departed, Danford rushed into the room. "I got here as quickly as I could. How's Jeff?" he said, taking her hands between his.

"Jeff's in surgery but he's going to be okay, thank the Lord. The bullet hit him only in the shoulder. Oh, Tom, I don't know how or why this happened. Jeff told me at breakfast this morning he had called the decorator and she could see him at nine o'clock. The next thing I knew, Frank was calling me from the ER saying Jeff had been shot." Susan's tears began to flow as she whimpered softly in Tom's arms.

"Shhh, don't cry," said Tom, cradling her head on his shoulder. "Jeff's a strong little booger. He'll be fine."

"Frank said this was all my fault," Susan sobbed. "That I was a rotten mother to involve my son—"

"Frank's an asshole, Susan. Don't listen to him. Jeff told me last night that this type of investigation is what he has always wanted to do. You want to hear something funny? His career choice has more to do with him watching *Perry Mason* reruns than anything else."

Susan managed a small laugh. "Really? I knew he liked *Perry Mason,* but I didn't know the show had affected him that deeply."

Tom pulled her closer. "Apparently so. His die was cast a long time ago and nothing you could say or do would alter that course. Although, he might change his mind after this. I've learned that being safe is just an illusion. Look at what happened to Beth: She lost her life just running a simple banking errand. God gives us one life to live. It's up to us to live it with all the purpose, all the meaning we can pack into it. Because when your time is up, it's up."

Susan knew how hard it was for Tom to talk about his wife's death. That knowledge made his words all the more meaningful. She had never heard Tom speak so philosophically before. His words comforted her deeply. And he was right: The world was cruel, unfair, dangerous.

But in his arms she felt safer than she ever had before in her life.

28

Phillip dashed into the ER as soon as he heard about his brother. His parents had called him separately. His father's call had been dire, full of recriminations toward his mother and even his brother. Fortunately, his mother had called afterwards with a levelheaded account of the situation. He saw his mother talking on her cell phone and, nearby, Danford conferring with a uniformed cop. He strode quickly to his mother's side and was instantly enveloped in a smothering hug.

"Jeff's in the recovery room," Susan said softly, stroking Phillip's hair. "He's going to be fine! We can go see him." Danford came over and shook Phillip's hand warmly. The three of them boarded the elevator for the 3rd floor recovery room.

"Okay, now that we know Jeff's going to be just fine, somebody please give me the straight poop on this bizarreness," said Phillip.

"All we know," volunteered Danford, "is that Jeff had gone over to see Jennifer, the interior designer that decorated Michael Freidan's study to get her take on the Remington piece."

"But how did he manage to get himself plugged?"

"No one knows for sure. The same cops who worked Freidan's murder are investigating Jeff's shooting. They think they're connected. I was talking with Joe Owens, Jay's son. He was asking me what Jeff was doing at Jennifer's office. All we know is, he talked with her, left her office, and within ten feet of her shop, he was shot. The lone witness, who called the police, didn't see who shot him or even where the shot came from. He just saw Jeff on the sidewalk, bleeding."

Susan shivered at the ghastly mental picture of her baby lying in a pool of his own blood. As they entered the recovery room, Frank was just leaving.

"Well, isn't this cozy? My wife, her lover, and my firstborn son going to see my other son, who got shot because of their recklessness." Frank fixed Danford in his malicious gaze. "Do you have another life-threatening mission for Jeff, counselor?"

Susan put a restraining arm on Tom's arm. "You two go in, I'll be right there. "Frank, I want to talk to you," Susan said as she grabbed his wrist and dragged him to a private corner, like a mother managing a disobedient child. "I want this public maligning to stop," stormed Susan in a fierce whisper. "If I hear you say one more negative thing about Tom or me, I'm going to sue you for defamation of character and sexual abuse. I'm sure everyone in this hospital would *love* to know how you coerced me into taking my top off while we were out sailing while you took Polaroid pictures. And I still have the pictures to prove it. I'll take you down, Frank, so help me. Now back off!"

"Who do you think you are, talking to me—"

"I should have talked to you like this years ago, you narcissistic, son of a bitch. You've crushed my self-esteem with your verbal abuse and bullying, but I'm through turning the other cheek. And another thing, I've kept quiet all these years about the time I had to call the police that night you got drunk and tried to rape me. The newspapers would have a field day with that little escapade. You'd lose your practice."

Frank was indignant. "Rape you? It's not rape when a man wants to have sex with his own wife. It's your wifely duty."

"*Like hell.* You just ask Joe Owens if it's rape or not when a woman—wife or otherwise—says no and the man—husband or otherwise—won't stop. I'm telling you for the last time, Frank, back off."

Frank was speechless; he felt like an utter fool. He remembered that night; one of the cops had taken his side, but the other one, Joe Owens, had sided with Susan. "You won't get away with this!" he cried feebly as Susan stalked away, a triumphant grin on her face.

Susan suppressed a gasp as she saw Jeff lying in the hospital bed with a bulky bandage on his right shoulder and an intravenous running into his left arm. She hugged him gingerly, kissing his cheek repeatedly and cooing endearments.

"What happened with Dad, Mom?" asked Phillip.

"Let's just say I told your father to go sit in the naughty chair." Phillip and Jeff tittered remembering her way of punishing them when they were younger. "How do you feel, darling?"

"I'm fine, except for having trouble keeping my eyes open from the anesthesia. Boy, that's good stuff. I didn't feel a thing. Now that the shock of being shot has worn off, I'm okay. That's always been my worst fear, doing this type of work. Well, I faced it like Paul Drake on *Perry Mason* and I survived. But I didn't even see it coming."

"So what happened? What do you remember?" asked Tom.

"Well, I was leaving the decorator's office and the next thing I knew, I was on the sidewalk with blood running from my shoulder. I did have the feeling, though, that someone was following me from home to her place. I thought I saw this black car drive away after I was shot. Looked kinda new; it might have been a Mustang. I'm not sure it had anything to do with the shooting, though."

"I can tell you're feeling better if you're remembering the make of cars. I'm so glad you're all right. I was so scared."

"I know, Mom. I'm sorry to worry you. I'm a big boy now. I can handle it."

"So what did Jennifer say that was provocative enough to get you shot at?" asked Tom.

"Not much. She didn't know a great deal about the Remington sculpture. Michael had bought it from someone else he knew, not through her. He showed it to her before he bought it to make sure it would fit into her decorating scheme. She recognized it immediately as a Remington and told him it would look great on the bookcase. She didn't know from whom he bought it. He emphasized to her he had gotten it for a great price. That's pretty much it. The next thing I knew, I was being shot at."

"Did you see or hear anything?" pressed Tom.

"No, not really. Just street noise. Nothing unusual."

"How many shots?"

"Just one, I think. But I'm not sure. It all happened so fast."

"I think this was a warning shot. If someone had wanted to hurt you, they would have aimed lower and more to the center," said Tom, regretting his remark immediately as Susan looked at him crossly.

"Now there's a comforting thought," said Jeff. "On my next assignment, Tom, I'll expect you to give me an adequate supply of Valium with a police vest."

"I thought you said you had faced down your worst fear," Phillip kidded him.

"The old ones, yes. He just gave me some new ones."

Tom laughed and proceeded with his rumination. "We're getting close to something and someone is scared. Obviously, someone wants us to stop checking on this figure. What could be so important about it? We know it was stolen, but somehow, I can't see Michael Freidan being the receiver of stolen goods. By all accounts, he was a solid citizen with some typical character flaws but no real blemishes on his record."

"Maybe Freidan found out the sculpture was stolen and confronted the person who sold it to him," offered Phillip.

"Very good, Phillip. I'll bet you are right on the money. All we have to do is figure out from whom Freidan bought that Remington and how he knew it was stolen."

"I'll bet it's the same person who put that picture in Freidan's hand," Susan conjectured. "I'm scheduled to hypnotize Ann Marie Harkins on Wednesday about that picture with her husband kissing the blonde. The doctor said Jeff can come home tomorrow. If he promises to stay put, I'll keep that appointment." Jeff was nodding his head vigorously. "If the session produces any new details, maybe Phillip can use them to find out where the picture came from and who had access to it."

Jeff settled back in his bed with a satisfied look on his face. "I love it when a plan comes together."

29

Susan had taken to sleeping in the guest room the last few days. Neither of the boys said anything to her, nor did Frank comment on her absence from their bedroom. During her usual morning run on this Wednesday morning, she was in a world of her own as the jigsaw pieces of her twenty-five year marriage tumbled apart and tried to put themselves back together in her tormented mind.

Normally she enjoyed her morning runs. Even though there were no sidewalks, she usually ran easily in this quiet neighborhood with its brick houses and beautifully landscaped lawns. She barely noticed the chrysanthemums that added color to the doorsteps in preparation for the fall. She waved distractedly to her neighbor, Carl Simmons, who was walking down his driveway to retrieve his morning newspaper from the street box.

"Susan, watch out!" Simmons cried as a black car suddenly accelerated and sped past Susan, narrowly missing her.

Instinctively Susan dove into Simmons' driveway as the car sped away.

Susan caught her breath on the stairs and waited for her heart to stop beating. The car was black with tinted windows. There was something odd about the rear tail lights, too, but it had all happened too fast for her to read the license plate.

"That idiot!" yelled Simmons as he helped Susan to her feet. "Are you all right?"

"Fine, I think," said Susan, examining her skinned knees. "Thanks for the warning. I was in la-la land."

"Don't mention it." Simmons looked at her with concern. "Anyone out to get you, Susan?"

Her gut feeling was someone didn't want her hypnotizing Ann Marie Harkins that morning, but she wasn't about to share that information with her neighbor. "Oh, probably just someone that didn't like the pie I made for the last potluck spring dinner," she said. "Thanks again, Carl."

Susan jogged home—facing traffic this time—with a new mystery to ponder. She checked on Jeff once home and showered. He assured her his shoulder felt fine and that he would turn on the alarm system when she left. Then she was on to her office to meet with Ann Marie Harkins.

Susan's office was located in an older house in the Dilworth section of Charlotte that had been converted into office space. It was a magnificent colonial with tall columns in front. Susan's office was on the second floor in the rear of the building, overlooking the garden. She had two rooms, a waiting room and her office. The waiting room was furnished with a large tan couch, end tables, lamps, and an overstuffed chair—all very traditional and comfortable. Her clients adored the large seascape, purchased on one of her beach getaways, positioned on the wall facing the couch. The soothing picture captured early morning beachcombers, barely distinguishable in the light fog, against a backdrop of crashing waves.

The office was simple and elegant. She had a small desk in the corner with a computer. A large recliner filled the opposite corner with a smaller chair, where Susan usually sat, at an angle to the recliner. A laptop computer and other pieces of equipment rested on the end table next to the recliner. Susan liked the office because it had a separate exit door to the hall. Her patients that way never saw each other with a separate entrance and exit to protect her clients' anonymity.

She set up her video equipment and waited for Ann Marie to arrive. When it turned nine o'clock and Ann Marie hadn't arrived, she began to worry. Susan's fear that her would-be assailant had gotten to Ann Marie was assuaged when Julie, her receptionist, showed her in five minutes later.

"I'm so sorry I'm late. My husband says I will be late for my own funeral."

"That's quite all right. Come on in. Sit down, please, and make yourself comfortable."

"As we talked about, I'm going to hypnotize you to see if you can remember where you saw the picture of your husband kissing his blonde receptionist. There's got to be some reason why that's not upsetting you."

"It just seems very innocent to me. I don't know why."

"Mm-hmm," murmured Susan, absorbed in her work. "Here is how this is going to work. The videotape is already on as I give these explanations in case we bring this to court. First, I'm going to have you describe your reaction to the picture of your husband and his former receptionist. Then I'm going to ask you the same question in hypnosis.

'While you are in hypnosis, I can watch your reaction on my computer monitor via these sensors I'm putting on the palm of your hands. As you can see, they are held in place by this black strap. Just pull it so it's comfortable. What this does is monitor your level of hypnosis. It's not terribly dissimilar to and EKG machine that monitors your heart rate. This sensor just measures relaxation. We're high tech here."

"As long as I don't have to operate the computer, I'm happy to cooperate."

"Just sit and relax now and bring up the image of the picture before I hypnotize you. Can you see it?"

"Yes, I can see it. I know it's Mary Lou but somehow it's a familiar picture. I know I have seen it before but bigger. It's not upsetting to me either so I know it's innocent."

"Great, Anne Marie, you're doing great. Now we'll see what you remember in hypnosis. Close your eyes and take a deep breath. Now exhale. Inhale to the count of three and now exhale to the count of six. Very good. I want you to use your wonderful imagination and picture yourself covered in a blanket of relaxation. You are feeling very calm and relaxed. Notice all the relaxation around your eyes in particular. Your eyes are feeling very heavy."

As Susan spoke in a soothing, singsong voice, the computer indicated Ann Marie had reached a deep level of relaxation and altered consciousness. "Ann Marie, I want you to focus on all the feelings you felt when you saw the picture of John and his former receptionist. Allow those feelings to enter your body and perceive them as strongly as you can. When you reach that plateau of feeling, nod your head."

Ann Marie nodded her head.

"Let those feelings carry you to the first time you saw the picture. Don't force an image; just let those feelings carry you. Tell me when you see something."

"Christmas," said Ann Marie with the difficulty of movement typical of hypnotized patients. Even more slowly now, she slowly said, "I see a Christmas tree."

"You're doing great, Ann Marie. Let the Christmas tree come into focus. Look closely at the tree. What do you see?"

"Presents and someone dressed like Santa Claus."

"Take a closer look around the tree. What else do you see?"

"I—I can't see very much. The tree is starting to fade."

But Susan could see the scene quite clearly. There was a large room, with about sixty people circulating with drinks in their hands while waitresses served appetizers. A large banner with the words "Rotary Club Christmas Party" swam into her view, followed by a crystal clear vision of John Harkins kissing his blonde receptionist underneath a mistletoe sprig. No wonder Ann Marie wasn't upset by the picture, Susan thought. The kiss might have been a little suggestive but it was in plain sight of everyone. Now it was Susan's task to help Ann Marie see the same scene without influencing her responses.

"Take a deep relaxing breath and go back to feeling the feelings associated with the picture. Just relax. Let the image come into focus."

"I see a party hat. It's red with silver. That's all I see."

Susan saw it was time to release Ann Marie from her hypnotic state. While she was still suggestible, she leaned close to her and whispered: "Sometime this week, your subconscious mind will reveal the information you seek about the picture. Perhaps it will come in your dreams, perhaps in a waking moment. But you will have the knowledge you need with crystal clarity. In a moment, I'm going to count from 1 to 5. On the count of 5, your eyes will be open and you will be fully alert and awake remembering all you need to remember from the session. 1, 2, 3, 4, 5, eyes open."

Ann Marie opened her eyes slowly and looked at Susan with the typical confused, sleepy look of someone coming out of hypnosis. There was no doubt in Susan's mind she had been in deep hypnosis from all the reactions she was showing.

"I'm sorry," said Ann Marie. "I can't believe I didn't see the picture. All I saw was a Christmas tree, presents, and Santa Claus."

"While that's true, what you did see are probably clues about the picture. What is the connection between the picture and the Christmas tree, the presents and Santa?"

Ann Marie thought a moment. "I'm not sure. Could the picture have been taken at a Christmas party? There's something in the back of my mind, but I can't quite bring it into focus."

"Don't force it. I gave you the suggestion during hypnosis that sometime during the week your subconscious mind will lead you to information about the picture you are searching for. Just let that happen. Call me when it does." Susan shut off the videotape and was about to walk with Ann Marie to the door.

"I don't know if I should say anything. You might think I'm a little touched if I do," Ann Marie began.

"What's on your mind?" replied Susan.

"Well, my father came to see me last night."

"Yes, go on."

"I was just about falling off to sleep and there he was. He was there in my room. It was different from a dream, but it's hard to explain the difference. Anyway, he was worried about my mother and wanted to make sure I took care of her. He also told me where he put an extra insurance policy. He had a fireproof safety box under the bed in their room. He also said 'John didn't do it.' Then he said something strange, 'Remington.' I have no idea what he meant by Remington. Isn't this weird? Was I dreaming? I'm going to go see my mother today and check for those insurance papers."

"Thanks for telling me, Ann Marie. I know that couldn't have been easy. I'm going to write down the name of a book for you. It's called *Hello From Heaven,* by Bill and Judy Guggenheim. It's the best book I've read on something called after death communication. Many, many people have had these experiences, according to the interviews in this book, so no, you are not whacked. Unfinished business or warnings are often transmitted by the recently deceased to those still living. There was a Remington sculpture in your father's den. He might have been trying to tell you it has something to do with his murder."

"I was so afraid I was going crazy with all the stress of my father's death, John's accident and police suspicions of him being the murderer. Do you think my father was trying to console me?"

"Could be. What seems to happen, too, is the personality of the dead remains. So, if your father was protective of you and your mother, he'd continue to act that way."

"Extremely so. He always took good care of us. He was a tough businessman but a caring father and from what I can tell a good husband to my mother. Do you think I'll see him again?"

"Could be. Do let me know, if you do. You also did very well in hypnosis, Ann Marie. Trust your subconscious mind to reveal what you are searching for.

With Ann Marie gone, Susan could now think about what she going to do about what she had seen during the hypnosis session. If Ann Marie doesn't remember the picture was taken at a Rotary Christmas party, should she say something to Tom about her vision of the party? Will he think she was whacked? She should tell Tom about Ann Marie seeing her father? Maybe she should investigate this Rotary party on her own. And what about the black car that almost ran her over? Was that a coincidence? Should she tell Tom about that, too?

30

The traffic lights were all in Danford's favor this Wednesday morning as he drove to his ten o'clock appointment with Marjorie Freidan, who had affably consented to allow him to examine her late husband's bank statements. Danford was confident there had to be a check—or, more likely, a withdrawal—for several thousands of dollars. Michael had paid someone for that sculpture. Once he knew who that someone was, Danford would be closer to finding his killer.

Marjorie answered the door. She was impeccably dressed, as always, but the emotional toll of her husband's murder showed on her careworn face. "Please do come in, Tom," she said in her mellifluous Southern accent, a honeyed drawl that even the recent tragedy couldn't weaken. "I've got all the financial papers here in Michael's office.

It was all I could to be in the room long enough to round them up. I can't bear to be in there for more than a few moments, but you are welcome to take as long as you'd like. Would you like some coffee?"

"Thanks. That would be great. This might take a while."

Marjorie walked Danford to the office and excused herself to fetch the coffee. As Danford anticipated, the bloodstains had been removed and the apple pie order Michael Freidan demanded had been restored. Michael sat at Freidan's desk, where Marjorie had neatly arranged the financial documents for his perusal.

"Here's your coffee," said Marjorie. "There's more in the decanter. Let me know if I can answer any questions. My husband was organized, but he had an unusual filing system. I could never find anything—not that I looked very often. This office was off limits to everyone in the family." She hurried from the room without acknowledging Danford's thanks.

As the hours passed, Danford grew frustrated with his fruitless search that revealed no suspicious transactions among Freidan's records. Fortunately, as a safeguard against the reality of his untimely demise, Freidan had shared with his wife the passwords to his online accounts. No surprise: The online statements matched Freidan's physical checkbooks to the penny. It was obvious to Danford that no one was going to take a dime of Freidan's pocket without him knowing about it. His IRAs and 401k accounts were in meticulous order, with no significant withdrawals evident.

Danford was about to throw in the towel when he noticed Freidan had a PayPal account. A few clicks later, there was the proverbial smoking gun: a $12,000 payment to stdismashouse@yahoo.com on May 22nd, two weeks after the robbery. Maybe it's just a donation but maybe it's more, thought Danford. As he jotted down a note to have Phillip follow up on the St. Dismas House organization, Marjorie appeared in the doorway.

"Marjorie, I found a payment from Michael's PayPal account to an organization called what might be St. Dismas House. Know anything about it?"

"PlayPal account? What's that? It sound s—sexual," Marjorie said demurely.

"No, PayPal. It's a service that allows people to transfer money electronically over the Internet. eBay users use it all the time." He could see by Marjorie's expression she wasn't familiar with eBay either. He didn't want to get hung up on explaining all that involved.

"Back in May, Michael sent $12,000 to what looks like St. Dismas House. Did your husband ever mention that organization?"

"My, $12,000. Electronic money transfer? I just can't keep up with all this technology. I just don't know what I'm going to do now that Michael is gone. I'm not familiar with that organization. Michael did all the charitable donations. I just went with him to any fund raising dinners. I just came to see if you wanted anymore coffee."

"How about in about ten minutes. I just have this stack of papers to go through and I'm finished."

Tom went through the last stack that had been on Michael's desk. It looked like a random collection of different papers. Nothing stood out until he saw this newspaper clipping. The story described objects that had been stolen from a house in the Meyers Park section of Charlotte, the same place the cops who visited Jeff had mentioned. On the top margin of the article, a scrawled comment in black ballpoint pen with the signature "Ron" read as follows: "Michael, this look like your sculpture. Are there more then one?" In the photo was a before the robbery picture of a room with many objects including what looked like the Remington statue. Tom went looking for Marjorie. He found her on the porch.

"Marjorie, thanks for the coffee. It was great. I did find something else that might be helpful. Did Michael ever mention anything about stolen goods to you?"

"Sometime in June, I think it was, Michael said he thought he had bought something that was stolen. Can't remember now what it was. I told him he had an overactive imagination. He couldn't quite let it go, though. I think he asked his lawyer to look into it. I never paid it much mind. Michael could get carried away at times."

"Who was Michael's attorney, Marjorie?"

"Tony Nesco. I'll call him and tell him to give you whatever information you need. Better yet, I'll call the office right now. There's no phone out here. I'll make the call from the living room," she said. She returned a moment later. "He's with a client, but he'll call here as soon as he can. I left a message to have him tell you anything you need to know"

"Marjorie, do you remember anything else about what he thought was stolen goods?"

"Not really. Although, it couldn't have been anything we bought for the house. I would have known about it. It must have been for his office at work or maybe his office here in the house. He was always buying Civil War memorabilia for both places." The phone rang. Marjorie looked appealingly at Danford. "Would you mind getting that, Tom?"

Danford nodded as he walked to the living room and picked up the phone. "Tom Danford here. Hi, Tony. Yes, that's correct I'm representing John Harkins. The family is convinced he didn't kill Freidan so they are fully cooperating. Marjorie said Freidan talked with you about being concerned something he had bought was stolen. Do you have any more information on that interaction? A Remington statue is missing from his office, was that involved? Do you know where he got that sculpture?"

"Can't say that I do. I vaguely remember seeing it, but I have no idea where it came from. There *was* something Michael had been concerned about. I'd have to check his file to refresh my memory. I vaguely remember he was upset about something. He said something about 'when it's too good to be true, there's something wrong. Let me get back to you on that."

"I'd appreciate that. We assume it was taken the day he was killed. Might be connected to his murder."

"Did anyone search your client? Maybe he took it or hid it if it was big."

Danford cleared his throat. "It's for certain he didn't have the sculpture on him. The police searched him rather thoroughly, plus it would be too big to hid on his person."

"Sorry about that. No, I'm afraid I don't know anything about it. Anything else I can help you with?"

"No, just whatever Michael might have been worried was stolen." Danford gave Nesco his cell phone number and hung up.

Nesco's questions did make Danford wonder. Could John have taken the sculpture out of the office and stashed it? The actual amount of time that elapsed between the moment he found the body and called 911 was impossible to define; conceivably, he might have had time to hide it somewhere in the house. Why would he get involved in selling Michael Freidan a statue? Seemed out of repertoire of his activities, but it's a loose end that needs checking.

Tom picked up his cell phone as he drove away from the Freidan house. "Phillip, got an assignment for you. Check on a place called St. Dismas House or something like that in the Charlotte area. Thanks. See you later."

31

"Lukowski, get in here!" shouted Captain Jay Owens from his private office at police headquarters.

Stan Lukowski looked up from his desk with a mock smile on his piggish face. "Yes, sir, *captain.*"

Jay Owens despised the sarcastic edge that was always in Lukowski's voice. Lukowski might be a proficient detective, but he had the attitude and demeanor of a common schoolyard bully. His retirement couldn't come soon enough for Owens' sanity. At least Lukowski's brother was not around any more. Two Lukowskis were more than Jay Owens could manage. Owens handed Lukowski the tip-off note Mark and Phillip had painstakingly crafted. "This arrived in today's mail. Is the date on this note the same day of the Bank of America robbery where Beth Danford was killed?"

"I'll double-check, but I think you're right, *captain.*" Lukowski pronounced the word "captain" as if it tasted like excrement.

"Check this for fingerprints and follow up on it. Let's see what our divers can come up with."

"Yes sir, *captain.*"

Owens leveled his wolfish eyes in a predatory stare. "Lukowski, can the sarcasm. Your brother got kicked off the force because he was taking bribes. Any captain would have done what I did. If you want to stay until you retire, you'll ditch the attitude. If I hear so much as a whisper about you getting out of line in the field again, you're out of here. No pension. You get me, mister?"

Lukowski nodded meekly. He would trade his soul for that pension.

"Oh, yeah, I want Joe working this case with you. He's due a major case and this will be good experience."

"Yes, sir, captain," said Lukowski briskly, as he spun on his heel and marched back to his desk. He knew the captain was pairing him with his son to make sure he minded his Ps and Qs, but there was no sense protesting. The threat of losing his pension had thoroughly cowed him, for the moment.

Lukowski parked his colossal bulk in the too-small swivel chair. "Asshole," he muttered. "I'll give the kid an experience, alright." He navigated to the unsolved cases folder on his computer, opened the Bank of America case log of three years earlier and printed it. Bingo! The bank robbery date matched the date on the tip-off note. He never doubted it; unsolved crimes bugged him and the details of this particular one were imprinted on his brain.

Lukowski sauntered over to the crime lab and dropped the note off with Dick Jennings to check for fingerprints and other identifying marks. He doubted there'd be any. Whoever fashioned the tip-off, using the tried and true ransom note technique, would be too smart to let that happen. Somebody had gone to an awful lot of trouble to compose the note and assiduously hide his identity. Why? What would they have to gain by the police finding the gun used in that robbery? Was someone trying to get someone back? Was it a pay-off gone bad?

Back at his desk, he picked up his phone. "Hi, Henry. Got a job for your guys out in Sesquicentennial State Park outside Columbia."

"Sorry, Lukowski, no can do. That's across state lines. You've got to call the Columbia Police Department directly."

"For Christ sake, this bureaucratic bullshit is always getting in the way. Can't you guys just go there and do the job you're supposed to do?"

"I'll tell you what I'll do for you, Lukowski. I'll call Columbia and see what I can arrange. Maybe if we offer to help out, it will happen faster. But you'll owe me big time!"

"Like shit, I'll owe you. That's what you get paid for. You think this is Disneyland where the fairy godmother rewards your ass for doing your job? Call me back when you know something."

Joe Owens had been standing near Lukowski's desk listening to his phone conversation. The sour look on his face made it clear he wasn't happy about being assigned to ride herd on the man he considered the biggest prick south of the Mason-Dixon line. "Hi, Stan," said Owens tonelessly. "I understand we're working together on this old murder case. What do you have so far?"

Sneaky bastard, thought Lukowski. *Didn't even hear him.* "Well, aren't you a ray of fucking sunshine? Pull up a seat. I've got the file here. You can read it later, but I'll go over the highlights. And don't lose anything."

Owens melted into the chair with a drawn out sigh. "I won't, don't worry."

"Here's the deal," Lukowski began. "Three years ago, this kid in a mask walks into the Bank of America branch in Myers Park and tries to hold it up. Beth Danford, Tom Danford's wife, was stupid enough to put her checkbook into her purse after the robber said for everyone to put up their hands. We're guessing he thought she was going for a gun and panicked. So, he's a stupid jerk, too. He shoots her dead and runs out the door. Witnesses say, based on his voice and size, he's a white male in his late teens, early twenties. We have no clues. Today, your darling pappy gets this note about the gun used in that robbery being dumped in a lake down near Columbia."

Lukowski shuffled through his notes. "Sesquicentennial State Park. I dropped the note and envelope off with forensics, but I don't expect they'll find anything. Someone wants us to dig up that gun, but it doesn't make any sense. Whom are they setting up?"

"Do we have any choice but to look for it?" asked Owens innocently.

Lukowski twisted his mouth into a dumbfounded smirk and shook his head slowly. "You eat a bowl of stupid for breakfast? *Of course we get the gun.* Our divers have to coordinate with South Carolina divers. Maybe sometime this millennium, they'll go looking for this gun. If I'm stuck with you, you might as well make yourself useful. Go down and meet with these cracker South Carolina cops. Find out if there's a way they keep track of who goes in and out of that park. I want to know everyone who stopped to take a piss in that park from the day of that shooting to this very frickin' moment."

"That's three years' worth of information. It will take weeks to get that," Owens protested.

"And you're waiting around here for what, a ride on Santa's sleigh? Get your ass in gear."

That will keep the prick tied up for a while, thought Lukowski, grinning like the cat that swallowed the canary as Owens ambled back to his desk. He glanced at the old case file. That Midland robbery had always bothered him. He might bust Danford chops whenever they met, but he respected the guy. He knew he would help any cop who got into trouble. It rankled Lukowski that Danford wife's murderer had never been caught. Not good for Lukowski's image as an ace detective, either.

32

Mark Everett nervously awaited the arrival of Phillip Kemper late this Friday morning in a rear booth at Anderson's, a popular breakfast eatery renowned for its bargain-priced hungry man platter consisting of three eggs, hash browns, toast, and a giant, artery-hardening slice of country ham served all day. The menu held not one jot of interest for Mark, whose right leg bounced up and down like a jackhammer as he sipped coffee and darted his eyes guiltily around the room, supremely regretful he had opened his big mouth about that goddamn gun.

"Hey, man, how's it going?" said Phillip with annoying cheer as he slid into the booth across from Mark.

"What you go to be so happy about? You get laid or something?"

Phillip laughed. "Something like that. It seems an organization called St. Dismas House seems to be involved in the murder of Michael Freidan. I'll bet it's the same place Tim was involved with. After a few hours of looking this morning, I found information about both the original Dismas House and this knock-off St. Dismas House group. The original Dismas House is a legitimate organization, helping former prisoners rebuild their lives. The St. Dismas House also takes in former prisoners, but they are not connected with the original Dismas house, which is strange."

"So what do you need me for if you found out all this info already?" said Mark grouchily.

"The St. Dismas House here in Charlotte is listed as a legitimate nonprofit organization. It even has a board of directors. The purpose of the organization is to provide room and board in a home-like atmosphere for young men between the ages of fourteen and nineteen. If the kids are younger than sixteen, they supposedly get parental or court consent to house the boys. In the greater Charlotte area, there are four homes with five boys in each home and a live-in, adult supervisor. These St. Dismas Houses are touted as a means to keep young boys who have no family support off the streets and away from the criminal element. They rely on fundraising for support. Very noble description.

"Now, here's where it get interesting. Because of their nonprofit status, they are required to publish an annual report that identifies the board of directors, which includes—get this—Jay Owens, the Chief of Police, and your father! What's not listed is the name of the manager or house supervisors. The annual report references the houses' adult leaders but doesn't provide their names. They do list the houses, though, and the addresses. Do you know where Tim lived?"

Phillip took out a map of Charlotte on which he had marked the locations of the city's four houses.

Mark scanned the map. "Let's see. I did pick him up a few times. He didn't live on Tyvola, I know that much. We went out to a bar on Fifth Street one night to meet some guys from work. I think I picked him up on the corner of West Trade and North Tryon. I remember thinking it was odd that he didn't want me fetching him at the St. Dismas House."

"So that would put him here, near this house on South Tryon," Phillip suggested. "Did he ever mention the name of the guy who ran the house where he stayed? It could be that this outfit is legitimate, but maybe there's a supervisor who is leading these kids down the road to ruin rather than enlightenment."

"I don't remember, really. I never met anyone from there. Wait a minute. When he asked me to get rid of the gun, he said something about he'd be in trouble with *Tony* if he didn't do the job right. Who Tony is, I'm not sure. Tim was always pretty vague about the place until he had the gun—then he totally panicked. I'd never seen him so ape-shit nervous before."

"Do you think Tim would be willing to talk more about this?"

Mark's hand shook as he raised his coffee mug to his lips. "Maybe, if there's something in it for him. You're not going to tell anyone what you know about Tim and the gun, are you?"

"No, of course not. Don't worry. I'll keep you out of this." Phillip paused before posing his toughest question. "Did your father ever talk about this place?"

"*What!* You think my father had something to do with all this?"

"Not in so many words. But he *is* on the board."

"Look, he's on the board of directors of a lot of places—probably more than he can keep track of. If I know him, he probably sends one of his flunkies to the meetings."

"So, who would he have sent?"

Mark's fingers drummed nervously on his mug. "Can't you just let it go? Why are you sticking your nose into this?"

"Because," said Phillip sternly, "this group is shaping up to be a major player in the murder of Michael Freidan. It's what Tom Danford is paying me to find out. Either that entire organization, or someone in one of the houses, is not only involved in petty larceny, but also in cold-blooded murder."

Mark bristled. "Other than collecting your loot from Danford, how exactly does this affect you? It's too close to you and me. Suppose they found out I hid the gun and we sent the note. We'll *both* be in deep shit."

"Whoa, wait a minute. *You* hid the gun. *You* sent the note. I didn't have anything to do with all that."

Mark stood up abruptly and flung a five-dollar bill on the table. "That's not what I'd tell the police."

33

When Terry put the call through to him from Jay Owens, Danford expected the worst: the further escapades of his nemesis, Lukowski, or dire news about Susan or the boys, for whose lives he now feared every waking moment. They were due at 2:00 PM for a roundtable to discuss their latest findings on the Freidan case. It was 1:55 now. As he put the call on speakerphone, Danford sighed with relief as Terry showed the trio into his office. "Hi, Jay," said Danford. "What's up?"

"Maybe something, maybe nothing. But I have to tell you, we got an anonymous tip about the gun allegedly used in the Bank of America robbery. The legitimacy of the tip's in question, of course, but we're bound to check it out. We'll be dredging the lake at Sesquicentennial State Park over in Columbia all week. I wanted to tell you before this gets out to the press."

Danford's spirit rejoiced. *Closure.* Susan smiled tenderly at him, her eyes alight with empathy. Phillip and Jeff, his arm in a sling, flashed thumbs up signs. "After all these years, a break in the case," said Danford softly, as if to himself.

"I certainly hope so," said Owens. "I don't have to tell you, Tom, we've been stymied for three years. Until now. It's unlikely we'll find the gun is registered to the killer, but it may yield other information. I'll keep you posted."

"You do that. And thank you, Jay. Goodbye."

"Man, that's great news," said Phillip. He longed to tell him the whole story, but it was too complex and the timing was wrong.

Susan squeezed Danford's palm warmly. "I'm happy for you, Tom."

Abashed, Danford cleared his throat and said, "Okay, the gang's all here. Let's go into the conference room. There's coffee there."

In the conference room, Susan poured Danford and herself a mug of coffee. "I'll start," she said. "I hypnotized Ann Marie Harkins. She didn't remember the picture but she did get images of a Christmas tree and presents. I gave her the suggestion that a clearer message will come to her during the week. It's likely that picture of John kissing his receptionist is part of a larger image taken at a Christmas party, which would explain why Ann Marie was so sure the kiss was innocuous. If that's true, someone had access to that picture. They could have been at the Christmas party and obtained a copy of it, which they manipulated for their own purposes.

Susan paused. She wanted badly to describe her chilling encounter with the speeding car that morning, but decided it was best discussed with Danford in private; there was no need to worry the boys. "I have an appointment to hypnotize Marjorie Freidan next week to delve into the noises she heard the morning of Michael's murder. Hopefully, under hypnosis, she'll recall more details."

Phillip spoke next. "I found out some information about the real Dismas House and the St. Dismas House here in Charlotte, the group Freidan sent that large amount of money to." For the benefit of Susan and Jeff, he explained that Tom had found the money in Michael Freidan's accounts. "St. Dismas House is an organization that rents houses to provide a home-like living environment for teens ages sixteen to eighteen. They have about four houses in the Charlotte area. Each house has around five boys living there with one or two adult supervisors.

"All the boys have had some minor skirmishes with the law. The boys are too old for foster care, but without adult supervision, they are prone to getting into trouble. The courts will often give them probation without jail time if they are willing to go to one of the houses. They are required, though, to live there and abide by the rules. As a nonprofit organization, the St. Dismas House annual report is a matter of public record. We know Jay Owens and Roger Everett are on the board of directors. But we don't know who the adults are or the managers, if there are more then one adults. I'm going to see what more I can find out tomorrow."

Jeff sat forlornly, with an uncharacteristic frown on his face, fidgeting with his cast. "I don't have anything to report, other than my shoulder is better."

"We're glad to hear that, Jeff. This investigation is getting even more dangerous. I want you two boys to be extra careful and limit your investigation to computer and record searches."

"Leave it to Jeff to get shot leaving a decorator's office. Talk about wimpy!" said Phillip.

"Phillip! Don't pick on your brother," chided Susan.

Tom continued the report. "As Phillip said, we did find out about the money Michael Freidan sent the St. Dismas Houses. What's possible is someone is using those boys to commit robberies and then fencing the stolen goods. I found something else in Michael's office." Tom passed around the newspaper clipping with the picture of the Remington sculpture along with other stolen articles and Ron's scrawled comment in black ballpoint pen asking Freidan about his sculpture.

"It looks like the person named Ron alerted Freidan about the possibility his sculpture might have been stolen. We know from the visit from the police, initiated by Jeff, that the sculpture was stolen," Danford continued. "Now we have proof that Michael Freidan later learned the sculpture he had bought was stolen. He might have confronted the person that sold him the Remington. Maybe the person he confronted killed him."

Danford paused to make sure his audience was with him. "This gives us some more information also about whoever stole the sculpture. He's not a smart crook. A smart crook wouldn't have taken that figure. A smart crook would stick to stealing and selling untraceable duplicate items, like plain diamond earrings, non- engraved watches, and so forth. This might be a maverick crook within an organized crime group."

"Wow. Makes sense," said Phillip. "What do we do now?"

"I'm not sure I want you checking out those St. Dismas Houses, Phillip. That might be dangerous. Jeff's shooting might have been just a warning. Ordinarily, I'd turn this over to the police, but I think someone there might be involved. Like you said, it's the crimes that are sending these boys to the St. Dismas houses. I'd like to see if we can learn something about the adults in these local houses. See what you can find out through the Internet and court records only. You hear me? I don't want you to go there if you find out anything. I'll go myself."

Susan was relieved that Danford was keeping Phillip out of harm's way. His concern, almost paternal, touched her heart.

"So what's my assignment?" asked Jeff hopefully. "I don't want to be benched."

Tom thought for a minute. "You and Phillip can go to the courthouse and bone up on recent burglaries. The cops who accosted you had their lips zipped tight on the matter. We could go to the police, but I don't know who I can trust there."

"You don't feel you could trust Jay Owens?" asked Phillip. "I know he's on the Dismas House board of directors, but you don't think he could be involved in the robberies, do you?"

"I doubt Jay is involved with a criminal activity, but I'm not taking any chances that someone close to him with access to his notes or files might be involved. Someone is doing a good job framing John. He or she knows police procedure and how to make him appear to be the prime suspect."

"Let me see if I have this right. Mom's hypnotizing Mrs. Freidan next week to see what she remembers the morning of the murder. We're waiting to see if Mrs. Harkins remembers anything more about the Christmas party during which Mr. Harkins kissed his blonde receptionist. Gimpy and I are going to the courthouse to check burglary records and see who sends whom to these St. Dismas houses." With that comment, Jeff swatted his brother with his good arm. "I'm going to check online or maybe even in the courthouse records to see if I can find out who the adult supervisors are at these St. Dismas houses. Have I got that right?"

"Right on, man," said Tom. "Make it so." Everyone laughed at Tom's reference to the captain of the Federation starship Enterprise, Jean-Luc Picard's, famous command and started leaving the room in good cheer.

Susan was the last going out the door. She turned to Tom as the boys went down the hall and said, "Tom, we have to talk."

34

Susan sat on the couch in Danford's office. Sitting in one of the comfortable upholstered chairs, he faced her, smiling enigmatically. With a little pang of fear, Susan thought his expression looked a trifle amorous.

"So, what can I do for you, Susan?" said Danford flirtatiously.

"There are two things I need to talk to you about. For the past few days, I've had a feeling I'm being followed. I've seen a black car in my rearview mirror a few times but didn't think too much about it. When I noticed it, it turned off so it seemed innocent enough. This morning when I was out running, someone in a black car tried to run me off the road. If it hadn't been for my neighbor, Clark, warning me, I might be in the hospital now—or the morgue. I'm not usually the paranoid type, but I'm getting nervous."

"I want you off the case immediately," said Danford sternly. "It's getting too dangerous. First Jeff gets shot and now someone is terrorizing you. I cannot risk your life with this investigation."

"I'm a big girl and I can take care of myself," said Susan assertively. "I just thought you should know. It's for certain we're getting closer and someone is trying to scare us off this case. Well, I don't scare that easily. I'll be extra careful and watch what is going on around me."

"Don't get your feathers ruffled, Susan. I just don't want you in be in danger. You mean too much to me."

Susan was touched by Tom's comment. "I'll be fine. Don't worry."

"So what was the other thing you wanted to talk about?"

"It's something I've wanted to share with you for the longest time. I have to warn you in advance, it's rather strange."

"I'm listening."

Susan took a deep breath. "When I hypnotized Anne Marie about the picture, I could see what she was seeing—only with more clarity and detail. I could tell that she was describing a Rotary Club Christmas party, although she couldn't. The picture was taken during that event."

"Run that by me again. You shared Ann Marie's subconscious mental image, even though you weren't there. That doesn't make sense."

"When a hypnotist hypnotizes a client, he or she also goes into some level of hypnosis. For some reason, when I regress witnesses back to a previous event, I can also see the event clearly in my mind's eye. Even when the witnesses can't focus, I can. It sounds farfetched, I know, but there is research into a phenomenon called shared consciousness that validates its existence between husbands and wives and parents and children. It's how wives seem to know when their husbands are cheating, for example. When Ann Marie talked about seeing a Christmas tree, presents and someone dressed up like Santa Claus, I could visualize the whole Christmas party scene, right down to a banner that said 'Rotary Club Christmas Party.'"

"Does this make you psychic or something?"

"I wouldn't go that far, but it is an unusual ability. It does create a small problem, though. We can investigate what I see or experience, but it obviously won't hold up in court. I also cannot prompt the subject into seeing what I see, because then opposing counsel can claim I was suggesting something that perhaps wasn't there."

"I hear you. How certain are you that what you are seeing is accurate?"

"I know in the kidnapping case, I could see the text underneath the letter E on the windshield sticker even though Mary Ford couldn't see it."

"So not only are you beautiful, smart, and nice to have around, you have a gift. What more could a man want?" Danford said with a playful leer.

Susan sighed with relief at Tom's reaction and warmed to his flirtation. "I'm glad you don't think this is too strange. The only other people who know about it are my friend, Peggy Hunter and Frank. I haven't mentioned it to the boys."

"So what did Peggy and Frank say?"

"Frank thinks it's freakish and that I should just stay home and be a housewife. Peggy thinks it's great. She's a wonderful friend."

"I'm glad you told me. I'm hoping it's one hundred percent accurate. It's a great advantage for our team. I'll keep it to myself." Danford paused for a moment. "Let me think about this a while. Off the top of my head, I'd say one of the things we need to do with this gift of yours is keep track of how accurate it is."

"That's what the people at the parapsychology centers in New York said, too. They also said I may develop more psychic abilities now that my 'psychic center' is open." Susan anxiously awaited Tom's reaction to this piece of news.

"If police can use psychic investigators, why can't lawyers?" With that comment, Tom walked over to Susan, gently pulled her up from the couch and into his arms. "I love everything about you, Susan," he said and they kissed for the first time.

35

While passing through the imposing phalanx of Corinthian columns across the façade of the neoclassical Charlotte County Courthouse, Jeff felt a heightened sense of importance and a oneness with the movers and shakers of the community. He was disappointed when the archive room turned out to be a nondescript, windowless room with absolutely nothing grand about it. With a promise from Phillip to take a mid-morning coffee break—it was Wednesday after all, hump day, a day that always called for more coffee—he allowed his big brother to play big boss man.

"You sit there like a good little second banana and look through these files," Phillip commanded. "We need to list the recent robberies in the greater Charlotte area and all the boys that got sent to these group homes. Type in your laptop all the names, dates, offenses, and locations of the robberies. If you come across any information about the homes, type it in."

"You got it, Herr Commandant," said Jeff, clicking his heels together and saluting.

"Don't be smart. Just get down to it."

Jeff settled down to the laborious task of poring over the court records, typing in data in an Excel spreadsheet program. With one arm in a sling, it was awkward and tiring work, but the discovery of an especially compelling tidbit made the mundane work worthwhile.

"Let's go get a nosh and go over what we've got so far," Jeff suggested, itching to share his breakthrough.

"We just got started, you clown."

"Au contraire, it's been over two hours. Besides, I've got an earthshaking revelation to impart."

"Okay, okay, you've convinced me. Let's go."

The brothers walked to the coffee shop around the corner, popular with lawyers, interns, and courthouse staff. They sat at a secluded outdoor table for privacy.

"Did you notice anything interesting about your cases?" asked Jeff.

"No, other than there has been a large increase in robberies in Michael Freidan's neighborhood in the last year. So let's hear it: What's your earthshaking revelation?"

Jeff looked smug. "Only this: Joe Owens' cases that involved teens ended up with them going to a St. Dismas House." He paused and took and savored a bite of his doughnut. "In fact, they ended up going to *his* St. Dismas House."

"*What?* Joe Owens supervises one of the houses?"

"You got it. Not only that, all the boys who go there had been hauled in for petty theft."

"Why the hell didn't you tell me this before?"

"I wanted to bask in your reaction, in a romantic setting like this."

"Ha-ha. Let's puzzle this out: Is Joe Owens trying to do a good deed or is he recruiting pint-sized bandits? His father is chief of police and also on the board of the St. Dismas Houses. So, is Joe a Good Samaritan, or is he taking advantage of his father being chief of police? For all we know, Jay Owens, Sr. could be involved as well. No wonder Tom didn't want to go to the police yet. When we go back to the courthouse, let's ferret out more dope on Joe's background." The boys looked up slowly as a wide shadow fell across the table.

"For a fat guy you sure are good at sneaking up on people, Lukowski.

What do you want? How'd you know to find us here? Have you had us tailed?" asked Phillip.

"Hah! There's not a lot you and your brother here do that's under my radar. You're taking a ride downtown with me, punk. We know you and your buddy Mark Everett were camping at Sesquicentennial State Park on the 2nd of June, 2005, when a certain gun was ditched in the lake."

Phillip's face went ashen. "You can't arrest me on hearsay—"

"I'm not arresting you, darling, I'm just hauling your ass in for questioning. Now come along like a good little mouthpiece."

Lukowski grabbed Phillip's arm in vice-like grip and trotted him to his unmarked police car around the corner. Phillip called instructions to Jeff over his shoulder as his brother followed along.

"Call Tom, but then finish what we started. I'll let you know what happens. Don't worry."

"How the hell am I supposed to get home?" Jeff protested.

"Here," shouted Phillip as he tossed Jeff his keys. "Now do what I said." Lukowski put his oven mitt-sized hand on top of Phillip's head and loaded him into the backseat as Jeff looked on helplessly.

Danford's phone rang. Caller ID identified Jeff as the caller. "Hi, Jeff. What's up?"

"Hang onto your hat. Phillip and I were taking a break at the coffee shop near the courthouse when Stan Lukowski showed up out of the blue and took Phillip away. They found the gun Chief Owens called you about last week. He said something about Phillip and Mark Everett camping at the park and took Phillip in for questioning."

"I'll be right there. I'll call your mother, too."

36

In the spartan interrogation room at police headquarters, Phillip was beside himself with relief when the guard admitted Danford and Susan. His mother sat down beside him and stroked his hair distractedly, her eyes welling with love and concern. Danford took a seat opposite Phillip and locked his hands together atop the cheap table, in a tight grip that turned his knuckles white. His mouth was set in a grim straight line. "Out with it, Phillip," he said in a harsh tone that took Susan and Phillip aback.

"I know I should have said something earlier but Mark Everett made me promise to not say anything. Mark and I had gone camping on my way back to law school. Unbeknownst to me at the time, Mark had gone out in the boat in the middle of the night and dropped the gun in the lake.

"I swear I knew nothing about it until Mark told me last week. He had been asked by our mutual friend Tim to get rid of the gun. It was part of an initiation so he could gain the trust of this group of criminals. I was the one who suggested he anonymously send the police the note telling them where the gun was. We were so careful. How did they know it was Mark and me that sent the note?"

"They didn't know you two sent the note. According to Captain Owens, all they know is you two were out camping right after the robbery. Your friend, Mark, filled out the registration form to get into the

park. He put his name and car license, as required, on the form. It
didn't take the police long to find out who his camping buddy usually
was. They are bringing in everyone who was at the lake within two
weeks of the robbery. They have no proof you were with Mark. That's
pure speculation on their part."

"I don't deny I was with Mark at Sesquicentennial State Park, but I
swear I didn't know anything about the gun. He threw it in the lake
while I was asleep."

Danford sighed with a world-weary sadness. "Phillip, I'm not the
best person to represent you. I'm too emotionally involved. Ballistics
has determined the bullet that killed my wife matches the gun in the
lake. I can't represent you because you are now connected to both a
bank robbery and a murder, albeit indirectly, it seems." He paused.

"It's hard for me to say this, but I don't know if I can believe everything you've said."

Susan and Phillip were shell-shocked. "Tom, you have to defend
Phillip," said Susan. "He's my son. If he says he didn't know what
Mark did, you have to believe him. He's honest to a fault."

The pained expression on Danford's face registered anger, hurt,
and distrust. "If he was that honest, he would have told one of us
about Mark and the gun long before now," said Danford brusquely.
"I'm sorry, Susan, I can't do this. Not when it involves the murder of
my Beth."

Susan's eyes blazed. "You mean you won't do it, don't you? Don't
all the times we've worked with you mean anything? You trusted Phillip then. My boys risked their lives working with you and this is the
thanks they get?"

"What can I say to prove I'm totally innocent?" Phillip pleaded.
"You're the best criminal attorney in the state, let alone Charlotte. I
need your help, please."

"I'm sorry. Here's Don Henderson's phone number. Tell him I
referred you."

Lukowski barged into the room, his hulking frame making the
small space feel uncomfortably claustrophobic. He leered at Phillip
like a gargoyle. "You ready to confess to killing your buddy's wife
yet?"

Danford got up and stood chest to chest with Lukowski. "You have
no evidence of Phillip committing any crime and you know it. Are
you going to arrest him?"

Lukowski gritted his teeth. "No, counselor."

"We're leaving then."

As Danford moved to take Susan's arm, she coldly shook off his touch and ushered Phillip from the room.

Lukowski sniggered. "Trouble in paradise, eh?"

"You insufferable prick," said Danford slowly. "You and I both know that I could lay you out like a rug with one hand tied behind my back."

"Tough guy, huh? As the man said: Go ahead, make my day."

Danford was tempted. It might just be worth risking disbarment to wipe the smirk off Lukowski's mug once and for all. "Tell the truth. Do you have anything on Phillip?"

"Maybe I do. Maybe I don't. I think you'd want us to be working our asses off looking for the perp who plugged your precious wifey."

Danford grabbed Lukowski's coat and slammed him into the wall with a loud thud. "Don't you ever mention my wife again, you bastard."

"Okay, okay...*counselor.*"

Danford loosened his grip and walked slowly away. If Phillip Kemper were involved in his wife's death, it changed everything.

37

Susan and Phillip arrived home to find Frank in his favorite chair, a ratty relic from his bachelor days that he refused to part with, watching *The Late Show With David Letterman.* "I can't believe someone is finally home," he said snidely. "I was beginning to feel I was the only one who lived here. Where's Jeff?"

"You mean he's not here?" said Susan.

"You got it, Sherlock."

Susan had come to detest the 'see what you did' tone in Frank's voice. Every time something went wrong, it was somehow her fault due to her professional aspirations.

"I guess it would never occur to you, Frank, to get off your duff and look for him?" she said coldly.

Phillip interjected. "I just remembered, Mom. I left him at the courthouse to keep doing research. I gave him to keys to my Civic when Lukowski took me in. He should be home by now; it's after midnight. Maybe we should call the police."

"They won't do anything unless he's been missing for twenty-four hours," said Susan fretfully. "I'll try his cell…He's not answering."

A low, sardonic laugh caused Susan and Phillip to turn towards Frank's chair. "See what all your foolhardy work has come to? Now our son is missing. Probably kidnapped by some pervert. It's all your fault, Susan."

Susan put her hands on either side of Frank's chair and shouted in his face. *"Shut up, Frank!* I've had enough of your accusations and put-downs. Anytime you want to leave, there's the door."

Frank was taken aback. Susan's tongue lashing at the hospital had gravely wounded his manhood, now here she was standing up to him at home. He opened his mouth to speak, shut it meekly, and sank in his chair.

"Come on, Phillip," said Susan, "let's go find Jeff."

"Uh, I'll go," said Frank halfheartedly, as he began to rise.

"You'll stay here," Susan commanded. The authority she heard in her voice came from some deep well of rediscovered self-worth. "Someone needs to be here in case Jeff calls or comes home."

With great pleasure, Susan watched Frank sink further down in his unsightly chair like a petulant child.

Phillip and Susan drove to the courthouse in worried silence. "There's my car," said Phillip, pointing, "right near the coffee shop with a ticket on it. Do you think Jeff could still be in the courthouse?"

"Let's see if we can find a guard to let us in and check," said Susan. Phillip and Susan walked down the long corridor to the conference room. The light was on. There was Jeff with his head on a stack of files, sound asleep. He woke when he heard them call his name.

"Hey, what's happening? So, they let you out of jail? I was hoping I could take over your room at home."

"Very funny. We were scared to death something had happened to you and here you doing the Rip Van Winkle bit, plus I got a parking ticket, dingy. You were supposed to take my car home."

"I was working. Look what I found out while you were goofing off at the pokey."

Bleary-eyed, Jeff began to shuffle through his notes as Susan enveloped him in a hug. "Can it wait until tomorrow, sweetheart? It's late and we've all had a difficult day."

"Sure, Mom," said Jeff warmly. "Tomorrow it is."

Susan picked up her cell phone. "Frank," Susan said. "We found Jeff. He's fine. We need to figure out for how many days he should be grounded for scaring us. We'll be home soon."

"Grounded? But I didn't do anything. I've been working."

"It's late. Let's talk about it at home. Phillip, you take Jeff home in your car and I'll follow."

As they left the courthouse, Susan noticed a dark car parked across the street. When she started her Acura and fell in behind Phillip's Civic, the black car's headlights blazed to life. Instinctively Susan reached for her cell phone. "Tom, it's me. I hope I didn't wake you. I think I'm being followed. I'm not sure, but I think it's the same one that tried to run me down. Phillip and Jeff are ahead of me in Phillip's car. What should I do?"

"Just keep your cool, maintain a safe speed. How far are you from home?"

"About ten minutes, I'd say."

"Good. I'll stay on the line with you until you're safely home."

"Thanks, Tom. Tom?"

"Yes?"

"I'm sorry about this afternoon. I know your emotions are on edge now that the police have found the gun that killed Beth." It felt awkward to Susan to speak her name aloud.

"Not as sorry as I am. Let's just forget it happened. You'll be glad to know the police have no evidence tying Phillip to Beth's death. His detainment was just posturing on Lukowski's part."

"That does not surprise me. Tom, we're just a couple of blocks from home. The car's still behind me."

"Is there anything unusual about the car, Susan?"

"Not that I can see. It's hard to tell the make of the car in the dark. Phillip or Jeff could probably identify it, but they're in front of me. Tom, the boys are pulling into the driveway. I'm just about to myself. The car's still—wait, it's pulling away."

Susan noticed that as the car accelerated it made a loud, guttural surge of power and disappeared down the block. "It's the same car as this morning. A sports car of some sort, maybe, with a loud engine."

"I heard," said Danford. He was ninety-nine percent sure it was a V8. "I'm glad your home safe, Susan. Sleep well."

38

Susan was glad to have the next day to herself this Friday morning. She had not scheduled any clients so she could spend some quality time working on the case. With no one else up yet, she savored the quiet as she brewed coffee and mixed up a batch of blueberry muffins from her grandmother's recipe. She knew the boys and Frank would be happy to find her cooking in the kitchen. She wondered if Tom liked blueberry muffins. He entered her thoughts more and more these days.

While the muffins baked, she sat down at the kitchen table with her pad, pen, and mug of coffee and started to organize her thoughts. Under the heading of "Known Facts" she wrote the following:

- Michael Freidan was shot between 7:00 and 7:30 AM.
- No forced entry
- Remington sculpture—The Sergeant—stolen worth $25,000? (Freidan paid $12,000)
- Victim had incriminating picture of John Harkins kissing blonde secretary in his hand
- Ann Marie Harkins said picture was familiar; I saw it was taken at a Rotary Club Christmas party. Call her today to see if she remembered anything else

- Under hypnosis unable to remember but may surface, did see it was at the Rotary Christmas party? TC today if Ann Marie remembered anything else

Unanswered Questions:
- Why steal the Remington? LCD television, Freidan's Rolex watch also valuable but not taken
- Who would have access to the picture of John and his former blond receptionist, Mary Lou?
- Who would Freidan know who would only want the Remington?
- Who would know John Harkins was coming there and could frame him?
- Who was in the black car following her?

Next to do:
- Interview with Michael's wife to determine what she knew about the possible visitor and what she heard the morning of the murder.

"Good morning, Mom," said Jeff, looking comically bushy-headed as he stumbled into the kitchen in his pajamas. "Whatcha doin'?"

"I'm trying to get organized. How did you sleep?"

"Oh, fine. Yay, blueberry muffins! Boy, do I have stuff to tell you and Phillip and Tom."

Frank entered, expertly tying his tie in a Windsor knot. "How about me, Jeff, do you have anything to tell your own father?" he said morosely. "I feel like an outsider in this house. No one talks to me. No one is ever around. My family gets shot at, thrown in jail, followed. I have no control over anything anymore."

"How about a blueberry muffin before you go to the hospital?" asked Susan, eager to avoid another family argument. "I made them fresh this morning."

"*You* made something fresh? I'll alert the media."

Susan ignored him and dutifully set a place for her husband. He ate in childish silence and left for the hospital with his usual self-important bluster. The tension in the air left with him.

"Do I smell blueberry muffins?" asked Phillip, yawning luxuriously and scratching his hindquarters with gusto.

"Yes, you do. And we also have a question on the table. Jeff has some information, but I'm thinking maybe we should wait until we get together with Tom before discussing it. What do you think?"

"Hmm. Do you think Tom likes blueberry muffins?" asked Phillip suggestively.

"Let's find out," Susan said. She called Tom on his cell phone, hoping to catch him before he reached the office.

"Hi, Tom. Glad to catch up with you. Jeff is about to share what he found out in the courthouse yesterday over some homemade blueberry muffins. Care to join us?"

She smiled at his answer. "He'll be right over." She happily set another place.

Danford arrived in five minutes. "Wow, something smells good. I haven't tasted a homemade blueberry muffin in ages. Nice of you to invite me."

"Can I tell you what I found now?" asked Jeff, champing at the bit.

"Go ahead before your burst," said Susan.

Jeff started with his report as Tom, Phillip and Susan listened intently around the kitchen table. Susan thought he looked so confident and official with his black notepad and pages of handwritten notes. "Okay, here's the thing. I went through all the robbery arrests in Charlotte for the last two years. Here are the names of the perpetrators, who and what they burglarized, and what happened to them.

There were forty-two burglaries during that time. As you can see, about half the perpetrators were first offenders. All but four of these burglaries were committed by young men under the age of eighteen. Joe Owens was the arresting officer in these thirty-eight cases. All of them were sent to various St. Dismas Houses in the Charlotte area. With the other cases, the offenders were sent to jail or other juvenile detention centers."

"That's not a surprise," said Phillip. "His father, Jay Owens, is on the board of directors of St. Dismas House."

"Hold your horses, I'm just getting to the good part. About eight months ago, a guy named Albert Swanson was convicted of several robberies. His fingerprints were on an antique watch that he had sold to an antique dealer named Norman Gallagher who lives in Chapel Hill, North Carolina. The antique dealer recognized him from his picture on the Internet. This antique watch was stolen from the same Charlotte judge from whose house the Remington sculpture had been stolen. That sculpture, as we know, was never recovered. Because Swanson had a history of burglary, he was an early suspect to that robbery and others. He was convicted and sent to Polk Youth Institution in Butner, North Carolina."

Jeff grinned broadly, delighting in the fact he had a captive audience. "Now get this. He was living at one of the St. Dismas Houses during the time of his arrest. From the description, the sculpture looks a lot like the one in Michael Freidan's office. Most of the items from the other robberies were common items like small LCD TVs, cameras, jewelry, and so forth."

"Good work, Jeff," Danford interjected. "Albert Swanson sounds like a promising lead. Could you tell from the reports if Albert Swanson is still at Polk?"

"He was sentenced to two years. It was his second offense, but he was unarmed or didn't show a gun if he had one. He should still be at Polk unless they paroled him early. But wait; here comes the pièce de résistance. About two weeks ago, there was an article in the *Charlotte Observer* about the judge and his outstanding collection of Civil War relics. The article mentioned that *The Sergeant* sculpture was stolen. According to the article, it was worth about $20,000. A picture of the sculpture was even in the paper." With a dramatic flourish worthy of Perry Mason, Jeff tossed a copy of the *Charlotte Observer* on the table, open to the article in question.

Susan was thoughtful. "We know Michael Freidan got a note from a friend about that article and the stolen Remington. Freidan was a Civil War buff and might have also read this article in the *Charlotte Observer*. He may have realized he had bought stolen merchandise." Susan tapped her coffee mug with her beautiful long nails. "I have a theory. Like we said before, it is possible someone at these St. Dismas Houses takes in youthful offenders under the pretense they will provide them with a home-like environment. The real agenda is to use them to commit robberies.

These young robbers, though, are instructed to take non-traceable, everyday stuff like TVs, jewelry, that could have come from a variety of places. Even if they have serial numbers, those can be removed. One of the kids robs a judge's house and maybe without authorization takes this Remington sculpture. Here now is an item that is unique. But who would sell the sculpture to Michael Freidan? It wouldn't be the person running the robbery ring. He'd be too smart to do that. Could it be the robber himself?"

Danford clicked into Susan's line of reasoning. "Michael could have gotten suspicious that the person who sold him the statue was trafficking in stolen goods and confronted him. Whoever that was, might have killed Michael to shut him up. Phillip, do you have time to come with me to check out Albert Swanson?

Ordinarily, I'd turn this over to the police, but I don't know who to trust there these days. I doubt that Chief Owens or his son, Jay, are involved but someone on the force may be hooking up these kids with the St. Dismas Houses. I just want to talk to this Albert Swanson and see if we can find out who he worked with. I have a hunch about this case, but I need proof."

"What about me?" said Jeff dejectedly. "I did all this legwork and he gets the plum assignments."

Danford ruffled Jeff's bed-head hair affectionately. "You, my resourceful friend, still have an arm in a sling. This could be danger-ous. I also need you to dig around some more. We know Freidan donated $12,000 to the St. Dismas House on July 23rd. The robbery at the judge's house was on June 15th. Somewhere between June 15th and before July 23rd someone contacted Freidan. Somewhere around July 23, Freidan got the sculpture. The newspaper article came out on August 11th, so after that he might have had contact with the person again. We need to find a paper trail from Michael Freidan's telephone calls and meetings at home that document who he was calling and meeting with that might have sold him the Remington. You'll need to talk with his wife, Marjorie, and ask if you can go through Michael's appointment book and their phone records.

"If I've told you once," groused Jeff good naturedly, "I've told you a thousand times: Lay off the 'do!"

39

Susan shook her head with a motherly resignation as her sons raced up the stairs to get dressed, still being as noisy about it in their twenties as they had when they were youngsters. She tried to remember: Had she and Frank been happy even then?

Her thoughts were interrupted by Danford's cell phone.

As he was speaking those words, Tom's cell phone went off. "Excuse me. Tom Danford here. What? Say that again. You're sure? Thanks, I appreciate you letting me know." He closed his phone and looked up at Susan with a stunned look. "That was Chief Owens. The gun retrieved from the lake had been stolen during a robbery at another private home. Along with fenceable goods, this robbery ring is stealing a small arsenal of weapons."

Susan pondered the new development. "So, someone involved in all these robberies gets their guns—including the one used to kill Beth—by stealing them from private residences. This particular gun had to be disposed of because of the connection with your wife's death. It's one thing to connect a gun with a robbery; it's another to connect it with a murder."

Back to your theory, it could be that someone in the police department is using young men with a history of robberies to commit more robberies as a trade-off for avoiding jail time. My wife's killing was an impulsive act, whereas Freidan's was premeditated. Some poor kid just got caught up in this robbery ring, panicked, and shot Beth. I don't blame him as much as I blame the mastermind behind the break-ins."

Susan picked up on the sadness in Danford's voice. She knew the talk about Beth's passing still tore at his heartstrings. She placed her hand on his brawny forearm and massaged it gently. "Penny for your thoughts."

Danford heaved a heavy sigh. "I know you want to prove your competence by working on these cases, but I'm worried about you. We're talking about robbery and murder investigations here. The danger quotient is high. Jeff's already been shot and that business with the car has even me spooked. I don't want anything to happen to you, Susan."

The warmth in his tone kindled a fire at the core of Susan's being. "I'll be careful. I promise. I'm meeting Marjorie Freidan in my office. We'll be safe there. I-I appreciate your concern."

Susan's thoughts were interrupted by the thunder of feet on the stairs. She watched admiringly as Tom counseled Jeff and Phillip with the same heartfelt concern he had shown her. "I want you two to be extra careful. Don't talk about what you are doing with anyone. We are on the trail of dangerous people and I don't want them to know we're getting closer. At the first sign of reckless behavior from either of you, you're off the case for good."

"My sentiments exactly," said Susan.

"What do you think about me talking with my friend Mark?" asked Phillip. "He might know something more about Dismas Houses from talking with Tim—he was living there when he was arrested. I could even visit Tim in prison."

Susan and Tom wore identical expressions of apprehension.

"Tom, what do you think about Phillip meeting with Mark?" Susan said. "They've been friends for years. No one would think twice about them getting together. On the other hand, if Phillip goes to the prison and talks with Tim, he'll tip our hand and it might be dangerous."

"Sound thinking, Susan," said Danford. "Okay, Phillip. Set up a meeting with Mark in a place that is part of your routine. Anything that even smells like danger, you get out. Hear me?"

"Yes, sir," said Phillip.

Phillip's delight with his assignment could not have been more evident.

Susan just wished she could be sure both her boys would be careful and stay away from dangerous situations.

40

Susan was a dedicated psychologist with an analytical mind, but she was not immune to the allure of haute couture. When she welcomed Marjorie Freidan into her office that Monday afternoon, the dowager's elegant ensemble—St. John's knit suit (black with red and white trim) topped off with a bag and shoes by Prada—inspired her to perform a little mental arithmetic. She figured the outfit had set Michael Freidan back at least two grand. Even in mourning, Marjorie looked chic.

"I hope I'm not late," said Marjorie, as she looked at her watch.

"Actually, you're five minutes early," said Susan. To her surprise, she noticed Marjorie's watch was not a Cartier or a Rolex, but a simple, drug store variety Timex.

Marjorie noted Susan's interest. "My grandchildren gave me this watch for Christmas. They picked it out themselves. It's my favorite piece of jewelry. Michael's success afforded me certain luxuries, but underneath these glad rags, I'm just a sentimental country girl at heart."

Susan smiled as she seated Marjorie in the recliner next to her computer and in front of the videotape equipment. For the subject's benefit, Susan briefly outlined the purpose and legalities of forensic hypnosis. "Before we get started, Marjorie, do you remember anything about the Remington sculpture that disappeared from Michael's office?" asked Susan.

"I remember when Michael came home with it. He was so happy. He couldn't wait to take it out of the box and put it on the shelf."

"Did he say who he bought it from?"

"Not that I remember. All I remember was, he said the decorator didn't get it for him. He bought the sculpture from a dealer he knew. Civil War stuff bores me silly, so I didn't pester him for details. I was just happy he found something he liked."

"What did the box that it came in look like?"

Marjorie thought for a moment. "The box had a red stripe on it—I do recall that well. It also had some lettering on it that I don't remember. I think I slipped back into my Catholic grammar school education, wondering how I could use that box. The nuns were so good about recycling everything. I still feel guilty when I throw stuff out."

Susan laughed. "I can totally relate. What do you remember about the morning of Michael's murder?"

"That morning, I vaguely remember Michael got up early like he usually did and I turned over and went back to sleep. The next thing I remember is a loud sound, like a car backfiring. I remember thinking I hadn't heard that sound in a while. I know I heard a car door slamming and a car engine. In my dreamlike state, I thought it was peculiar that the car door needed to be shut. For a car to backfire, it had to be running. Usually you shut the door before you start the car. Then I went back to sleep. The next thing I remember is John yelling up the stairs, calling my name." Marjorie sniffled and daubed the corner of her each of her eyes with a lace handkerchief. "I don't know if there's much more to remember."

"That's where the hypnosis comes in," said Susan. "You'll be amazed at the details that can emerge." Susan used a progressive relaxation to put Marjorie under hypnosis. She had her take some deep breaths and then relax all the muscles throughout her entire body. Susan watched her computer screen as a graph displaying the level of Marjorie's relaxation progressed slowly downward to a deep level of altered consciousness. "Marjorie, I want you to first go back to the time when Michael came home with the box containing the sculpture. Visualize him walking into the house with the box."

"I can see him walking into the house. He's smiling and so happy."

"Focus on the box, Marjorie. What do you see?"

"It's not a big box—grayish in color with a red stripe. I can see that there are letters on the box, but I can't make them out."

"Marjorie, I want you to use your wonderful imagination and imagine you have a magnifying glass in your hand. Now take that magnifying glass and hold it up to the box."

"Okay, I'm trying. The letters keep going out of focus."

Susan clearly saw the letters Marjorie could not visualize. The letters, executed in beautiful calligraphy, were unmistakably ED.

"Marjorie, sometime during the week, your subconscious mind will help you see those letters more clearly. Let's focus now on the morning of August 12th the morning of Michael's murder. Go back to the time you knew he was getting out of bed."

"Is it morning, already?" murmured Marjorie sleepily.

Susan smiled. Marjorie was clearly reliving the event as if it were just happening. "What did Michael say, Marjorie?"

Marjorie's voice acquired a masculine aspect. "Go back to sleep, hon. It's only six o'clock. Too early for you to get up."

"And how did you respond, Marjorie?" prompted Susan.

"Mmmm, okay, darling."

"You're in your bed on the morning of August 12th, Marjorie. You're in that twilight space between sleep and wakefulness when a series of sounds prevents you from dropping off."

"Damn that car backfiring. Why can't people keep their cars in good running condition? God, that's a loud door slam. What a noisy engine. Maybe it's the tiger in the tank, like they use to say. Wasn't that a cereal ad?"

The masculine voice again: "Marjorie, Marjorie! Are you awake? Wake up!"

"John, is that you? Why are you waking me up? Go find Michael."

"Get up! Get up!" Marjorie's voice was husky, urgent. "Something awful has happened!"

"Marjorie, go back for a moment," said Susan softly. "Tell me about the loud engine and the tiger."

In response, Marjorie made a growling, guttural sound.

Susan could tell from the computer graph that Marjorie was beginning to emerge from hypnosis. "Anything else you remember?"

"No, that's all."

During the waning minutes of the session—when a subject is still in a suggestible state—Susan reinforced the idea that Marjorie would remember the initials on the box later during the week.

"My, that was quite an experience! So relaxing at first, but then it was like I was there that morning Michael died," said Marjorie, as she looked about Susan's office to reorient herself. "I hope some of this is helpful. I know John didn't kill Michael. I so hope the real killer is found."

"Every clue helps. At this point, it's hard to know what information will create a trail of evidence. If anything turns up, you know you'll be one of the first to know."

"Thank you, Dr. Kemper," said Marjorie. "I have the fullest confidence in you and Mr. Danford. There is one other thing that I'm not sure I should mention..."

"Go ahead, Marjorie. I'm listening."

Marjorie laughed at Susan's reference to Kelsey Grammer's character, the psychiatrist, Dr. Frasier Crane. "Even Frasier Crane would have been surprised by this story. The other night, as I was dosing off to sleep, I swear I heard Michael's voice. It wasn't like a dream. It was like he was there in the bedroom. He kept saying, "Everett Concrete, Everett Concrete." I have no idea why he would keep saying that. It's not like we knew the Everetts well or had a lot to do with their company. I've been to their new design store a few times but that's about all the contact I've ever had with them. Do you think it means anything? Maybe I'm just losing it. I just feel lost without Michael."

"No, you're not losing it, Marjorie. It's not unusual for someone who has lost a loved one to experience a connection with them after death. I've had a number of clients who have had that experience. It's quite common and normal." Susan wasn't sure Ann Marie had told her mother she had seen Freidan, too. It was unethical for Susan to discuss one client with another even under these circumstances. She gave Marjorie the same book reference she had given Ann Marie. She did feel comfortable, though, in suggesting Marjorie may find someone else in her family or someone who was close to Michael may also have seen or heard him.

"Thank you, Dr. Kemper. "You've been very helpful."

Susan could hardly wait to phone Danford. She shared with him her theory that the backfire Marjorie thought she heard was in actuality the gunshot that killed her husband. The door slamming and revving car engine seemed to indicate that the killer had come and gone before John arrived for his seven o'clock appointment.

"Great work, Susan," said Danford. "The car sounds like it had either a V8 engine or was altered to make that sound. Either way, we're talking about someone who has a car with plenty of giddy-up. The possibilities are endless: Could be a man or a woman of any age or description. We should have the guys check to see what kind of car everyone involved in the case drives."

"Here comes what you might think is the more weird stuff. Marjorie said the sculpture was delivered to Freidan in a box with a red stripe and some letters. In hypnosis, she couldn't see the letters but I could. The letters were ED. She also said Freidan talked to her. I know that sounds weird, but it happens to a lot of people. He kept saying Everett Concrete to her. Marjorie didn't understand the Everett Concrete reference."

"So now we have a box with a red stripe on it and the initials ED that only you saw in hypnosis and a suggestion from the dead that we check out Everett Concrete?" replied Tom.

Susan was relieved that Tom's tone contained surprise and playfulness but lacked sarcasm.

"That's what we've got, counselor," agreed Susan.

"I think this needs a lot more discussion. How about dinner tonight? Maggiano's?"

The schoolboy hesitation in Tom's voice let Susan know he intended the dinner to be as much social as business. She felt herself teetering on a moral precipice; but really, what harm was there in it? Besides, with Frank working late at the hospital that evening, there was no chance of the Chips fiasco being repeated. Aware that she was crossing an invisible line she had created for herself, Susan heard herself stammering out her acceptance.

"Great. I'll meet you there at six."

Susan grabbed her purse and dashed home to change. She tried on four different outfits, finally settling on a three-quarter length black skirt, a blue blouse with her favorite Chico's belt, and her black, open toe shoes with three-inch stiletto heels. She left the rejected outfits in a heap on the bed and checked her look in her cheval floor mirror.

The beautiful, clear-eyed, confident woman who peered back at her was barely recognizable. She felt transformed, empowered, and more than a little bit excited.

"Hello, the new Susan," she said laughingly, and danced to her destiny to the beat of a different drum.

41

Renowned for its southern Italian cuisine, Maggiano's Little Italy in Charlotte's South Park Mall was a popular rendezvous for romantic couples. Coincidentally, Nordstrom, one of Susan's favorite department stores, was in the same mall. Before meeting Tom, she made a perfunctory purchase of a single lipstick and a bottle of her new favorite perfume, *Angie ou Demon* by Givenchy. Should she meet an acquaintance, she could honestly claim she had been shopping and had happened to "run into Tom." She was amazed at how her mind was beginning to work in a frighteningly new and different way. Joining Tom in a secluded corner booth, Susan placed the bag atop the table with the Nordstrom logo conspicuously in view.

Susan always thought Maggiano's had that wonderful happy Italian family feeling, especially when it was crowded and the piano player was there like tonight. Yet the seating arrangements provided a sense of intimacy. It was definitely the place for happy couples. That thought made Susan nervous.

Painfully aware that Tom must know she was trying to cover up her profound nervousness, Susan instantly began chattering away. "Oh, by the way, I got a call from Ann Marie. She said she didn't get a clear vision, but she's almost sure the picture of her husband John kissing his receptionist was taken at a Christmas party. She's going to go through her old pictures to see if she can find it."

Tom flashed a mischievous smile. "You know, Susan, you look even more beautiful when you're flustered. You've forgotten, we already know it was at a Rotary Christmas party thanks to your uncanny insight."

Susan felt her cheeks turning crimson. "All I can do is encourage her to look at all the pictures from public parties since Ann Marie knows it wasn't taken at her house. Maybe someone can go to the Rotary Club and check their archive of pictures. What do you think?"

"Why don't I do that? I don't want you to get involved any further than you have to. I'll go over there myself tomorrow." Impulsively he took Susan's hand. "What do you say to some champagne?"

"All right," said Susan in a choked whisper.

The waiter fetched a flavorful spumante and poured two glasses full of the sparkling liquid.

"A toast to a most excellent case, a most excellent team, a most excellent night and most excellent company," said Tom, extending his glass.

Susan felt herself loosening up as her guilty feelings scattered to the wind. "I'll drink to that!" she said heartily, clinking his glass, and taking a nose-tickling sip. She giggled helplessly as the bubbles ignited a contagious spark of mirth that had Tom laughing, too, without knowing why.

Just then a braying laugh that carried throughout the dining room emerged from the back of the restaurant.

"What's the matter?" asked Tom. "You're as white as a ghost. Are you feeling all right?"

Susan felt her heart race. "Frank is here. I'd know his laugh anywhere."

"It's all right. We're just here having dinner and discussing the case—same as that night at Chips. You've been shopping. What's wrong with that?"

"I don't know what he's doing here. He's supposed to be at a meeting at the hospital. Can you see him?" Susan was nervous, curious, and suspicious all at the same time. It was hard to tell which emotion was the strongest.

"Could you tell from what direction you heard his laugh?"

"I think it came from the back."

"Good. That's where the restrooms are. I'll go check."

Before Susan could object, Tom got up and starting walking toward the rear of the restaurant. Susan took a sip of her wine. She took a series of deep breaths to quell the panicked tightness in her chest.

When Tom returned to the booth the look on his face confirmed Susan's suspicion. "It is Frank, Susan. I hate to be the one to tell you this, but he's with another woman."

The color drained from Susan's face. *"What?"* she said incredulously.

Tom hesitated. "I'm pretty sure she's a nurse at the hospital. I've seen them together before."

"What? Why haven't you said something before?"

"It's rather common knowledge that Frank is having an affair with this nurse."

Susan reached for her wine glass and took a most unladylike gulp. It was almost a relief—no, it *was* a relief—to have her longtime suspicions about Frank's penchant for infidelity confirmed. All those late meetings, the unexplained charges on his credit cards, the odd, organic stains on his clothing she'd rather not think about. She had been a fool. "Frank and I haven't been happy together for a long time. It's no surprise to me that he is seeing another woman. We both have a need for a connection with someone else." Susan's eyes and voice dropped. It was at once scary and liberating, admitting to herself— and Tom—that there was an opening in her life for another man.

"That's no surprise. Everyone knows about you and Frank not getting along. It's all over town."

"Oh, my God! What have you heard?" Susan needed a minute to process the implications. How could the state of their relationship have become public knowledge? Certainly, she hadn't said anything to anyone but Peggy, and Peggy wasn't a gossip. It was horrible to contemplate that their estrangement probably showed in their mannerisms, the tone of their voices, no matter how brave a face they had tried to put on.

The incidents at Chips and the hospital were just outrageous proof of the private hell they'd struggled to keep secret for years.

"I had heard about you and Frank not getting along even before we started working together. I think I first heard about you about a year ago—and then about Frank—from a friend of mine who was referred to Frank for a consultation. In his opinion, Frank was an arrogant jerk who didn't deserve a sensitive, beautiful wife like you. Even then, why you stayed with Frank was the million dollar question around town. I hate to say this, but he also mentioned he knew Frank was having an affair with a nurse in the hospital."

Susan couldn't believe what she was hearing. She couldn't believe her marriage to Frank was fueling the gossip train. "I'm shocked and bewildered. How could anyone know? I have not talked to anyone about my marriage except for one good friend."

"People have eyes and ears, Susan. You know that. They love to talk—particularly about professional people in the public eye. I don't know that Frank is as discreet as you are. I have seen him myself out with this nurse. I'm sorry to bring this up to you, but you have to know I'm glad you and Frank aren't getting along."

Susan blushed. She knew where this headed. "I'm glad everything is out on the table."

Tom smiled and took her hand. "Me, too. I think I've been in love with you since the first day we met. I never thought I'd feel that way again after Beth died. I was just filled with hate and could only think of revenge. You changed all that."

Susan was aware her breathing had all but stopped. The restaurant's festive chatter faded away, leaving the two of them alone, soul mates in the eye of a hurricane.

"I feel like a fool. Here I was worried about keeping my marriage vows and my responsibility to my husband, when in reality there was no marriage. You've been on my mind a lot, too. Every day I can't wait to see you, can't wait to talk with you. I haven't dared to think about anything more than that."

"So what do you want to do?"

"I need to talk with Frank and file for a separation. Our marriage is over. I just didn't want to face it."

"Whatever you need from me, Susan, is yours. I'm here for you."

§ § § § §

When Susan got home from dinner she went into her bedroom to find Frank swaying like a pine in the wind and staring at the clothes she had left on the bed. He had obviously been drinking.

"What the hell is all this? Did you have a hot date with what's his face and couldn't decide what to wear?"

Susan looked with disgust and loathing at the pitiful shell of the man she had married for better or worse. There was a limit to the amount of "worse" even a good Catholic girl should be expected to bear. On the instant, a devil on her shoulder whispered an insidious plan in her ear.

"Frank," she purred, fondling the lapel of his coat suggestively, "how would you like to go to the bar at the Hilton, have a drink, and listen to the piano player? Maybe we could get a room for the night? We haven't done that for a while."

Frank grinned lasciviously and allowed Susan to guide his reeking carcass out the front door. At the Hilton, she tipped the valet parking attendant a hundred dollar bill from Frank's wallet and proceeded to register Frank in the honeymoon suite using his Visa card. With the help of an amused bellman, she loaded Frank into an elevator and installed him in the room. For his trouble, Susan tipped the bellman two more hundreds from Frank's wallet.

Frank looked around the grand room, his rolling eyes finally settling on the king-size bed. He beckoned to Susan with outstretched arms. "Come on, baby, let's get it on."

With a mild flick of her right index finger, Susan sent him reeling backwards on the bed, where he immediately passed out. "Not tonight, tiger. Not any night."

As Susan put the key card on the bureau, she noticed a pad of Hilton stationery.

A few moments later, she put the 'do not disturb' sign on the outer doorknob and quietly shut the door behind her. The smile on her face could have lit Broadway.

It would be mid-afternoon of the next door before Frank would find Susan's note: "I can't take it anymore. Welcome to your new residence."

42

On her morning run this Tuesday, Susan's mind was more clear and resolute than she could ever remember as she mapped out her busy day. First on the agenda was a call to a divorce lawyer recommended by Tom to file for a legal separation from Frank. The thought of Tom made her smile like a lovesick teenager. She realized she was happy now and hadn't been for a long time. She couldn't believe how she had agonized over keeping the marriage together and here was Frank, stepping out on her for who knew how long.

The arduous task of breaking the news to the boys lay ahead of her, too. They wouldn't notice he wasn't there this morning, since it wasn't unusual for him to leave for the hospital before they got up. Her personal finances were another consideration. She had never worried about finances while married to Frank. Yes, she had her career, but her income was always secondary. She and Frank had used her money to splurge on household amenities and getaways and, fortunately, savings. She had to go to the bank today to take out the money and open her own account.

She looked to her faith to get her through the hard weeks and months to come. Once the Freidan case was over and the boys were back in school, she and Frank could finalize the divorce proceedings.

With a firm plan in place, she looked forward to hearing Peggy's take on her situation over lunch. Slowing her pace, she loped homeward to find Jeff busy in the kitchen, making pancakes, as a fresh pot of coffee filled the room with a homey smell.

"Hi, Mom. I figured you could use a good breakfast today."

"Thanks, Jeff. You're so right."

"Dad called while you were out. He wanted to talk with you. He said you dumped him at the Hilton last night and left him a nasty note. Phillip and I figured you finally threw him out."

So much for telling the boys, thought Susan.

"I wouldn't say I threw him out. Where is Phillip? I'd like to discuss the situation with your father and I with the two of you."

"Someone looking for me?" said Phillip. "Here I am." He stretched his arms out like a stage actor taking a curtain call. "So, I hear you finally threw Dad out, Mom?"

"No, I didn't *throw him out.* As you two wise guys obviously know, your father and I haven't been getting along. We decided a trial separation would be the best thing."

"We, huh?" said Jeff teasingly. "Dad said you took advantage of him having too much to drink and put him in the honeymoon suite." It was all both boys could do to keep from bursting out laughing.

"Took advantage is a strong word. I just—"

"Look, Mom," said Phillip equitably. "We know that Dad has not been the best of husbands. Jeff and I have both heard lots of rumors about him seeing other women. Jeff and I knew this day would come eventually. Now that it's here, we're relieved. We love Dad and always will. He's our father. But you deserve someone who is good to you."

Susan sighed in mock exasperation. "And I thought *I* was the psychologist here. Thanks, you two. Your understanding means a lot." Her eyes filled with tears. She felt a surge of relief flood over her and tried to compose herself.

"It's okay, Mom," said Jeff cheerfully. "Sit down and have some coffee and pancakes."

Susan could see both boys were handling the impending separation with remarkable maturity. She guessed that, long ago, they had emotionally prepared themselves for the moment when the proverbial sword of Damocles would fall. Susan couldn't believe they had known about Frank's infidelity. *Everyone knew but me,* she thought. *What a fool I have been. Here I was having all this angst over my marriage and Frank was out cheating on me.*

In a fog, Susan caught snatches of her sons' conversation: Jeff was going to spend the day at the Freidan house taking a look at Michael's phone records and appointments. Phillip and Tom were going to try to track down Albert Swanson. As for herself, Susan knew only a long, hot, luxurious soak in the garden tub would recharge her batteries before she could concentrate on the Freidan case. "Phillip, how did your dinner with Mark go yesterday?" asked Susan.

"Well, it went all right, but at the same time, it was rather strange," said Phillip with a mouthful of pancake. "Mark and I kidded around like we always did, but when I asked him about Tim and the St. Dismas Houses, he took the Fifth on me. I didn't tell you, at one of our previous get-togethers he threatened to tell the police I was in on disposing of the gun. There's been a strain in our relationship since then.

He knows something—I'm sure of it—but he's not saying. I did find out he knew that Jay Owens was on the board and that his son, Joe, lobbies for sending youthful offenders there for rehab as an alternative to prison. He thought it might be a former cop—maybe even Lukowski's brother—that actually manages the places. Mark's just acting funny. Something's eating at him, I can tell, but he can't or won't discuss it. I'll mention it to Tom and see what he thinks."

"When are you meeting Tom?" Susan asked.

"Nine," said Phillip." Wow, look at the time! Better run."

"What about your pancakes? You left half your stack."

"Got a date."

"What? With whom?"

"Later, Mom."

"Yeah, later Mom," echoed Jeff. "Sorry to leave you with the dishes."

"I'll just bet you are. Be careful out there you two. Love you." Susan stood in the kitchen doorway with her hands on her hips, her expression wistful as her fine young men dived into their cars and drove away. She admired their resilience. The separation was a small bump in the road of their young lives. Good for them!

She bounded up the stairs two at a time. The garden tub was calling her name.

43

Susan was just getting out of the tub when she heard the doorbell chime. She quickly threw on her terry robe and ran down the stairs. She was surprised to see Tom standing on the doorstep, wearing an unfathomable expression that reminded her of nothing so much as her junior year prom date, who had turned out to be all hands.

"Good morning," said Tom. With a gallant flourish, he presented her with the bouquet of fresh cut flowers he had been hiding behind his back. He had nearly driven the florist to distraction as he agonized over his decision, finally settling on a mixture of soft pink daisies, white alstroemeria, and hot pink roses. To Tom, the soft pink represented the tenderness Susan had reawakened in his heart, while the hot pink symbolized the passion her gaze, her touch, her very nearness, stirred in him.

Susan was stunned. No one—certainly not Frank—had given her flowers in a coon's age. "Oh, they're beautiful, Tom, thank you so much. Come on in. Can I make you some coffee?"

"That sounds great. Phillip called about our meeting and told me you had kicked Frank out. I figured I'd beat the other suitors to the door."

Susan decided it was futile to argue with the consensus that she had kicked Frank out. Now that Tom had made his intentions clear, she was self-conscious about being in her robe with nothing on underneath it except black lace panties. "Let me put these flowers in some water, get you some coffee, and put on some clothes."

In the kitchen Susan took a vase from the pantry and walked to the sink to fill it with water. She could feel Tom's hands on her shoulders and smelled his musky cologne as he bent to kiss her neck. With a thrill of anticipation, she calmly finished the arrangement and turned towards him. Gently, he drew her body to his, gazing into her eyes as he slowly lowered his face until their lips met. It was the softest, gentlest kiss Susan had ever felt. She responded in kind.

Susan's mind was racing. It was so soon! She was barely—and not actually legally—separated. By now, Tom had opened her robe slightly and slipped a hand underneath it, touching the bare skin of her waist and back. He pulled her toward him and kissed her again, more passionately this time. As the tips of their tongues met, Susan's last reservation died.

Every particle of Susan's body was alive and every inch of it ached for Tom to caress her. Without conscious thought, she engaged the deadbolts on the front and back doors and, taking his hand, led him upstairs.

There would be no ghosts to haunt them in the guest room; she and Frank had never slept in its majestic queen-size bed. Susan barely had time to fold down the red and gold comforter and satin sheets before Tom pulled her down beside him.

She deftly unbuttoned his shirt and undid his belt buckle and watched, fascinated, as he doffed his shirt and pants and tossed them cavalierly on a chair. Susan drank in the manly beauty of his body: the broad shoulders and trim waist, the washboard stomach and the brawny chest with its forest of dark hair, the corded muscles of his arms. Her desire intensified as he leaned over her, naked save for his boxers. The outline of his massive erection at once startled and thrilled her.

He untied her robe and opened it, revealing her supple breasts and her black lace panties. He kissed her lips again, then her neck and shoulders, at last settling on her right breast. His tongue gently stimulated her nipple, tracing slow circles around the areola and flicking the stalk until it swelled to an aching point of desire. He cupped the engorged breast in his hand, kneading it sensuously while his hungry mouth moved to the other nipple, sucking and nibbling it until Susan feared she would climax.

Facing each other on their knees, she pulled down his boxers and ran her hands along his buttocks, gently massaging them. He groaned in delight as she kissed his abdomen and ran her tongue along his inner thighs. Ever so gently, he pushed his shoulder against her, until her back was against the bed. Straddling her, he slipped off her panties while his tongue traced a straight path from the flat plane of her belly to her moist delta. He stimulated her slowly at first, building to an intense fluttering motion that made her arch her back in ecstasy. She snaked her fingers through his hair, pulling him closer and closer until she could bear the pleasure no more. Moaning, she let herself go as an electric current of rapture coursed through her body.

With her hips still quivering from the echoes of her orgasm, Tom got on top of Susan and entered her gently, completely. His thrusts were long and slow at first, building to a rapid pile driver motion that shook the headboard and caused the bedsprings to whine for mercy. They rocked together, two parts of a mighty machine oblivious to everything but the moment. Susan could feel a small tremor spread across Tom's back as he came with a final sequence of deep, rotating thrusts. Susan climaxed again and again. She clung to Tom desperately, never wanting to let go.

At last Tom rolled off of her and lay with his head on Susan's breasts, smiling at her in rapt delight. "Guess I need to buy flowers more often."

Susan smiled back, still in the throes of carnal bliss. "You can come empty-handed anytime if you promise to do what you just did."

Tom laughed heartily. Someone rang the front doorbell repeatedly and pounded on the door. Over the din, a strident voice cried out, "Susan, open this door immediately!"

"Oh, God, it's Frank!" said Susan. "He usually comes in through the garage but his car is in there and the door's down. I'll bet he doesn't have a key to the dead bolt on the front door with him since he never uses it." Susan allowed herself a moment to admire Tom's Adonisian body and kissed him lustily. "Until next time!"

Tom fumbled for his clothes while Susan ran to her closet and threw on the first outfit she saw. Once dressed and downstairs, Tom said, "I'll get the door."

"Thanks, but I'll do this—with pleasure. Just watch."

Tom sat at the kitchen table, pad and pen neatly laid under the pretense of working on the case. He wrote some general legal terms on the paper to complete the deceit.

As she opened the door, Frank pushed her aside and strode into the house with autocratic bravado. "Who are you to lock me out of my house?" he shouted at Susan. "What is *he* doing here?"

Frank started to walk over toward Tom, his fists clenched at his sides.

"Just a minute, Frank. You're forgetting something. *This house is in my name, remember?* You wanted to protect it in case someone sued you. I heard about you and your nurse. In fact, I saw you out to dinner with her at Maggiano's last night," said Susan, stretching the truth a little. "Your affair is all over town. I'm having the separation papers drawn up today. You come anywhere near this house again, I'm calling the police. I'll pack up your stuff and have the boys drop it off for you. You can call the boys on their cell phones to let them know where you will be living. I'll open up the garage and you can get your precious Beemer. *Now get out and don't come back.*"

Susan put her both her hands on Frank's chest and pushed him toward the door as his legs and feet bicycled backwards to keep from falling. As he stood outside on the steps, his mouth open wide enough to catch flies, Susan slammed the door so hard, there were vibrations throughout the house.

Without a word Frank walked dejectedly to the garage, got into his BMW, and drove away.

Susan walked to the kitchen where Tom waited.

"Remind me not to get you mad at me."

44

After Tom left, Susan collapsed in a living room chair, emotionally spent but wondrously happy. The whirlwind of events—making love to Tom for the first time, giving Frank the old heave-ho—energized her. She thought Frank's ouster would bring with it at least some measure of sadness, but right now she was feeling anything but sad.

Face it girl, this is what happy's supposed to feel like! Tom was on her mind when the phone rang.

"Susan," said Marjorie Freidan in her pleasant drawl, "I'm sorry to be calling you at home, but your office message said you'd be out of the office until next Tuesday. You said to call if I remembered something else: It just popped into my head as I was making bread. I always make bread when I need a pick-me-up. Do you like home-made bread, dear?"

"I love homemade bread, Marjorie," said Susan patiently. "But please, tell me what you remember."

"Do you recall asking me if I remembered anything else about the box the sculpture came in? I remembered what I hope is an important detail as I was kneading the bread. Isn't that funny? I'm just standing here, kneading the bread, when up pops this memory. Is that how hypnosis works? You'll have to explain that to me sometime."

"I gave you what is called a posthypnotic suggestion to prompt your subconscious mind into remembering any significant information regarding your husband's death. When you perform a routine task, like vacuuming or kneading bread, your conscious mind is occupied with completing the chore, but your subconscious mind is more open and free. Memories or ideas will often pop into your head in such unguarded moments. What you experienced is not unusual. Do tell me though what you remembered."

"I remembered that the box with the red stripe had letters on it. I think the letters were ED, but I'm not 100% certain. They were in a fancy script. What do you call it? Calligraphy? I hope that's helpful."

"ED in calligraphy letters. Thanks, Marjorie. That information could be important in the future. I'll keep you posted."

"Please do that. I'm so happy John is out on bail. Tom must have friends in high places, since suspects in a murder case don't often get bail."

"I think it was due to Tom finding the picture in the Rotary Club archives of one of their Christmas parties. That's where John innocently kissed his receptionist. Ann Marie thought that kiss happened at a Christmas party. Tom followed a hunch and found the picture in a file at the Rotary Club. With that picture 'out of the picture,' so to speak, the motive the police planned to use against John flew out the window. I think the district attorney is thinking of dropping the murder charges altogether. In the meantime though, the least they could do is let John out on bail."

"I hope you and Tom will continue to pursue Michael's killer. He was no saint, but he was a good husband and I miss him."

The grief in Marjorie's voice was heart-wrenching. "We're still on the case. Don't worry."

"I'm glad. Thank you, Susan. I'll let you know if anything else pops up."

As soon as Susan hung up the phone, it rang again. An enthusiastic voice immediately began talking a mile a minute. "Hi, Susie-Q, what say we skip lunch and go to the grand opening of Everett Design instead? The first hundred customers get a free gift, and you know me, I'll stand in line for three days to get a freebie. They also are offering free packing in gift boxes just today. After today, there will be a charge for them. They've got some primo deals on birdbaths, wind chimes, garden statuary—all that artsy-fartsy stuff you like. Whaddaya say, galfriend?"

Susan had to laugh. Peggy came from a wealthy family and had married a surgeon with a great income who lavished her with gifts, but she could never pass up a bargain. "Thanks for the offer but I have to work today. Let me know what gift you get. Call me when you're done shopping—we can hit Chick-fil-A for lunch." Susan settled down to organizing her case notes but something kept nagging at her. She had a sudden epiphany and called Peggy back. "Everett Design at noon. Meet you there," she said without further explanation.

Susan had a strong hunch the ED she, and now Marjorie, had seen on the box during Marjorie Freidan's hypnosis session stood for Everett Design. It was unlikely that a shopping excursion with Peggy during the business's grand opening would arouse suspicion, even that of whoever had been dogging the Danford team's investigation in recent days.

When Susan arrived, Everett Design was overflowing with curiosity seekers and bargain hunters. Peggy beat her there and was enthusiastically waving her ticket entitling her to a free gift.

"I'm one of the first hundred and you're not!" she crowed, sticking her tongue out.

Susan shook her head and laughed. "Do you even know what it is?"

"No, I just know it's free and that's all right by me," said Peggy. "Let's look around and see if they've got anything interesting. I could use a statue or something for my backyard. I'm tired of looking at the same old same old."

They idly roamed the aisles of the new store, oohing and ahhing over the wide array of decorative outdoor wares. There were the typical birdbaths, bird feeders, some outdoor furniture, whimsical figures for gardens, angels, too. Susan particularly liked the four feet ceramic pots in multiple colors. She was momentarily distracted from her quest into thinking maybe one of the red ceramic pots would look good in her garden.

Regaining her focus, she kept an eye out for boxes being carried by customers or stacked up around displays. As most of the customers had not made their purchases yet, she realized she might not see what she was looking for until checked out.

Susan convinced Peggy that a sculpture of a frog with a fishing pole, at the end of which dangled a hapless fish, was the perfect piece of whimsy to enliven her backyard and steered her toward the checkout stand. Susan put her senses on full alert. The woman in front of them requested a box for her garden fairy. The clerk brought out a small 12-inch square box with E D rendered in calligraphy across the lid. There was no red stripe.

Peggy put her frog sculpture on the counter to be checked out. The clerk reached for a large shopping bag in which to put froggy.

Susan asked the clerk for a box for Peggy's purchase. The clerk searched under the counter, emerging at last with a large box, approximately two feet square, again with the ornate E D, but absent the red stripe. "Are these the only boxes you have?" asked Susan.

The clerk was nonplussed. "The smaller boxes aren't big enough and we don't have anything bigger," she said, doing her best to satisfy the customer.

"No, that's not what I mean," said Susan. "Do you have any boxes with a *different design?*"

"No. Those are the only ones we were given. We can gift wrap the box for you if you like; anything to make you happy, ma'am."

The line behind Susan was growing restless; she was loath to draw further attention to the transaction. "This box will be fine. Thanks."

The clerk also handed Peggy a four-inch basil plant in an off-white, antique stone looking ceramic planter as her free gift. Peggy was all smiles!

Over lunch at Chick-fil-A, Peggy bombarded Susan with questions. "Spill it, kiddo. Why the sudden interest in boxes at Everett Design? Does this have anything to do with the case? Why do you look so happy today? Inquiring minds want to know."

"A witness in the Freidan case recalled an important detail about a box with the calligraphied initials E D and a red stripe on it. The box I got at Everett Design today seems to match the witness's description—except for that pesky red stripe."

Peggy thought for a moment. "If the box was used before this grand opening, it could have been a prototype design. Maybe whoever is running Everett Design decided against using the red stripe on the final design."

"That's a pretty off the wall theory, Peg. What do you base it on?"

"Well, when I went to The Treasure Shop's grand opening a few months ago," Susan shook her head and smiled at her friend's devotion to grand openings with free gifts, "they had a few of their prototype boxes left over and were still using them along with the final design they settled on. I figure they were too expensive to just throw away. For some reason Everett Design isn't using their prototypes, but I bet they still have them."

"Are you saying Everett Design might have some of those sample boxes in the backroom or someplace like that?"

"Don't even think about it. First of all, you don't know if Everett Design is in on this business. If they are, you don't want to be caught snooping around their backroom. That could be dangerous."

"You're right. First, I'm going to see if the lettering is the same as what the witness saw. If it is, then I'll see about getting into that backroom."

"Okay, Miss Marple. I get the cloak and dagger stuff, but there's something else going on with you. You're beaming today like somebody who just figured out the sweet mystery of life. Fess up!"

Susan knew Peggy would nag her until she told her about Tom. Without going into intimate details, Susan described her dramatic showdown with Frank and her "morning ride" with Tom.

"So you finally got rid of that snake Frank and got your dance card punched to boot! Way to go, girl!"

Susan blushed and changed the subject. "I've just got to find a way to get into Everett Design's storeroom."

Peggy shook her head ruefully. "Okay, but if you get caught, Lucy, you've got some 'splainin' to do."

45

"Yes, that's definitely the lettering I saw," said Marjorie Freidan when Susan showed her the box from Everett Design later that afternoon. "I'm almost positive now that I'm looking at the box that the letters on Michael's statue box were ED. Except the box had a red stripe right directly underneath the letters—I know that for sure. I remember thinking it was not a very attractive combination. The plain lettering looks much better, if you ask me."

"Marjorie, did you or your husband have any contact with Everett Concrete?"

"Oh, yes. They put in our patio last year. Michael got very friendly with one of the young men, a fellow Civil War buff, who supervised the project. They did a wonderful job. I'd certainly recommend them."

Just then, Jeff came into the living room. "I thought I heard a familiar parental unit voice."

"Jeff! What are you doing here?"

"Don't you remember? I told you this morning: Tom asked me to go over Mr. Freidan's phone records and appointment book."

Susan felt herself blush at her son's mention of Tom's name. "That's right, I completely forgot. It's been a very hectic day, you might say. How is your research going?"

"Well, fortunately there weren't many appointments or phone calls from home. He must have kept another appointment book at the office. Marjorie shook her head yes to Jeff's comment. "I do have a number of phone calls and appointments with Everett Concrete. There's one notation in February that just says 'delivery.' Do you remember anything about that, Mrs. Freidan?"

"No, not really. I do remember the box with the red stripe and the lettering came around February 12th, though. I was suspicious it might have been my Valentine's Day present. Michael always made such a..." Marjorie's voice broke.

"Marjorie, I know this has been so hard on you. We'll get out of your hair now. We'll be in touch as soon as we know something definite. I feel we are getting closer to solving your husband's murder."

"Yes, I believe you are right. Just be careful. Who ever killed Michael is a cruel and heartless person. I wouldn't want anything to happen to either one of you."

"We'll be careful, Mrs. Freidan," said Jeff, nearly tearing up himself. "I promise. And we'll catch the bad guy, or my name's not Perry Mason."

"It's not," said Susan.

The levity lightened the tense mood in the room. Marjorie Freidan hugged Susan and Jeff in turn. "Just a moment," she said, holding up an index finger. She went to the kitchen and returned with a package wrapped in tin foil. "Homemade bread. You said you were fond of it, dear."

Susan almost cried. She could smell the delicious bread through the wrapper.

"I appreciate it so much, Marjorie, but you don't have to—"

"Land sakes alive, child, it was no trouble! And the least I could do for my favorite detectives. You need your nourishment!"

Jeff took a deep whiff of the bread. "Mmm, mmm, thanks, Aunt Bea!"

"You rascal!" said Marjorie as she showed them to the door. "Y'all come back."

Outside the Freidan house, Susan called Tom to arrange a late afternoon confab of the investigative team. When Tom suggested four o'clock, Susan looked at her watch. It was only two-thirty—plenty of time for a return visit to Everett Design.

"Jeff, I'll meet you and Phillip at Tom's office at four. I have a quick errand to run."

Inside Everett Design's showroom, Susan was completely above suspicion as just another browser in the bustling grand opening crowd. Meandering through the long aisles, she made her way casually toward the back of the store. Just beyond a display of outdoor concrete fountains, she spied a "Restrooms" sign pointing down a hallway and followed it toward two public restrooms with the universal symbols for male and female. Further down, at the end of the hallway, there were two rooms: an apparent storeroom with a pair of swinging doors to permit the unimpeded passage of employees with merchandise-laden carts and a second room with a standard door marked "Employees Only." Her curiosity piqued, Susan opened the door marked "Employees Only" and locked it behind her.

Susan found herself in the employees' restroom. Stealthily, she walked toward a pair of metal cabinets against the far wall and opened the narrower of the two; it contained only bathroom supplies and cleaning solutions. The second cabinet, much wider, was packed full of mops, brooms, a floor polisher, and a vacuum cleaner.

Cursing her luck, Susan heard footsteps approaching. The doorknob jiggled and there was a loud knock on the door. "Are you going to be in their long?" asked an urgent female voice.

Susan found her voice and said, "In a minute." Thinking quickly, she flushed the toilet, ran the tap, and unlocked the door. Susan was nearly bowled over as a young woman about seven months pregnant ambled in.

"Sorry to rush you. My bladder's my worst enemy these days, know what I mean? Hey, you don't work here, do you?"

"Uh, no. The customers' ladies room was occupied so—"

"Say no more! When you gotta go, you gotta go." The girl scurried into the stall. A satisfied "ahhh" reached Susan's ears as she ducked out the door.

In the hallway, Susan fell against the wall and let out a cleansing breath. When her heart rate was nearly back to normal, she debated braving the room with the double doors. It was now three-thirty. Tom's office was only ten minutes away, which gave her fifteen to twenty minutes to hopefully discover the cache of prototype boxes. There was no one in the hallway and all the employees seemed busy with customers. If she got caught, she could just say she wandered in there by mistake. Maybe she should wait until another day and think this through? Searching this backroom might be dangerous.

46

The minutes crawled by as Tom, Phillip, and Jeff waited for Susan to rendezvous with the team. The unspoken fear that the mysterious black car had assailed her again tortured Tom's mind. At four-fifteen, he broke the uneasy silence.

"Jeff, you were with your mother when we agreed to meet at four, weren't you?"

The boys were surprised at the skittishness in his normally steady baritone.

Jeff nodded. "Mom is always on time, if not early. She's rarely late for anything. If she is late, it's always something beyond her control, like an accident or something."

"Jeff's right, Mom's a stickler for punctuality," said Phillip. "Do you think we should call the hospitals? Maybe we can turn on the television and see if there are any accidents in the area."

"I think it's a little early to call the hospitals," said Tom. His face erupted into a widescreen grin. "Speak of the devil!"

"Well, I've heard friendlier greetings than *that* before!" said Susan.

"How come you're late, young lady?" asked Jeff. "Tom's been looking so nervous, I was sure he was going to have kittens any minute."

Tom tugged embarrassedly at the neck of his shirt. "Never mind that. You'd better have a good excuse for keeping the rest of the fantastic four waiting."

"Oh, a semi jackknifed on the highway. It took me forty-five minutes to get here. Of course, my cell phone was out of juice and *someone* had taken my portable charger out of the car." Susan glared at her two sons. "I couldn't call to let you know I was going to be late. Did I miss something?"

"Sorry, Mom," confessed Phillip, raising his hand. "I didn't have time to charge my cell phone last night before I left for dinner with Mark, so I kind of borrowed your charger. I need to get one of my own."

Tom was relieved and happy again. He hadn't realized how tense his muscles were until he felt them relaxing by degrees. Susan meant the world to him now; he wondered if the boys could tell. "All right, then, the mystery of the lost mother and," said Tom, struggling for a neutral way to refer to Susan, "invaluable colleague has been solved. Let's get back to the case and go over what we know. Some of this may be repetitive, but I need to make sure we have everyone's information on the board."

Tom stood beside an erasable white easel on which the case notes had been painstakingly transcribed. "This is what we know. On August 15th around 7:00 AM, Michael Freidan was shot to death by a gun once owned by his son-in-law, our client, John Harkins. The gun contained John's fingerprints because, as he has said repeatedly, he moved it out of the way to turn Michael over to perform CPR. The fingerprints, however, were only on one side of the gun and on the top of the barrel. The location of the fingerprints was consistent with someone moving a gun and not holding it in a shooting.

The victim held a picture in his hand of John kissing a blonde woman. The picture was authentic, all right, but it didn't tell the whole story. The blonde turned out to be John's former receptionist and the kiss occurred at a Christmas party. As I told your mother earlier, I stopped at the Rotary Club on a hunch and checked their archives. I found a large Christmas party photo that showed not only the infamous smooch, but also John's wife, Ann Marie, standing next to him and exhibiting not one iota of jealousy. The picture found at the crime scene had been cropped down to only John and his receptionist and did not show the mistletoe above their heads, nor any other Christmas trappings. I turned the picture over to Jay Owens.

Initially, the police thought John had killed Michael with his gun because the father-in-law caught him cheating on his daughter. Now that the motive has been disproved and the forensic evidence clears John as the shooter, he was let out on bail. He's still not out of the woods as a suspect, but the police will need more evidence to charge him. Any thoughts about all this?"

Susan picked up the story. "Marjorie Freidan's story supports someone shooting Michael and fleeing the scene. She was awakened by what she thought was a backfiring car. Cars don't backfire these days, so the noise that woke her was undoubtedly the fatal gunshot. Then she heard a car door slam and a car drive away. The car's engine had a growling sound, she said. Then she fell back asleep until John's voice woke her."

"Can we back up a little?" said Phillip. "Where did you get the idea that the Christmas party was a *Rotary Club* Christmas party? That seemed like an awfully good hunch, Tom old man."

"Let's just say there are many ways of getting information that are not completely understood as yet," suggested Tom cagily with a sly wink at Susan.

"I get it," said Phillip. "Mind my own business. Moving on. If Mr. Harkins, our client, did have his gun stolen in the robbery, then whoever murdered Mr. Freidan knew the guys doing all these break-ins. The murderer needed to know the robbers to get the gun. He needed to be a Rotary Club member or know someone who was to have a copy of that Christmas party picture. In fact, he could have been at that party during which the picture was taken."

Tom rubbed his chin contemplatively. "Good reasoning, Phillip. I agree. Jeff, how about getting a list of all the people at that Christmas party?"

"Okay, but only if I do something more exciting the next time. Too much computer wizardry and no legwork makes Jeff a dull boy."

"Before we move away from evidence that John Harkins is not the shooter," Susan interjected, "I'd like to add one more piece of information to support that position. John Harkins also does not fit the profile of someone who could kill someone else. To quote numerous people with regard to John's personality, he's simply too wimpy.

Mind you, sometimes people can have a wimpy persona, but harbor hostile or aggressive tendencies underneath their exterior. If that violent component exists, the anger and aggression manifests itself in close personal relationships. In John's case, he's timid through and through. If need be, I can testify to that assessment in court."

Tom paced the room. "Okay, good. We have evidence to show John is not guilty. Now, what evidence do we have that could point to someone else? Remember, we just need to show reasonable doubt in court. We do not have to track down the killer, just provide the police with evidence so they can do their job. This is a warning to all of you." Tom looked at each of them in turn. His steely gaze lingered the longest on Susan. *"Don't put yourself in jeopardy by doing anything dangerous or foolish."* He paused to let his admonition sink in. "Phillip, bring us up to date on the St. Dismas House connection."

Phillip put his hands in his pants pockets and moseyed around the conference room in a lawyerly fashion. His voice acquired the entreating tone of a closing argument. "This crime seems to be connected to the increase in robberies, which in turn seem to be connected to some of the houses in the St. Dismas House program. We know the Remington sculpture that Michael Freidan acquired had been stolen. Michael Freidan could have confronted the person who sold him that piece and threatened to go to the police. That could be what got him killed.

"According to Mark Everett, Tim, our former classmate, got into trouble because the house father at the St. Dismas House he was assigned to forced him to commit robberies. When Tom and I met with Tim in jail, he said talking was too dangerous and he didn't want to see us again."

Jeff frowned. "Okay, drop the Matlock imitation, bro, and get to the point."

Phillip scowled at him and resumed in his normal voice. "I was thinking if we got a list of all the kids that were sent to the various St. Dismas Houses, we could see which of them had the greatest rate of recidivism."

"Recidi-*what?*" asked Jeff.

"Recidivism, Sherlock. Meaning the tendency of convicted criminals to habitually reoffend. I know it's a long shot, since a lot of these kids end up committing more crimes regardless of where they are sent. But one or two of these St. Dismas places might just have higher rates then the others."

"You sure have your thinking cap on today, Phillip," said Tom. "Go to the courthouse and get the list of kids sent to those St. Dismas Houses. That's public information. It will be harder to get information on the addresses of those recently arrested for burglary. You're going to have a lot of data to go through. I'm feeling good about all this. We're making headway on a very complex case."

"Wait a minute here!" put in Jeff. "You haven't heard my information yet. When I went through Michael Freidan's phone and appointment records, I discovered he was waiting for a delivery on February, 12th, just a few weeks after *The Sergeant* was stolen. It was the only delivery notation is his home appointment book."

Seeing Tom was about to reach out and tousle his hair, Jeff waggled a warning finger at him. Tom shrugged apologetically. "Brilliant, my boy, just brilliant. I just love it when a case comes together."

"I have one loose end," said Susan. "Marjorie Freidan remembered this delivery. This was the time the Remington sculpture showed up at the house. She did not see the person who delivered *The Sergeant* but she remembered it came in a box with a red stripe and the letters E D in calligraphic script. Today, she confirmed that the boxes Everett Design currently uses are identical to that box—only *sans* the red stripe. My theory is the red stripe was an element of a prototype design that was discarded in favor of a simpler motif."

Tom hesitated for a minute. "Susan, that sounds like a dead end. The evidence seems to be pointing to the St. Dismas Houses and the rash of robberies. Like I said, all we need is some reasonable information we can give to the police or use in court if it comes to a trial. But pursue it if you want."

Feeling a trifle dismissed, Susan nodded her head obediently. She had the nagging feeling their evidence, though compelling was somehow too pat and contrived.

Something told her the truth lay beyond the double doors at Everett Design.

47

As the meeting wound down, Tom lightly touched Susan's hand as a signal for her to remain. After the boys were gone, he closed and locked the office door.

"Should I be afraid?" asked Susan.

"Most definitely," Tom replied. He took her in his arms and gently kissed her. When he pulled back from the kiss, he looked admiringly at her. "I can't begin to tell you how much you mean to me. The only thing that got me out of bed in the morning was anger toward the person who killed my wife. My life had no purpose other than to inflict revenge. Now I wake up with a wonderful feeling of joy knowing I'm going to see you."

Susan was taken aback. In all their years of marriage, Frank had never spoken such loving words. She thought she knew what love was but realized she had only experienced a pale imitation in her sham of a marriage. Frank saw her as his possession, a prized object to own and control; she might as well have been one of his damnable coins. She had dated a little in college, but Frank had been her only serious relationship. Apart from Frank, she had never been with another man until Tom. He was so very different from Frank's bombast and empty swagger; so utterly masculine, yet with a vulnerability he wasn't afraid to show the world.

Susan heard her words spill out in an emotional torrent. "I don't know what to say. I've never heard such loving words from a man. I still feel like I'm protecting myself, though. It has nothing to do with you; it's because of my marriage. I'm always happy to see you, too, Tom. I just have a hard time letting go and trusting."

"Take all the time you need to trust me. We need to get to know each other. I can't wait to find out everything about you: all your interests, your favorite movie, your favorite food, your favorite flower. There's no rush. I just need to know you feel something for me, too."

"Oh, yes, I do. Without a doubt. I just can't tell, yet, how much is love and how much is lust."

"It's five-thirty and everyone has left the office. We're alone." Tom shut the window blinds and removed the papers and the flower arrangement from the conference table. Both Susan and Tom started to undress.

Susan felt more at ease this time even though 'doing it' in the office made her a little nervous. There was no doubt about wanting to make love to Tom, none of the hesitancy she had felt the first time. She was free of guilt now that she and Frank were not living together. This freedom had unlocked her passion. She was inflamed with a desire she hadn't felt for years.

Tom came up to her and kissed her sweetly at first. Susan returned his kiss with passion. Tom's jacket and shoes were off and his collar and tie were loosened but not off. Susan had her black lace bra and matching panties on, partially covered by an unbuttoned red blouse. She gingerly took Tom's tie and pulled him toward the conference table. Sitting on top of him, she removed the tie and shirt and then his pants.

He had now removed her blouse. He unsnapped her bra and gently massaged her breasts. She could feel her nipples contract. They kissed passionately. Tom's hand moved down her back, gently massaging her buttocks. Susan massaged Tom's inner thighs.

Susan had never made love anywhere but the bed. Making love in Tom's office heightened her excitement. Even though the door was locked and everyone had left the building, Susan's adrenaline was elevated by the potential of being caught. There was a feeling of naughtiness and risk having sex on the conference table.

Susan had surprised Tom by getting on top of him. She kissed his lips passionately, then kissed his neck and his nipples. With her pelvis, she put rhythmic pressure on his lower abdomen, gradually moving downward on his body. When she knew he was hard and erect, she lowered herself on him, engulfing him.

"Ah," said Tom. "You feel so good on top of me. I love feeling you, looking at you."

Susan could feel her passion increasing. That warm, pre-orgasmic feeling swept over her and then she climaxed uncontrollably. Tom came seconds later. They collapsed in each other's arms, smiling in post coital bliss. Tom gently stroked Susan's face. Susan started to talk but stopped. They both heard the sound of voices in the hallway and then the sound of a key in the door.

"The cleaning service!" Tom whispered. "I forgot about the cleaning service. Don't come in!" he shouted. "Come back later, Consuela."

A stout Hispanic woman cracked open the conference room door about six inches and peered inside warily. Spotting the naked couple shielding themselves with handfuls of clothing, she cried "*Caramba!* Your pardon, *Señor* Danford!" and gently closed the door.

Susan and Tom burst out in hysterical laughter. In the hallway, a babel of excited voices speaking in Spanish let them know Conseula was already getting good mileage out of her latest gossip.

"It's not usually the way I end lovemaking," Tom said. "I guess this will be one memory for the scrapbook. We're two for two with someone interrupting us. Next time, let's go to my house."

Susan kissed him lightly on the lips. "I haven't had this much fun in years. What a wonderful way to end the day."

"It's not over yet. How about dinner?" asked Tom.

Susan checked her watch. She didn't want her time with Tom to end. "That will be great, but let's go somewhere quick. I promised the boys I'd pick up some pizza for them tonight."

"Let's go to Anthony's Pizza. We can eat there and then get some takeout for the boys. As much as I hate to suggest it, it makes more sense if we each drive our own cars there. It's less time that I get to spend with you, though." Tom lowered his head in exaggerated sorrow.

Susan purred seductively. "I'll make it up to you, big boy."

"What a day!" Susan sighed aloud as she followed Tom to Anthony's Pizza. Susan was so happy she failed to notice she was being shadowed yet again by a mysterious black car.

48

Susan timed her morning visit to Everett Design to coincide with the noon lunch break, a time when employees would be unlikely to frequent the storage area. Browsing among the garden statuary, her eyes lit on a reproduction of *Bird Girl,* the statue popularized by *Midnight in the Garden of Good and Evil,* one of Susan's favorite novels.

Ever since she had seen the book's cover showing the forlorn looking girl in the simple dress holding a bowl in each of her outstretched hands, Susan had fancied the piece and often thought it would look nice in her English garden. Pretending to be a customer, she casually turned the price tag over in her hand and nodded in approval of the reasonable cost.

She slowly made her way toward the concrete fountains in front of the hallway that led to the restrooms and the storage room with the swinging doors. After a cursory examination of the fountains, she continued down the empty hallway. With no sounds coming from the storage room, she quickly stepped inside.

When her eyes had adjusted to the dimly lit room, she saw it was much larger than she had anticipated. The door to the outside on her far left was open to a loading dock where a few workers sat eating their lunches and shooting the breeze.

Susan tried to identify a pattern to the room. There were large boxes of figurines to the right of her. On the left were tall shelves that reached almost to the ceiling. Further down, on the same side, she saw what looked like a stack of flattened boxes. Constantly looking over her shoulder, she slowly made her way down the aisle. Just a few yards shy of her prize, a hushed conversation between three men froze her in her tracks. Heart pounding, she ducked into an opening between the shelves and hid behind a large box straining to listen to what the men were saying.

"What do you mean it will take a few days?" a man's voice rose in anger. Another man answered, but his voice was low and unintelligible. A third voice bellowed, "You had better take care of it!" Presently, Susan saw the three men walk toward the open door where the workers lunched. Even in the dim light, Susan thought one of the men looked familiar, but they were at least forty feet away and she could only see their backs.

Desperate now, Susan quickly formed a plan. Stealth was out; she would openly search for a box large enough to hold the *Bird Girl* statue under the pretense the clerks were too busy—or lazy—to help her.

She left her hiding place and strolled nonchalantly down the aisle toward the stack of flattened boxes she had observed earlier. As she dug through the stack, she caught sight of the Holy Grail: a scattering of already assembled boxes with the prototypical Everett Design motif with the elusive red stripe, tucked in behind a sea of wooden pallets.

Susan felt like a kid in a candy shop. It would be impossible for her to steal behind the pallets without making a racket and calling attention to herself. What she needed was an unsuspecting pawn to fetch the box for her. Right on cue, a dull-looking young man in his late teens, clad in dirty jeans and an Everett Design t-shirt, approached her. Susan already had a plan.

"Well, hello there, sugar" Susan said in a syrupy Southern accent.

"You're not allowed back here, ma'am. This section is for employees only. I'm afraid you'll have to leave."

"I'm so sorry, sugar, I didn't know that. The clerks are so busy. I just need a box for a gift. It's that Savannah *Bird Girl* statue, don't you know. It's about yay big." Susan held her arms about two feet apart. "If you will kindly get me one of those boxes in the back with the red stripe on it, I'll be on my way."

"We don't use those boxes anymore, lady. Those are going to be thrown out. I'll get you one of our current boxes that are about the size you want," the young man said. With gentle firmness, he started ushering her toward the showroom.

"Oh, I'm so disappointed," Susan drawled. "It's a housewarming present for my friend. I was going to tie a big red bow around the box. The red stripe would look absolutely *perfect* with the red bow, don't you think?"

"I don't know nothing about that, ma'am. I just know you're going to have to leave before I get in trouble."

"I do declare, young man, you obviously have never heard the expression, 'the customer is always right,' have you? I would have thought your mama raised you to be a Southern gentleman who would go out of his way to help a woman in distress."

Bingo! Susan saw she had struck a nerve.

"Okay, okay, I'll get you one of those boxes, but then you'll have to leave. I could get into a lot of trouble for this. Those boxes were supposed to have been destroyed last week. But why anyone would be such a big a hurry to get rid of perfectly good boxes, I have no idea. They don't pay me to think, though, just lift and tote."

The young man worked his way behind the obstacle of pallets to the boxes with the red stripes. He held one up for Susan to see. She nodded her head vigorously in approval. He made his way back to Susan, hugging the box to his chest to protect it.

"Thank you, sugar pie," said Susan in a voice thick and sweet as sorghum syrup. She patted his cheek and slipped a five- dollar bill in his hand. She exited the storage room and went into the restroom at the end of the hallway to figure out how she was going to get out of the store with her trophy. Inside a stall, she folded the box to hide the red stripe on the top panel. When folded, she could keep the red stripe toward her body so no one would know it was the rejected prototype.

Susan could feel herself getting more anxious as she thought about trying to get out of the store without being seen with the box. She did some self-hypnosis. She closed her eyes, took three deep relaxing breaths and imagined herself on her porch, totally relaxed, looking into her peaceful garden. She was ready then to try to make a clean getaway with the box, without making a purchase.

With all the people around, what could possibly happen?

49

That same morning, Phillip woke up early. Down in the kitchen, he read the note Susan had left him and Jeff saying there were fresh bagels in the breadbox and cream cheese with walnuts in the refrigerator. If they needed her, she'd be at Everett Design later during the day.

By seven-thirty, he had made coffee and was munching a bagel. Finding the criminals who had been at the St. Dismas Houses and then arrested for another crime would be a monumental challenge today. Fortunately, North Carolina was one of twenty-nine states that listed every criminal on a public access database. But in order to search the courthouse database, he needed *names.* The only way to get them was to go to the library and search the back issues of the local newspapers for recent arrests. When the library opened at eight-thirty, he would the first one in the door to get started on what promised to be a tedious promise.

"Hey, bro, you're up early," said Jeff, stumbling into the kitchen with his hair in disarray. "Where are you off to?"

"The library, my friend, the library. What are your plans for the day?"

"I called Mr. Harkins last night. I'm going over to the Harkins' house to find out whom those people are in the party picture with Mr. Harkins kissing the blonde. There might be more people who had

221

attended that party, too. I need the whole list. What we don't do for evidence!"

Phillip thought Jeff's day sounded even more tedious than his own. At least he had lunch with Mark Everett to look forward. The grand opening of Everett Design had drawn nearly 500 customers each day, twice the anticipated figure. As Mark was the proud manager, a celebratory lunch was in order.

"Call me if you find anything worthwhile. Chances are, though, that it will be me finding worthwhile stuff," Phillip teased.

Jeff raised his right hand showing his brother his three middle fingers. "The tallest man to you, bro," he laughed.

At the library, Phillip immersed himself in the newspaper archives. By eleven forty-five he had compiled a list of arrests in the Mecklenburg county for the last six months. Most of the articles only gave the names of the criminals, what they attempted, or what they had stolen. Some referenced the criminals' workplaces, but only a few articles indicated where they lived. Phillip put all the information he collected on the Excel spreadsheet on his computer.

Phillip left the library just in time to meet Mark at the Rusty Rudder by noon. He was glad Mark had elected to dine outside. A sailor at heart, Phillip loved gazing out over Lake Norman at the blue expanse of water dotted with pleasure craft and fishing boats. "So, how's the budding entrepreneur?" Phillip asked.

"Business is so good, I'm going to hire you as my lawyer when you graduate," said Mark. "We had another record day and can hardly keep the place stocked."

"That's great. How's your father taking all this success? Have you gotten any credit for the good response?"

"He's happy, I guess. You know him; he's just a tough old bird that has trouble saying anything positive. He hasn't disinherited me yet, so I guess that's a good sign. He's still reluctant to let me into the inner sanctum of his business. I'm shut out of the meetings with his financial advisors. I don't even get to meet with the general accountant, just the one who is specifically responsible for Everett Design."

"Hang in there. It may just take some more time for your father to appreciate your business acumen. Believe me, I know what it's like to have a jerk for a father. My mother finally kicked the good doctor out of the house. She found out about his fooling around and that clenched it."

"Sorry to hear that. I had heard rumors about your old man, but didn't know if they were true or not. Raising parents ain't easy, is it?"

Phillip laughed. "Mom deserves someone who treats her better," he said thoughtfully. "I think she and Tom Danford have something going on, but they're playing it close to the vest. He's been a great guy to work with. I can see him and my mother together."

"I've only heard good things about him. I'm glad we tipped the cops off about the gun that creep used to shoot his wife although that was a close encounter with those cops. Thank God Lukowski's off our asses. I couldn't believe he dragged us into the police station just because they found out we had been camping where they found the gun. It was stupid on my part to not remember I had signed in that day. Heaven help the guy who pulled the trigger and killed Tom's wife. Lukowski will be merciless."

Phillip didn't want to think about that day in the police station. He looked wistfully at the lake, daydreaming he could ditch his duties and idle away the afternoon catching a mess of striped bass. "Think your old man will let you take your nose up from the grindstone long enough to go fishing next week?"

"Deal. Just promise me one thing."

"Yeah?"

"We don't go anywhere near Sesquicentennial State Park!"

Phillip arrived at the courthouse, refreshed and ready to scan through the forty-three names he acquired from the newspapers. His high school friend, Jake, who worked in the records division, set him up with a computer and the access codes for the database. Four hours and one measly coffee break later, he had all the information he needed and then some. Examining the spreadsheet printout, his palms sweated profusely as a startling revelation came to light.

Frantically, he tried to reach his mother on the phone. She didn't answer.

50

Susan slowly left the restroom with the folded box under her arm, partially covered by her purse. She was feeling more relaxed, but not completely. Her fingers were tense around the box. Once inside the main showroom, her calm returned now that the main exit was in sight. She paused to feign interest in a fountain with a cherub frolicking in its basin, smiling approvingly at the design for the benefit of a fellow customer. With studied nonchalance, she continued to browse as she inched her way toward the exit.

"Hi, Dr. Kemper. Nice to see you here," said a voice behind her. Susan started; it was all she could do to quell the urge to make a mad dash for the door. She was relieved when she turned to meet the smiling face of Mark Everett.

"Hi, Mark. So good to see you. Phillip told me you were managing this part of your father's business. Your selection is just marvelous. Congratulations on your successful grand opening!"

"Thanks. It's been a lot of work, but business is excellent. I was just telling that to Phillip over lunch. It's nice to see all the customers." Mark glanced at the burden under her arm. "I see you haven't found anything you like, though. What's that, just a box?"

"Oh! I bought a birdhouse here two days ago and came back today for a box. It's a gift for a friend. One of your clerks was kind enough to get the box for me."

"I'm glad to hear our clerks are being helpful. You have a good day and thanks for coming."

"My pleasure, Mark."

As another customer beckoned to Mark, Susan felt her frozen smile gradually melt. She took a deep breath, wondering if she had breathed at all while talking to Mark. Susan had made up her mind to get while the getting was good when a hand grabbed her shoulder and spun her around. Her mouth dropped open. She thought she was hallucinating, but the sad, red-rimmed eyes that bore down on her were all too real. Every head in the store turned in her direction as a strident voice rang out.

"I thought I would find you here! I stopped at the house to pick up some things. Jeff let me in. I saw the note you left the boys. We need to talk. You can't do this to me!"

"Frank, this is not the time or place," Susan hissed in an urgent whisper. "Let's go outside."

Frank's voice rose in a hysterical crescendo. "You won't answer my phone calls. I don't care who hears me. I love you, Susan. I want you back."

Susan hung her head, mortified, as the store became as silent as a tomb. She felt the eyes of the rubbernecking customers on her, straining to see the sideshow.

Mark sized up the situation and intervened. "Would you two like someplace quiet to talk? You can go in my office."

"Thanks, Mark, but we can just go outside and talk."

"I think Mark's office is a good idea," said Frank. "That way you can't run away."

"Okay, thanks, Mark," Susan sighed resignedly. "You're office might be better."

They had to pass the main exit to get to Mark's office. Susan had a sudden impulse to dash to her car and make a clean getaway. As if reading her mind, Frank put his arm around her, giving her a squeeze. *"Damn!"* Susan muttered.

"What did you say?" asked Frank.

"Nothing, Frank."

Mark graciously sat them down in his office and shut the door behind him.

"Frank, this is not a good time to hash out our differences. You don't understand what's going on."

"Why, are you meeting your boyfriend here? Is that why you're in such a hurry to leave?"

"No, it's nothing like that. It's just important that I leave this store now with this box. I'll explain later."

"Explain now."

"I can't explain now. It's about the case."

There was a rap on the door—shave and a haircut, two bits—before Roger Everett stuck his head in. "Oh, I'm sorry. I'm Roger Everett. I was looking for Mark. Are you waiting for him? Say, aren't you Phillip Kemper's parents?"

"Hi, Roger," answered Susan. "Yes, Phillip is our son. I was shopping when my husband, Frank, came in. We were having a rather loud discussion and Mark was kind enough to let use his office."

"Sorry to interrupt then. Mark's probably on the floor. Hope you found something you like."

Susan watched in mute terror as Roger's gaze went to Mark's desktop where, in the confusion, Susan had set down her purse and the box. The red stripe was in full view.

"Looks like someone gave you one of our sample boxes," said Roger as he started sliding the box off the desktop. "We don't use them. Let me get you a new one."

Susan's hand shot out; her trembling fingers closed on the box's edge. "Never mind, Roger. This box is perfect for what I want."

"I have to insist. We can't have a box with our rejected logo in circulation. Bad for our image."

"I don't want you to go through any trouble. Let us finish this discussion and I'll find you and we can trade boxes."

Roger's tone was cold. "No, I'll take it now."

"You heard my wife," Frank snapped defensively, rising and getting in Roger's face. "She'll find you later or she'll keep the damn box. She needs it for her case. Isn't that right, honey?"

"What case?" Roger asked. "What's going on here?"

Susan grabbed her purse and the box and got up. "You two can stay and fight it out. I'm leaving."

Roger moved to block her exit. "No, you're not."

Frank was livid. "Who are you to tell my wife what she can and cannot do? If she wants that damn box, she can have it. If she wants to leave, she can."

As Susan tried to nudge her way past Roger, he grabbed her arm.

"Take your hand off my wife!" Frank bellowed. He seized Roger by the neck of his polo shirt and landed a hard right to his chin. Reeling, Roger fell across the desk but rebounded instantly and lunged headlong at Frank. They crashed against a file cabinet and tumbled to the floor.

Susan grabbed her purse and the box and made her escape. The noise of the melee followed her down the hall. With a wry smile, she gave Frank credit. It sounded like he was giving a good account of himself.

Halfway to the exit she nearly collided with a burly figure.

"What the fuck's going on here? I happened to be pulling into the parking lot when one of the clerks came running out saying there was a fight in here," groused Stan Lukowski, reaching out to grab Susan's shoulders. "Trouble seems to follow you around like a stray dog, lady. What's that racket down the hallway?"

Susan thought fast. "Stan, thank goodness you're here!" she shrieked. "Roger Everett and my husband, Frank, are fighting. Please, you have to go stop them!"

As Lukowski trotted down the hall with all the clerks and a curious knot of shoppers in his wake, Susan strolled nonchalantly into the parking lot, smiling triumphantly.

"I'll take the box," a voice said behind her. "Get into this car."

51

When Susan didn't answer her phone, Phillip called Tom. "Unbelievable news, Tom," said Phillip. "We've been barking up the wrong tree this whole time. I'm afraid Mom may be in danger."

"Jeff just called with his information and is on his way over to my office, Phillip. Come on over here and we'll pull all this information together," said Tom. "I'll keep trying to get your mother on the phone."

Within fifteen minutes, the two Kemper brothers were in Tom's office.

"I got what we were looking for," said Jeff. "Here's the picture from the Rotary party and a complete guest list of everyone who was at the Rotary Christmas party."

"Excellent, Jeff. Anything else?"

"Here's the list. Nothing really jumped out at me. Roger and Mark Everett are on the list. I don't know if that's relevant. So is the decorator, Jennifer Houston, and the *deceased*, Michael Freidan." Jeff had uttered the word deceased with the utmost seriousness trying hard to maintain an air of professional police decorum.

Phillip gave him a look that said, "Give it a rest." "Any word from Mom?" Phillip asked Tom.

"No, not yet. What's the problem? What did you find that has you so upset?" asked Tom.

"It's my fault. I was set up and didn't even know it. Here look at this." Phillip pulled the spreadsheet printout with comprehensive information he had compiled between the library and the courthouse. "Here are all the robbery arrests in the last six months where the convict was sent to the St. Dismas Houses instead of to jail. As you can see by the addresses, there is no single St. Dismas House that they came from.

However, look at their places of employment. Seventy percent of them worked at Everett Concrete. I'm thinking Mark set me up. He's the one who put us on the scent of the St Dismas Houses and suggested it was a few of the house fathers that were leading these young guys back into crime. But it's not them. It's someone at Everett Concrete. Mom said she was going to Everett Design today."

Tom examined Jeff's Rotary party list. "I'd say you were right, Phillip. Jeff said Mark Everett and his father, Roger Everett, are both on this guest list. Let's review the scenario. Someone at Everett Concrete hires these young guys who go to St. Dismas Houses for rehab. They have to get a job and Everett Concrete fits the bill for young guys with limited education and skills. Once on the payroll, they're coerced into committing robberies. But can we prove that? It could be that Roger Everett, being a civic-minded Rotarian, is just giving these guys a break. One could argue, too, that these guys have a high recidivism rate and are prone to reverting to their criminal ways. We have nothing substantive linking Everett Concrete to these crimes."

"What about the box with the red stripe and the Everett Design logo?" asked Phillip.

"I'm afraid I dismissed that notion out of hand when your mother brought it up, but there may be something to it. How do you figure Everett Concrete and the Remington statue are connected?"

Phillip pondered the question. "When I looked at what was stolen, it was mostly untraceable stuff: TVs, computers, DVDs, cash. The Remington statue would have been an unusual object for these guys to steal. It's not something they could fence easily; they would have to sell it to an individual."

"Hold the presses!" shouted Jeff. "Mom came to the Freidan house while I was there. I heard her ask Mrs. Freidan if her husband had an association with Everett Concrete. She said he had hired them to put in a sidewalk. Mr. Freidan struck a friendship with the young guy supervising the project, a fellow Civil War nut. Mr. Freidan even showed him his collection."

Tom grinned broadly. "Gentleman, as my grandpa used to say: I think we've got'er if she don't jump."

"Huh?" the Kemper brothers chorused.

"Hear me out. If this young guy had been involved with robberies, he could have taken the sculpture, thinking he could sell it to Mr. Freidan. Maybe this kid took the sculpture on his own hook. He sells it to Michael Freidan without telling anyone who was involved in the robbery. He stupidly delivers it in one of Everett Design's prototype boxes. Most damning of all, Freidan *knows* the kid works for Everett Concrete. When Freidan reads that his statue was stolen, he calls his contact at Everett Concrete and tells him one of his workers is a crook and threatens to involve the police. His contact convinces him to wait until he can come over to discuss the situation."

Danford paced the conference room as keen deductive mind clicked into high gear. "Michael Freidan knew both Mark and Roger Everett through the Rotary Club. It could have been either one of them; as fellow Rotarians, they would be welcome in Freidan's house anytime and they would have access to the photo from the Rotary Club party."

"Yeah, but which one knows how to shoot a gun?" Jeff queried.

"They both do," said Phillip. "I've been to their cabin in Highlands near Harris Lake. Both Roger and Mark go there duck hunting. It's one of the few father and son things they do together."

"Do either one of them own a black car with a loud, powerful engine?" asked Tom. "A V8 might make the growling noise Mrs. Freidan heard the morning of the murder."

"I don't know what Roger Everett drives. Mark has a Toyota Tundra. It's big, but I don't think its engine makes a growling noise," Phillip said a little impatiently.

Tom put his hand on Phillip's shoulder. "Why are you so worried about your mother, Phillip?"

"She was fixated on the Everett Design box with the red stripe," Jeff chimed in.

Phillip nodded his head. "I'm afraid she might do something crazy like prowling around at Everett Design, trying to find evidence. If Mark or his dad is involved, that could be dangerous."

Jeff was more alert and anxious now. "Mom had brought a box she recently acquired from Everett Design to show Mrs. Freidan. Mrs. Freidan said the lettering the Remington figure had come in was the same as the lettering on the Everett Design boxes being used now, except the box she had seen had had a red stripe on the side. Mom was convinced that was an important clue and wanted to find the box with the red stripe. I'm with Phillip: Maybe she went back to Everett Design to look for it."

"She also thought a black car had been following her," said Tom. His car keys were already in his hand as he bolted for the door. "Let's go!"

52

Tom drove like the proverbial bat out of hell, his knuckles white on the steering wheel. A large vein on his forehead pulsed in time with the jackhammer beating of his heart. Phillip sat beside him, goggle-eyed with terror. In the back seat, Jeff, muttering prayerfully to himself, had curled himself into a protective ball. Fortunately, there wasn't a lot of traffic this afternoon which lessened the chances of an accident.

"Uh, Tom, can we slow it down a bit?" asked Phillip, his voice cracking. "I'm sure Mom's alright. Her cell phone is probably just out of juice again."

Tom glanced at the speedometer. He was doing eighty-eight in a forty mph zone. He eased off the accelerator and eased the Lexus down to sixty. He couldn't endanger the boys' lives. But he couldn't lose Susan, either. If something happened to her, he didn't want to live. It had taken him years to recover from Beth's death. He couldn't go through that again.

As the Lexus squealed into the parking lot, they saw Susan getting into the passenger seat of a black car.

"There's Mom!" exclaimed Phillip. "Who's the guy behind her? Why is she getting into his car? I wish the car was any color but black."

"Holy shit, there's Stan Lukowski!" observed Jeff in astonishment. "And Dad and Roger Everett in handcuffs! *What the hell is going on here?*"

Tom screeched crookedly into a parking space. The trio spilled out of the car, leaving the doors open as they sprinted toward the black car. Tom pounded on the driver's side window as the Kemper brothers did the same on the passenger side. Suddenly the tinted windows opened to reveal Jay Owens at the wheel. Beside him, relaxed and unharmed, Susan sat, smiling. She held tight to her prize: the elusive box with the red stripe.

As Danford's confused mind raced through a thousand scenarios, he was overcome with relief that Susan was okay. "Jay, for the love of Mike, what the hell's going on here?"

Owens' mouth twitched into a guilty grin. "You fellows meet me in my office and I'll explain everything to all of you."

Tom and the Kemper brothers followed Jay Owens' car back to the police station. Once in his office, seated comfortably, with Susan looking much more relaxed, Jay began his explanation. "We've been trying to break up this robbery ring for nine months now," said Owens. "We knew these robberies were connected with Michael Freidan's death. When you four got involved with the case, we were afraid you'd screw up our investigation or get hurt. Stan Lukowski can be obnoxious, but on my orders he's been turning in an Academy Award performance to try to scare you off the investigation. All the stunts he pulled were designed to make you back off. We had Stan or one of his boys follow you to make sure you didn't get hurt."

"I don't understand then why Stan or one of his guys would try to run me over. That's kind of extreme, don't you think?" responded Susan.

"They wouldn't have done that," said Jay Owens. "Lukowski did mention something about one of the men seeing some idiot who almost hit you. The officer thought it was just one of our typical bad drivers. Lukowski chewed out the cop tailing you for not pursuing the bad driver just in case the near hit was intentional."

Susan now was more concerned.

Jay Owens went on explaining. "Mark Everett was also helping us. Phillip, all that stuff about the St. Dismas House was just smoke and mirrors to put you off the trail. When we had him in for questioning about the gun, he admitted he had thrown the gun in the lake. He also told us he suspected someone at Everett Concrete was involved with setting up these robberies. He talked with his father about all the ex-cons working there. His father said when business had been bad, he borrowed money from a loan shark. When Roger Everett couldn't pay the money back because of the vigorish, or excessively high interest, he made a deal with the loan shark to hire these ex-cons. In order for the ex-cons to stay in the St. Dismas Houses, they needed to get a job within thirty days of being placed there. No problem: Their employment at Everett Concrete was guaranteed and flexible. These crooks could now get their boys out of prison into the St. Dismas Houses with no restrictions placed on their time and a job where no one questioned their comings and goings. Roger Everett agreed to help us put the kibosh on the robbery ring in exchange for immunity from prosecution. You four got in the middle of our investigation."

"So how did Michael Freidan get involved with all this?" asked Susan.

"Joey Barnes, the kid who supervised the installation of the Freidan patio, was one of these guys from the St. Dismas House. He robbed the house with the Remington sculpture. We think he sold the figure to Freidan on his own, but we're not sure. Generally they only stole untraceable items: TVs, DVD players and recorders, coins, jewelry—stuff that could be easily sold.

"When Freidan read in the paper the Remington was stolen, we think he went looking for Joey Barnes. We also have Freidan's phone records. He knew Joey was staying at one of the St. Dismas Houses. Because Freidan had donated money to this organization, he knew where all the houses were located and had their phone numbers. According to Joey, Freidan found the house Joey was staying at and left a message on his answering machine saying he knew the Remington was stolen and wanted his money back. We have Joey in custody, but he's not talking beyond that. We don't think he killed Michael. We figure someone he told did it."

"What about my wife?" asked Tom.

"A victim of the same robbery gang. We're questioning all the cons to see if we can get someone to own up to that robbery and murder. There's a young man, named Henry Michaels, who fits the description of the would-be bank robber who killed your wife. He's back in prison again for burglary. He also was a St. Dismas house tenant around the time of the bank robbery. We need someone to roll over on him to make the case. We're working on offering Joey Barnes a deal. Now what kind of evidence do y'all have?"

Tom responded. "Here's what we have so far on this investigation. We figure whoever killed Freidan had access to the incriminating picture of Harkins from the Rotary Club Christmas party." At this point Phillip open his laptop computer while Tom continued. "Here's the list of names of everyone at that party who received a copy of this picture. Here's a list of all the guys released from prison who are staying at the St. Dismas Houses and working at Everett Concrete."

Owens took the proffered documents. "Thanks. So, tell me Susan, what's so special about this box?"

Susan recounted the evolution of the red-striped box's significance, from Marjorie Freidan's first recollection of it, through the widow's hypnosis session and post-hypnotic remembrance of the letters ED, to her clandestine recovery of the sample box and the ensuing fight between Frank and Roger Everett. She discreetly left out the salient detail of her special cognitive gift that allowed her to see the letters on the box.

"Wow," said Jeff, "imagine Dad in a knock down, drag out brawl!"

"I guess the old man finally grew some balls," mused Phillip, somewhat admiringly.

"Phillip!" Susan scolded

"It gets even better. He took a swing at Lukowski. We had to put him in handcuffs to get him to calm down," responded Jay with a smirk on his lips.

"I do have to hand it to Frank: If he hadn't stood up for me, I would never have made it out of Roger Everett's office with the box."

"Jay, where does the investigation stand at this point?" asked Tom.

"We know from Roger Everett who loaned him the money. Now, thanks to the work done by Team Danford, we have a list of all the St. Dismas House cons that were working at Everett Concrete. Because of this box, we can connect Everett Concrete with the murder of Michael Freidan. We're missing the identity of just one person before we make arrests. We're convinced there was an insider because somebody knew when the victims' houses would be empty and that the houses contained desirable goods. We also suspect that some of the objects were sold to ordinary citizens, not just fences. We think it's the insider who killed Michael Freidan. Freidan probably knew him and put all the pieces together."

"Can I see the picture of the Rotary Christmas party and those lists again?" asked Susan.

"Sure," said Owens. "Dr. Kemper, you've got a gleam in your eye that scares me, frankly."

An impish grin blossomed on Susan's face. "Suddenly it all makes sense. Gentlemen, we've got a trap to set and I know just what bait to use."

53

A week later, Susan watched through the kitchen window as the sports car pulled into her driveway, its throaty, high performance engine thrumming lustily. *Bingo!* She was sure it would be a black Mustang with a V8 engine with dual exhausts. She peeked through the window and could see she was right. She waited until the doorbell rang before she went to answer the door. "Hi," Susan said. "So good of you to come at such short notice."

"No problem, Susan," said Jennifer Houston. "Decorating your house was one of my favorite assignments." Jennifer was dressed in high fashion clothes. Susan guessed she spent a lot of time at Neiman Marcus. She recognized the Christopher Deane camisole top she had seen there with the black bodice and black and white striped design and green and blue octagons on the bottom. The top looked great on top of the dark knee length jeans and black heels on Jennifer's shapely size six body.

"Thank you. Come on in and I'll show you the space that needs your expertise." Susan led Jennifer into the living room. "I love the Roger Deering seascape oil painting you helped us pick out over the fireplace, but there's a nagging lack of symmetry on the mantelpiece. I've got my grandmother's heirloom mantel clock in the middle and the candlesticks on the left. I just need a sculpture or vase, or some-

thing on the right for balance. I hope I'm not being too anal reten-
tive."

"Not at all! I see what your problem is. Do you have a budget in
mind?"

"I would love a Galle vase—that is, if I could keep the cost under
$2,500. Something simple and understated."

"Susan, you have such exquisite taste. I think I can help you out. In
fact, I have a new Galle vase in the design gallery. Are you going to
be here for a while? I could bring it here after lunch for a test drive, so
to speak."

"That sounds marvelous. I'm writing an article and it's keeping me
chained to my computer."

"I'll be back in an hour."

Susan showed Jennifer to the door and watched her drive away. "Can
you guys hear me?" she said, fingering the microphone concealed in the
broach on the lapel of her blouse. In her ear, she wore a tiny clear ear-
piece virtually invisible to the naked eye. "She took the bait."

"So we heard," said Jay Owens. A block away, he waited with the
Kemper brothers in his car. Lukowski and Danford had insisted they
be in the house and were within hearing range. They remained in their
places just in case Jennifer came back unexpectedly.

"If it's the same Galle that was stolen a few weeks ago, we've got her
for robbery. We know she got that stolen coin for your husband, but that's
not the only one available. This Galle is rare. Hopefully, we'll get her for
Michael Freidan's murder, if you can get her to admit to having the Remington. As you know, we have a lot of circumstantial evidence, but we
need something more conclusive, but don't do anything to provoke her,
Susan. I don't want you in any danger. This vase stuff is bad enough."

"I hear you," said Susan. "I'm starting to get nervous now that you
mention danger. Give me a few minutes to do some self hypnosis
before speaking to me again."

Jennifer Houston returned after lunch as she had promised. The
Galle vase she had brought was the blue/green one that had been stolen a few weeks before.

"Oh, Jennifer, it's beautiful. Would you mind positioning it on the
mantel while I see how it looks from back here?"

"Certainly."

"Move it a little to the right. That's a little too far."

Susan winced at the sound of Lukowski's voice blaring in her ear,
momentarily distracting her. *What the fuck is she doing? Who cares
where the stupid vase goes?"*

"M-maybe a little more to the left," she stuttered. "Just a little more. Almost there. Perfect! I love it. How much is it?"

"Because you've been such a good customer, Susan, I can sell it to you for $2,250. Does that work for your budget?"

"It sure does. I'll get my checkbook in a minute. How about a cup of tea? I've got some herbal flavors I think you'd like. I can boil the water in a jiffy."

"Don't mind if I do."

Ignoring Lukowski's ranting in her ear, Susan prepared the tea and took a tray with cups and scones to the coffee table in the living room.

"Isn't it hard to part with all these beautiful pieces, Jennifer? I know I'd have trouble letting them go. I hope you are managing to make enough of a profit to buy an occasional piece for yourself."

"Oh, yes, of course. It's up and down, but business, in general, has been very good."

"I'm so glad to hear that." Susan's heart was beating a mile a minute. She put both hands on her cup to steady it. "You have such wonderful design skills. I'm sure some of the people you work with don't appreciate your talent. You deserve to make a comfortable living and enjoy the good things in life. I guess the profit depends upon what price you pay for the item, right?"

Jennifer cocked her head and narrowed her eyes. "Of course. I'm always keeping my ears open for bargains. What are you getting at, Susan?"

"I've heard rumors there might be a Remington sculpture for sale at a good price on the gray market. I've always loved Remington. One of his sculptures would look so wonderful in the den."

Owens' voice murmured in her ear. "Hold back, guys. Susan's baiting her. Let's see if she bites."

Jennifer set down her teacup and looked Susan straight in the eye.

"A Remington might be harder to come by and more expensive."

"For a Remington I would be able to pay around $15,000. Would that work?"

"I have a Remington sculpture of *The Sergeant* at my studio. I think we could work that one into your budget. Would you like to make an appointment to see it? I'd love to show you some of the other pieces I have, too."

Susan stood up. "Sounds marvelous. Let me get your check and my appointment book from the bedroom. I'll be right back."

Susan walked calmly to the bedroom and partially closed the door. Her purse was on the dresser. As she rummaged through it, a chorus of anxious voices assailed her ear. "Guys, if I can just keep her talking, she might spill the beans," she pleaded sotto voce. "Give me just a couple more minutes!"

"Who are you talking to?"

Susan nearly jumped out of her skin. When she looked up, she could see Jennifer Houston in the mirror with a .38 caliber Smith & Wesson in her hand. "Just to myself," said Susan. She knew her voice had a telltale catch in it. "I do that some—"

"How did you know?"

Susan heard the voices buzzing in her ear. She had to keep Jennifer talking. "How did I know what?"

"How did you know I had the Remington sculpture from Michael Freidan's office?"

"It just all fit together. You were the perfect inside person for all these robberies. You'd know who would be away at certain times and who would be interested in buying certain goods. You even sold my husband, Frank, a coin you knew he'd wanted for years. You had a Ford Mustang V8 with a distinctive sound like the one Marjorie Freidan heard the morning of the murder. You knew Michael would be interested in the Remington. You were the one he could finger. That's why you had to kill him."

"I was so careful. If he hadn't seen the article about the Remington being stolen, I would have gotten away with it. I wouldn't have had to kill him."

The faintest of smiles played across Susan's lips. "Case closed," she said, enunciating with elaborate precision.

"We got her. Go! Go!" yelled Jay Owens.

In a flash, Lukowski and then the police stormed the house, surrounding Jennifer Houston with weapons drawn.

"One move and the sharpshooter on the roof next door drops you, Jennifer," Lukowski said coolly. "He's mighty good. Drop your weapon. Hey, Chief, can you get someone to get a warrant to search her house for that Remington sculpture?"

As Jennifer was led away in handcuffs, Susan sat down heavily on the bed and exhaled luxuriously. It was good to breathe again.

Phillip and Jeff burst into the room and smothered Susan in a group hug. When they separated, Tom scooped Susan into his arms and kissed her long and well.

He smiled at her admiringly. "You did great, but don't you ever do that to me again!"

Susan sighed and looked at her three beloved men. "I love you guys," she said.

"Susan, I'm impressed," said Owens. "You were so calm even with her pointing the gun at you."

Susan got off the bed and opened her nightstand drawer. She opened her hand where the bullets from Jennifer's gun nestled. "I heard you say 'She's got a gun, take out the bullets,' so I took the gun out of her purse and the bullets out of the gun while she was positioning the vase." She turned to Lukowski and said, "That's what I was doing."

Jay smiled. "I never said 'She has a gun, take out the bullets.'"

"Me, neither," said Tom.

"Don't look at me," said Lukowski, hands in the air like he was not guilty.

"Do, do, do, do," hummed Jeff to the tune of the Twilight zone theme song.

Susan looked at Tom who instantly knew what she was thinking. "Thanks, Mr. Freidan," she said to herself. "I appreciate the helpful advice." Susan thought she heard her wind chime even though the air was still this August afternoon.

She was feeling exhilarated. She had come through her baptism of fire without a scratch. She thought about how Frank had her under his thumb for years and what both Peggy and Tom had said about the importance of living a life with purpose. Well, brother, she intended to do just that from now on! "We make one helluva team, don't cha think?" she said to Tom and the boys, and then paused. "Oh my God, I just remembered something!"

She called to Jay Owens. "Jay, don't forget to drop the charges against Frank for taking a swing at Lukowski. I think you kept him busy enough in court so he couldn't mess up the case any more." Yes, sir, it had been a very good day!

CPSIA information can be obtained at www.ICGtesting.com
Printed in the USA
LVOW061733270911

248102LV00006B/8/P